MOKANSHAN

For Trish Saywell
And the Irwin boys,
Mackenzie and Thomas

MOKANSHAN

A Tale of Wallis Simpson's Naughty Shanghai Postcards

James H Irwin

iUniverse, Inc.
New York Lincoln Shanghai

MOKANSHAN

A Tale of Wallis Simpson's Naughty Shanghai Postcards

iUniverse books may be ordered through booksellers or by contacting:

iUniverse
2021 Pine Lake Road, Suite 100
Lincoln, NE 68512
www.iuniverse.com
1-800-Authors (1-800-288-4677)

ISBN-13: 978-0-595-36201-1 (pbk)
ISBN-13: 978-0-595-80646-1 (ebk)
ISBN-10: 0-595-36201-X (pbk)
ISBN-10: 0-595-80646-5 (ebk)

Printed in the United States of America

From the *North-China Daily News*:

REDS GIVEN LESSON IN MODESTY

Chengdu, August 8, 1936

A group of Reds numbering about 600, who took refuge in the mountains near Menningshun recently, hoping to prepare the way for the reception of Communistic preaching and to secure the support of the Lolo tribesmen against the Government troops, had the tables turned on them in an unexpectedly tragi-comic manner. One of the most popular slogans of the Communists is "Down with modesty!" This apparently so outraged the sense of propriety of the Lolos, or perhaps stirred their sense of humour, that they determined to do something about it. They rounded up all the Reds in the vicinity, disarmed them and stripped them of their clothing, and then headed the naked mob towards the Government lines, where the Lolos handed over to the Government troops the clothing and equipment of the Communists. As the naked Reds approached the Government troops, followed by the laughing Lolos, Government officers report that the sheer amazement of the soldiers gave way to the highest hilarity at the surprising denouement.

CHAPTER 1

Eli Swan sat motionless, head on forearms, lathered in sweat. If I ever go back to the States and want to remember what Shanghai was like in the summer of 1936, he thought, all I have to do is put on a heavy woollen suit and sit in a Turkish steam bath for an hour or two.

Percy Finch, the city editor, sprawled over his desk nearby, sleeping off a long lunch at the Shanghai Club. The ring of a telephone caused him to lurch upright. The daily siesta in the *North China Daily News* came to its usual end as Swan, no longer the newspaper's junior reporter, began idly eavesdropping on Redvers Witherspoon, who was.

'I don't recall...' said a puzzled Witherspoon. 'In Japanese...and German? Well, no...no, no....'

Swan, eyes closed and with a slightly wicked satisfaction, identified the caller as a nautical engineer he'd met at a bar in Blood Alley some days before. When the man, clearly loopy, discovered Swan was a newsman he had launched into an explanation of how the fillings in his teeth picked up messages in German and Japanese, usually at night when he was deep in the recesses of a ship's hull.

Swan encountered such odd types in bars and nightclubs almost weekly and kept a supply of his colleague's name cards in his wallet for precisely such occasions.

He had gripped the engineer by the elbow while slipping him one of Witherspoon's cards, he remembered. He'd taken a quick look around the bar, ostensibly for spies, then lowering his voice, had asked him to call him at the office when something interesting came up. As the man spoke not a word of Japanese or German, Swan thought maybe Witherspoon might be spared a call.

A few floors below hummed the riverside Bund, Shanghai's imposing face to the world. The tinny sound of moneychangers clinking coins against cups competed with the strident cries of hawkers and food sellers and the muted toots of ships making their way up the Whangpoo River to the nearby Yangtze, the main artery to the country's vast interior. A whiff of frying bean curd seeped through the closed windows and rekindled Swan's hangover.

Witherspoon hung up the phone. 'My word, they're getting worse,' he said in a voice tinged with awe and alarm. 'Last week it was that religious chap rabbitting on about Sodom and Gomorrah and the flooding of the Yangtze.' Swan remembered him too, an American missionary left too long in the hot sun in a remote corner of China.

'This time it was some deranged chap convinced not only that I was an American he'd met at some place called Lucy's. He claims to have a radio transmitter in his fillings that picks up military channels. He laughed hollowly. 'Said it's driving him mad.'

Swan made a note to sound more British when handing out Witherspoon's cards. His prank was not without its perils. A month earlier he had heard a vaguely familiar voice arguing with the Chinese doorman, Lolly, demanding to be let inside the newsroom. Few Chinese in Shanghai would deny Europeans entry anywhere, unless they were mad, Russian or both. Most foreigners either ignored Lolly or threatened to thrash him with their canes.

The man, an Australian, insisted he be allowed inside to speak to his mate Witherspoon as Swan quickly legged it for the toilet. Safely there, he heard him enter the editorial room and ask for Witherspoon. 'I'm he,' Witherspoon had said falteringly. 'No you're bloody not,' the man had snapped, turning on his heel and leaving poor Witherspoon as perplexed as ever.

Swan wasn't really malicious, nor was he even original. He himself had suffered at the hands of other reporters during his first few weeks at the paper until he had finally caught on to the prank. What was amazing was that after a few months Witherspoon seemed to regard it as normal that much of Shanghai's deranged population regarded him as a personal friend. The telephone rang again. Swan glanced over at Witherspoon who shuddered slightly. Taking this as a sign he should leave the newsroom, Swan made for the door, muttering to Finch that he was off to court.

Stepping on to the street he was hit by the full brunt of the late July heat, intensified by the smells of frying food and raw sewage. Eschewing the ubiquitous rickshaws, Swan began the block-and-a-half stroll north along the Bund to the municipal courthouse on the grounds of the British Consulate.

Despite the heat, Swan loved Shanghai and was entranced with its raw capitalism, loose women and sense of danger and exoticism. There was virtually no limit to the city's debaucheries. He hoped he might have servants forever. He gave thanks to his temporary housemate, Luther Flood, for getting them to China's biggest city, still foreign-controlled and prosperous despite a recent economic downturn. Compared with the rest of the world, Shanghai was still humming along nicely as a hopelessly divided China continued to pay big dividends to the foreign interests that controlled the city.

Across Soochow Creek loomed the Soviet Consulate, an object of such hatred to the city's 25,000 White Russians, stateless since the 1917 revolution, that on more than one occasion they'd tried burning it to the ground. The British Consulate, as befitting Shanghai's top colonial power, occupied the choicest piece of property in the city, bordered by Soochow Creek, the Bund and a large public garden that had recently opened its gates to any Chinese willing to pay a tiny entrance fee.

The fee discouraged rickshaw coolies who had taken to using the park benches as beds when the municipal authorities, quite uncharacteristically, had voted in favour of allowing non-Europeans entry to the park. Much to the consternation of pet owners, however, dogs were still forbidden. There were never any signs forbidding dogs and Chinese. It hadn't been necessary.

Swan flashed his press pass and entered the chambers, taking a seat in a booth reserved for the press. Glancing at the docket, he saw that it was a going to be quiet day. A gang of Chinese kidnappers were being tried en masse by the municipal advocate. Doubtless they would be sentenced to death and hustled along to the Chinese authorities for a prompt public execution at a place well removed from foreign eyes. This was virtually a monthly event, even a weekly one in the period leading up to the Chinese New Year when poor Chinese made desperate attempts to clear crippling debts.

Already bored, Swan gazed up at the dark outline on the wooden panelling above the judge's bench where, until recently, a large and much observed clock had hung. A couple of months earlier, between trials but in full view of the judge, two Chinese workers dressed in identical blue smocks had entered the room with a ladder and removed the timepiece. The clock and the two workers had then promptly disappeared.

Swan had interviewed the judge, Penrhyn Grant-Jones, about the brazen act. The short, bombastic Welshman had sworn revenge against the bandits, promising Swan and his readers that 'if it was *time* they wanted, it would be *time* they would be getting, but in *years*, not seconds and minutes.' The story had been published in newspapers around the world, giving Swan his first taste of overseas success.

Nodding to Mike Nenchew, the White Russian photographer who also worked at the *Daily News*, Swan decided to slip home for a few hours before returning to the office later that night to help sort and edit the news from Europe and America.

Bowing to the court, he returned to the Bund where he gestured to the strongest rickshaw puller in sight then barked out his address in pidgin, an act that invariably gave him a gratifying sense of worldliness, fuelling a pride that he could hold his own in a strange tongue.

He settled in his seat and tilted his Greens Super Fur Felt Fedora down to block the sun, better enabling him to ogle passing females. He played his usual game, giving himself ten seconds to pick the woman he would most like to fondle, then upgrading as the trip progressed towards his flat off the Avenue Joffre in the heart of the French Concession.

The rickshaw driver jogged down Thibet Road alongside the racetrack, alongside soccer, cricket and lawn bowling pitches, as well as tennis courts and a baseball diamond where he and Flood sometimes played with the US Marines. Swan thought how satisfying it was to work in the International Settlement but live in the more relaxed and sophisticated French Quarter with its continental architecture, lush gardens and Indochinese policemen.

Swan's apartment occupied the first two floors of a three-storey house on a dead-end alley overlooking the gardens and childhood home of the famous Soong sisters. Soong Ching-Ling was the widow of the saintly Sun Yat-sen, the first president of the Chinese Republic, while Soong May-ling was the wife the current ruler, Generalissimo Chiang Kai-shek. The third sister, Soong Ai-ling, was married to H.H. Kung, reputedly a direct descendent of Confucius and one of the richest men in China, if not the world.

Swan's housemate, Luther Flood, was drinking coffee in the kitchen.

'How're things at the paper?' he asked, figuring it was easier getting his news straight from Swan than buying a paper.

'Well,' said Swan, sitting down and stretching out his legs. 'Here's a good one. It seems that pack of swells that go horseback riding in the countryside went through a Chinese cemetery last weekend. Their hounds, which they don't need as it's a paper chase—but I guess gives the thing a proper tone—laid into some graves and started digging up bones.'

'Yeck,' said Flood, sipping his coffee. 'Cause a ruckus?'

'Sure did. Letters piled into the office this week, hand delivered of course.' He affected a British accent. 'I say, why don't the Chinese put *fences* around their beastly graves? What diseases might our dogs be *catching* from these beastly bones?'

Flood's father, the Reverend Augustus Flood, had procured for them ill-paid jobs with a YMCA mission to China, in the scant hope that doing the Lord's work would somehow keep his son on the straight and narrow, a move the reverend would come to regret.

Once in Shanghai and enticed by the opportunities the city offered, Swan and Flood had promptly quit their jobs teaching salesmanship at the YMCA. Swan landed a job with the *Daily News* while Flood became a representative of the Kool-Flo Air-Conditioning company. Flood was currently in semi-retirement, having sold enough air-conditioners with guaranteed service to make a tidy sum of Shanghai dollars. Unfortunately his makeshift Chinese crew hadn't a clue of how to fix the unwieldy beasts once they inevitably broke down, resulting in Flood's strategic exit from the world of business.

Swan, on the other hand, liked his job at the *North China Daily News*. It appealed to his sense of romance and paid three hundred and sixty Shanghai dollars per month, not a bad wage considering that rent was a mere sixty dollars. He helped edit overseas news bulletins, wrote court stories, advertising copy and sports reports. Swan was considering bolstering his income by doing more freelance work. Publications back home were becoming increasingly eager for news about China and paid quite well.

'How's the world of business look?' asked Swan, hoping Flood would pick up the burden of conversation until he went for his afternoon nap. 'Things should be dying down with your old customers by now.'

'Well, I plan to keep my options open,' replied Flood expansively. 'I'm thinking about joining the volunteers, there's a big ball coming up and…'

'The army? That's fine if Shanghai gets attacked by an army of groundhogs and they need a groundhog shooter.' Flood prided himself as a crack shot.

'Oh the volunteers are just part-time anyway, it's the people you meet and you need to meet people to get on with business. I'm thinking about all of China out there—there's parts of this country just ripe for the picking."

'The only things that would get picked are your bones with all the bandits, warlords, communists and Lord knows what else out there,' Swan said drolly.

'Well, signing up with the volunteers would show I've got the right spirit; I could meet some people and get a few business prospects lined up, test the waters—maybe find some big company looking for a man here in the Orient.'

Their cook, a round-faced young Chinese girl named Chen, entered the room with eggs, toast and coffee then bowed and returned to her lair off the kitchen. Flood eyed her retreating form speculatively. 'Maybe I should set up a little nightclub, hire a band, cater to the needs of visiting sailors…'

'I believe it's been tried,' replied Swan, yawning. 'I'm off for a bit of a nap. I've got to help Hoste with the news tonight. Could you ask Chen to wake me up around eight?'

Flood, munching toast and returning to an old copy of *Fortune* magazine, nodded absently.

Swan moved towards the stairs, removing his tie as he went. 'Given any thought about going to that wedding next weekend in Mokanshan?'

'Hmmph," grunted Flood. 'Big trip like that for a bunch of bible thumpers? Fat chance. I'll hold down the fort here, look after the place while you're gone.'

'I was afraid you might,' replied Swan.

Swan's bedroom was the finest room in the house, featuring a fireplace and arched windows overlooking a small walled garden. He even had a gardener, an old man who seemed to exist on fresh air and scraps from the kitchen. Swan, a bird lover, had asked the man to build a bird feeder but unfortunately the gardener netted whatever birds were attracted. Swan had ordered that the back garden be off limits to hunting but still had his suspicions.

Kicking off his shoes and removing his trousers, braces, shirt and socks he collapsed heavily onto his bed. Gazing idly at the ceiling he wondered how long Flood would be staying with him as he wasn't showing any evidence that he was looking for his own place. Still, it was Flood who had got them to China in the first place and it wasn't too bad having company either, someone to shoot the breeze with about baseball, girls and other topics of importance. Maybe he'd even offer to help pay the rent one day.

The flat was a fairly big one, and if it wasn't Flood then it would probably be some other homeless body in the spare bedroom. Lord knows he and Flood had certainly overstayed their welcome with other Americans after arriving in Shanghai the previous summer.

Swan thought back to their trip to China aboard the *SS Hoover*. They had sailed from San Francisco with a load of YMCA workers overjoyed by the prospect of spreading the word of God to millions of heathen Chinese. The bible stuff hadn't lasted long for Swan and Flood though, given the choice they'd had of attending prayer meetings or playing cards in the ship's hold.

Still, some of their fellow passengers had been nice enough, despite their high moral tone. The upcoming wedding in Mokanshan, a mountain town about two hundred miles away, involved two people who had sailed with them, Bert Porter and Dot Wattie, two earnest young Southerners.

He had arranged with his managing editor to take a few days off and write some articles while he was up in Mokanshan, perhaps an update on how the resort had grown since Generalissimo Chiang Kai-shek, then briefly retired from politics, had built himself a mountaintop eyrie there some ten years earlier. As he drifted off to sleep he hoped that Mokanshan, at an elevation of some 2,500 feet, would be considerably cooler than Shanghai.

A soft tap on his door woke him at eight. After showering and dressing he descended to the kitchen where he found a note from Flood saying he would drop by the newspaper later on. Chen handed him a package of sandwiches and pointed to the door, indicating that a rickshaw was waiting for him.

Though the streets were now dark, Swan was soon dripping with sweat. Reaching the office he found the night editor, Dickson Hoste, a former British army officer, sorting news cables from *Reuters*, the *Associated Press*, the *International News Service*, as well as the French *Havas*, German *Transocean* and the Italian *Stefani* services. The local agencies received the news by radio then typed out duplicate stencils for Shanghai's newspapers.

'This Berlin Olympic stuff is good,' said Hoste without looking up. 'The British team is the biggest ever…not that that means anything…the fighting in Spain is heating up…catch whatever stuff there is about Asia for me to look at…look for good things to say about the Japs…actually anything that's not overly critical of them.'

Swan accepted a sheaf of cables and sat down, wiping the sweat from his eyes.

'What about the local war stuff?'

'Look for whoever is slaughtering the communists; highlight the yellow peril....

'Aren't they all yellow......

'The Japs and the nationalists certainly aren't—not at this paper anyway.'

Swan began reading. The German press agency, *Transocean*, had an item about a high-ranking German minister helping fight a fire in Berlin.

'An unexpected thrill,' he read, 'was provided when General Goering himself arrived on the scene and helped the fire-fighters. The firemen were assisted by the Blackshirts, Brownshirts and police and as a result of their combined efforts, the conflagration was subdued.'

Swan set this one aside, followed by another report that Tokyo had been awarded the 1940 Olympic Games. That can't offend anyone, he thought, pausing to check what movies were showing on Sunday night, the big night for cinema in Shanghai. An advertisement for *'White Eagle'*, starring Buck Jones, pictured a mean looking and heavily preoccupied Indian muscleman in a war bonnet throttling what appeared to be a small bear. On closer inspection the bear proved to be a large cat of some kind. That looked all right.

Another, *'The Pride of the Marines'*, featuring Charles Bickford, pictured a wasp-waisted hero, complete with a black eye, dancing with a young, equally wasp-waisted woman while a series of smaller drawings had him either drinking with his pals or happily punching out a host of bad guys in bars. Bickford looked nothing whatsoever like the marines of Swan's acquaintance, although the drinking, dancing and brawling were certainly accurate.

Swan picked up a cable from the French agency *Havas*. Runners were relaying the Olympic torch across Europe from Athens to Berlin. The Czech portion of the journey had featured a massive anti-fascist demonstration in Prague while soon after Vienna had erupted in an equally massive pro-Nazi demonstration. Swan thought how much he would love to visit Europe one day.

A Charlie Chan movie, though it didn't say which one, was showing at the Circus Theatre. Charlie Chan was immensely popular in Shanghai amongst the foreigners, much to the bewilderment of Swan who found him completely unlike any Chinese he'd ever met.

He returned to work. The defection of 149 aviators, some with airplanes, from the Kwantung Army to the Generalissimo was obvious front page material, as was the capture and execution of 62 bandits by Shantung troops on the border of Kiangsu Province, not far from Shanghai as the crow flies.

A press release from *Asahi*, the Japanese press agency, quoted a Japanese general saying the best way to save China from Bolshevism was collaboration between the British and Japanese. Swan added this story to a pile for Hoste. The owners of the *North China Daily News*, the Morriss family, had the attitude that the Japanese were the only foreigners actually doing anything to prevent the communists from taking over Shanghai, even if the Reds were now seemed something of a spent force anyway.

The American community in China was divided over the simmering Sino-Japanese conflict, with some, generally businessmen, approving of Japan's willingness to take on the communists. Their main argument was that the Japanese around Peking and Manchuria—or Manchoukuo as they now called it—represented a buffer against the Russian Bolsheviks. The Japanese show of strength in Shanghai, they argued, protected foreign investment. But most Americans, particularly the powerful religious community, were fervently opposed to Japanese aggression in China.

The Japanese were actually quite comical little fellows, thought Swan, while the Communists were little more than pajama-clad bandits. The Nationalists under the Generalissimo were often described in the American press as the Chinese equivalent to America's founding fathers, particularly since Chiang Kai-shek had converted to Christianity.

A story from Hong Kong announced that the first typhoon of the season was approaching Southern China from the direction of the Philippines. This, and another story concerning an outbreak of Bubonic plague in Tsingkiangpu, two hundred miles north of Shanghai, Swan decided to take to Hoste immediately.

Hoste, who had been talking on the telephone, looked up at Swan.

'Dear God,' he said sombrely. 'I've just been talking with Davis. The newspapers in the States have run this,' he indicated a telegram. 'It seems the King intends to marry a twice-divorced American woman by the name of…' He paused to read the telegram. 'Err…Wallis Simpson. This is embargoed in England and most of the Empire but it's front-page news in your country. Davis is trying to learn if the blackout applies to us—he thinks it does but is trying to get the official word from the consulate.'

Davis was the managing editor. The telephone rang again and Hoste picked it up before the second ring, listened then returned the instrument to its cradle.

'Davis received word that we can't do anything about it without all kinds of trouble raining down on us from the British Legation. The biggest story in years. What have you got?'

'Olympic stuff, demonstrations for and against the Nazis; locally we've got captured-then-executed-bandits and 150 airmen defecting from the Kwantung army over to Chiang Kai-shek and these—a typhoon heading towards Hong Kong and an outbreak of bubonic plague 200 miles north. Can the King marry her?'

'A typhoon *and a* plague?' said Hoste with some exasperation. 'Well, he could but he'd probably stop being King. I think he'd have to abdicate—hell of a mess I'd imagine. Figures it would be an American woman who'd wobble the throne.'

'Don't the people in England know what's going on?'

'I'm sure it's fairly widespread in some circles,' said Hoste, with a touch of asperity.

Witherspoon and Ralph Shaw, both Englishmen, arrived at the newsroom together. Being British subjects they were asked their opinion of the latest news from America.

'He's the most popular king in centuries,' said Shaw numbly. 'He's a modern royal; the people love him—it would be mad to force him to abdicate. Who'd replace him? His brother can't string a sentence together…'

'He's not just the King; he's also head of the church,' interjected Witherspoon. 'And he's not Henry the Eighth. It would be madness to allow him to marry this divorcee…this American,' he added, looking at Swan as if he were responsible for introducing the wildly mismatched couple.

'Calm down,' said Hoste tiredly. 'The fact she's American is hardly Swan's fault—I imagine the King's old enough to know what he's doing…we're not running the story anyway so let's get to work.'

Witherspoon and Shaw went off to inspect the galleys, paying special care to the typesetting of the local news. A couple of weeks earlier all hell had broken loose when a story reporting the arrival of a prominent American religious figure from Salt Lake City had as a headline: *Prominent Moron Visits City.*

Swan was chewing on one of Chen's mysterious sandwich variations and looking for typos and other irregularities when Flood arrived. He helped himself to a sandwich and a magazine, knowing better than to interrupt the night's work. The less of an intrusion he made, the sooner they'd be out enjoying the town.

Just before one a.m. Hoste announced that he was satisfied and the tension in the room drained away. Flood stood looking at the main cartoon for the next day's paper. It depicted a Japanese airplane dive-bombing a pack of wolves with the caption: 'Hunting Communists in Manchoukuo'.

The cartoonist, Sapojnikoff, or Sapajou as he was widely known, had been offered positions with newspapers around the world but had chosen to remain in Shanghai at the *Daily News*, an undoubted coup as his drawings were easily the most popular feature of the paper. A former cavalry officer with the Imperial Russian Army, Sapajou's lofty position in Shanghai society was evidenced by the fact he was the only White Russian member of the ultra exclusive Shanghai Club, home of the world's longest bar.

His only strong passion was a fierce hatred of communists, a trait shared with virtually all of the White Russians in the city. At the *Daily News*, of course, this sentiment was not only tolerated but actively encouraged.

Shaw, an oversexed former British army clerk, asked what their plans for the rest of the evening were. Shaw was an invaluable guide to Shanghai's fleshpots but his obsession with having sex and worse, talking about it, never failed to make any undertaking, even visiting a restaurant, seem slightly seedy.

'Grab some drinks at the New Ritz,' said Swan. 'Maybe drop by the French Club for a late dinner, do some dancing. Come along if you want.'

Chapter 2

Patrick Givens, a large, former rugby-playing Irishman of long service to the Shanghai Municipal Police, was now superintendent of the force's political branch. He was also developing an ulcer trying to cope with the demands of his job.

Bolshevik mischief makers operating out of the Soviet Embassy; communists plotting the overthrow of the Nanking government; wild Russian royalists; Korean nationalists throwing bombs at Japanese generals; the Japanese, in turn, ferociously warring with China and tightening their grip on Shanghai; German and Italian fascists up to no good; Chiang Kai-shek the blood brother of Shanghai's most powerful gangster and a longstanding partner with him in the enormous opium trade. A Opium Suppression Bureau that was pushing heroin. And now this.

The Wallis Simpson who was trying to become Mrs. King of England had a thin but interesting file in the records of the Shanghai Municipal Police. Given's counterparts in England had enlisted his help in digging up additional information on Mrs. Simpson, a one-time resident of the city's International Settlement.

Known then as Mrs. Winfield Spencer, wife of an American naval officer serving with the US Asiatic fleet, Simpson had wiled away her time at the Cathay Hotel on the Bund back in the mid-twenties by painting her nails, learning about silk, smoking opium, peddling heroin, posing naked for a photographer specialising in smutty postcards and learning the myriad tricks of the trade at a high-class brothel.

Poor Edward didn't stand a chance once she had him in her clutches, Givens thought, musing over her exotic resume. It wasn't clear why the British Secret Service wanted him to gather all the information he could on Simpson, particularly the negatives of the dirty postcards.

Would they use the information to try to scare Edward off? Blackmail her into renouncing him? Were they simply trying to protect their King as loyal servants of the Crown or were there other forces at work?

Givens had just heard from the British consul that Emily Hahn, a somewhat wilful reporter who worked occasionally at the *North China Daily News* and as a stringer for the *New Yorker* magazine, was also hot on the trail of the Simpson negatives.

Taking a slug from the large container of buttermilk he kept on hand, Givens briefly pined for the happy days when he had rattled around town in bullet proof armour, trading shots with Chinese bandits and kidnappers. Life had been so simple then. Gunfights, rugby, then beer with the lads.

Although he hadn't met Simpson during her stint in Shanghai, Givens had crossed paths with Hahn on a number of occasions. He figured she was probably cut from the same cloth as Mrs. Simpson. Women who used all the weapons in their arsenal to get what they wanted.

Hahn was also reported to be tight with Soong May-ling, wife of the Generalissimo and one of the world's most famous women.

He'd rue the day he tried locking horns with that bunch, thought Givens, particularly since the entire clan had as a godfather none other than shadowy Tu Yue Sheng, nicknamed Big Ears Tu, head of Shanghai's notorious Green Gang and possibly the most powerful man in China.

Hahn had enchanted men ranging from Sir Victor Sassoon, the city's richest and most eligible bachelor, to a rich Chinese poet by the name of Zhou Sinmay.

The latest rumour had Hahn living with him as his concubine and devotedly preparing his opium pipes. Was opium was the key to locking up Hahn's ambitions?

She had burst upon the city the previous year with a pet gibbon ape named Mr. Mills on her shoulder and almost immediately,had Shanghai in her thrall. The prospect of dealing with a threesome made up of Hahn, Mrs. Simpson and Madame Chiang Kai-shek made him reach again for the soothing buttermilk.

Could the government of Chiang Kai-shek profit from information that was damaging to the British Royal family? Under the influence of the American-educated Madame Chiang Kai-shek the Chinese government was assiduously wooing American policy makers, angling for more financial assistance, as well as increased military support to bolster their efforts against the evil communists and perhaps soon the Imperial Japanese Army as well.

The British government was far more concerned with problems within their Empire than with the chaos in China and were traditionally allied with the Japanese anyway. Could Chiang Kai-shek use the negatives to influence British policy or gain British support? Perhaps drive a wedge between the British and the Japanese?

Doubtful, thought Givens, but then Chiang Kai-shek was capable of doing almost anything to stay in power. His hugely expensive military campaigns against the communists had drained the treasury dry. To pay for them, he and his financial geniuses, brothers-in-law T.V. Soong and H.H. Kung, had been forcing Chinese banks to buy their valueless government bonds for hard cash. When this ploy failed they simply took over some of the banks.

In addition, they had a lock on the lucrative opium trade and were now wooing American criminals on the West Coast of the United States with hopes of selling them high-grade heroin. A similar deal had already been established in Marseilles through contacts in Shanghai's other foreign settlement, the French Concession.

To the world the dapper little Chinese leader with the funny shaped head was a heroic figure, dashing hither and yon, forever proclaiming one thing then doing precisely the opposite. In reality, Chiang Kai-shek was a whiny-voiced, vengeance-loving little criminal who was, along with his gangster cronies, sucking the lifeblood out of China. Years before Givens had foolishly arranged for Chiang to be given a pass from the municipal government allowing him to wander at will throughout the International concession with an armed guard. Since then he had been a frequent visitor to the settlement.

The government's much-vaunted Opium Suppression Bureau, established to impress American missionaries and other do-gooders, was headed by the shadowy Big Ears Tu. The bureau had been urging addicts to give up opium by taking up heroin, a much more expensive and powerful drug. Like trying to give up beer by drinking absinthe, thought Givens.

The bureau, amazingly, also made it a crime punishable by death for addicts to smoke opium unless it had been bought from the bureau. The most comical effort to get the Yanks on side had been the 'New Life Movement', inspired somewhat by the American New Deal. Its main thrust had been through the efforts of thousands of local Boy Scouts who'd been encouraged to publicly accost spitters, smokers and drinkers, as if they were the main evils besetting China.

Their big brothers, the secretive 'Blue Shirts', took this one step further, ganging up on so-called 'degenerates' and beating the bejesus out of them.

Chiang Kai-shek had even become a Methodist, as had old Big Ears. There's a Methodist to their madness, thought Givens ruefully. The Americans were of course lapping it all up, comparing Chiang to George Washington and all the rest. But would a true Chinese patriot allow the Japanese free rein to rip and tear their way through the country, annihilating fellow Chinese, even if they were communists? Givens had devoted years of his life to fighting communists but for the life of him couldn't understand why Chiang didn't focus on the real threat to China: the Japanese.

Perhaps because he had made a deal with the Japanese that would better enable him to feather his own his nest and that of his wife's family, he thought, turning to Hahn's file.

A graduate with a degree in mining from the University of Wisconsin? Wild West trail guide? Congo explorer? Author of a book on seduction? A stint at Oxford? Givens read on, growing steadily more impressed. Occasional visitors at her flat included none other than Mao Tse-tung and his sidekick Chou En-lai. This was not the usual type of person employed at the *North China Daily News*, he decided, although he'd heard she didn't work there much anymore.

He retracted his earlier thoughts about her being cut from the same cloth as Simpson. That one had simply caught the eye of a king. Hahn, who also attracted her fair share of men, was a force to be reckoned with.

Still, the International Settlement was run jointly by the British and the Americans, and Givens was not without some strings of his own to pull. The head of the Shanghai Municipal Council, fat old Stuart Fessenden, was a Yank. Perhaps he could be approached for some help.

In the meantime, how could he go about laying his hands on the negatives? Trust the British to turn to an Irishman for help in a mix-up involving the bloody King of England, he thought bitterly, reaching for the buttermilk.

Chapter 3

'Fancy a silver taxi?' asked Shaw. The Silver Taxi Company, in cahoots with the Green Gang, provided four-wheeled brothels.

'You go ahead Ralph. I think we'll just take rickshaws,' replied Swan.

'All right then.'

The trio piled into separate rickshaws and gave directions for Blood Alley. As usually happened when the night got off to a late start, the trip turned into a race with the winning rickshaw puller getting double his normal fare and his passenger riding for free. Shaw, the lightest of the three, got there first.

Officially known as Rue Chu Pao-san, the French Settlement's Blood Alley was the source of Shanghai's global reputation for licentiousness. Situated on a street in which, ironically, most of the buildings were owned by the Catholic church, the area was immensely popular with sailors, soldiers and slumming local Shanghailanders. On the road outside the bars was the usual little army of ragged children, begging for money, offering dope for sale and darting after used cigarettes.

Jazz music from half a dozen bars spilled onto the dimly lit street as they arrived at the New Ritz, owned and operated by 'Yen' Yenalevicz, a former U.S. marine with a shaved head and massive physique. His bar was a favourite hangout for American servicemen, the highest-paid soldiers and sailors in Shanghai. While this made them popular with the girls it also created problems with the poorer British Tommies, French Poilus and Italian Savoia Grenadiers. Fights were common although most barmen were expert at quickly moving them on to the streets where the military police could take over. Most patrons were highly mindful of Yen, whose immediate response was to come down hard with a large wooden club he kept handy.

'What will it be fellas, three whiskies?' he asked, shifting his bulk behind the counter. He began pouring without waiting for an answer, whiskey being the drink of the house.

Heavily made-up girls of half a dozen nationalities, in various stages of dress and hopefulness, sat around the walls facing the dance floor. Shaw had no sooner sat down before bouncing off in the direction of the dance floor as though he had springs in his heels.

Offering his hand to a young Chinese girl, Shaw was soon swooping his way around the dance floor, grinding his partner tightly. In some Blood Alley bars, girls were paid commissions on the number of drinks they encouraged men to buy. In other cabarets, dances were arranged on the four-dances-for-a-dollar ticket system, hence the name 'taxi-dancers'. Yen preferred to sell tickets, figuring his customers needed little encouragement to buy drinks.

Shaw's dance partner delicately raised her forefinger, signifying to the other Chinese girls that she was being prodded by an erection. The gesture made the Chinese girls laugh discreetly into their hands while Swan and Flood exchanged amused looks.

'Shaw looks like he's been welded to that girl,' said Flood, sipping his whiskey and watching the dancers.

'Englishmen,' snorted Swan, who went on to relate the story of the King and Wallis Simpson and how solemnly his fellow newshounds had reacted to the news.

'He can have pretty much whatever woman in the world he wants, or as many of them as he likes,' pondered Flood, nodding at a swirling Shaw. 'So he must love her more than he does the whole Empire and everything. I guess he just wants to settle down and take it easy—I'd imagine he's pretty tired of being the King.'

'Hey,' he continued. 'I've been thinking about maybe coming up to Mokanshan with you next weekend after all, though I'll probably skip the wedding—there's a business idea that I got from a magazine in your office tonight about a guy up there who likes to fish.'

Swan waited patiently for his friend to begin making sense, signalling for another round of drinks.

'There's an old British guy, retired from the army or something and he's been trying to teach some locals how to make split bamboo fly rods. Mokanshan's got the finest bamboo in China on account of the soil and how the wind there gives the bamboo this natural flexibility—you know how important flex is to a fly rod?'

Swan and Flood had become friends a couple of years before when both were briefly enrolled at the University of Michigan. They had much preferred hunting and fishing to the academic life and no one was unduly upset when they'd flunked out, their families finding it hard to come up with money for their schooling anyway. Having at least attended a university was good enough, particularly when the Reverend Flood had arranged jobs for them with the YMCA in China.

Having endured an endless litany of zany business prospects from Flood, ranging from gold mining to opium smuggling, and hopeful that he might join him in Mokanshan, Swan encouraged him to continue.

'Well I think I know something about fly fishing and I'd like to get out of the city for a while, get some fresh air, maybe do some hiking or fishing if we could get a hold of a couple of those rods…'

Swan was warming to Flood's salesmanship. 'I could try to see if I can get a couple more days of holiday. I'll ask on Monday…maybe write something about this old guy…where did you find this article?'

'Some magazine in your office—here it is.'

Swan tilted a crumpled page to the weak overhead light then examined a blurry photograph of a tweed-clad man by the name of Brigadier Western, solemnly tying a fly. Swan squinted and read the caption out loud:

'Brigadier Hugh Western (ret'd) is encouraging the manufacture of split bamboo fishing rods at his home in Mokanshan, south-east of Shanghai. Brig. Western is hoping to create a new business venture in the mountain resort. Said the Brigadier: 'The local bamboo here is much more whip-like than any I've ever come across, in China or anywhere else in Asia. A combination of good wet soil plus the steady effect of the wind off the plain nearby produces a most satisfying form of the grass. Once split into thin strips, tapered and glued, it has produced a splendid rod.'

'Splendid rod. Absolutely,' A flushed Shaw had finished dancing. 'If you chaps will excuse me I believe I'll slip upstairs. Won't be a jiff. Don't wait for me though, ha ha.' He was gone.

'Well, that takes care of him for a while,' said Flood absently, eyeing a tall Eurasian girl with long brown hair who had just arrived at the club. Catching a closer look, he hurriedly excused himself and shot off in her direction.

Swan sat back and let his thoughts flow loose, enjoying the music of the Harry Fischer Trio. Fischer was an Austrian refugee and a superb violinist. Swan felt himself mentally slipping into the weekend, happily anticipating the pleasures that lay ahead.

'Did you know that the King of England has a girlfriend who used to live in Shanghai?', said Yen, wiping the bar in front of him.

Swan snapped out of his reverie, realising as he did so that all the secret telegrams and hush-hush phone calls to and from the consulate were miles behind Yen's more effective means of gathering information, that is, simply standing behind the bar and keeping his ears open.

'What?'

'Yeah, sure. Some of our navy guys, officers, were in here this week and they were talking about it,' said Len, filling glasses. 'She was married to a Navy guy before she was married to some other guy that she was married to when she met the King. She lived here and......'

Len moved closer to Swan and continued, *sotto voce*.

'...she was a prostitute. The navy guys were laughing about it. About ten years ago somebody found out where she was working so a couple of guys went to this place to see if it was true. She didn't bat an eyelid when she saw them, they said.'

Swan digested this wild piece of news, already thinking that there could be big money in a story like this. There was no way it would run locally but maybe back in the States or Europe...

'These officers, Yen. How do you know they weren't pulling your leg?'

'Because they were ignoring me the whole time they were talking about it except when they ordered more drinks. I didn't hear all of what they were saying but I caught that much.

'What ship were they on?'

'The *U.S.S. Omaha*, the flagship, here for provisioning.'

Flood and his dance partner joined Swan at the bar and introductions were made. The girl was called Sally and was very good looking. Shaw, who had just returned from upstairs *sans* partner, was standing next to her, practically begging to be introduced.

'Miss Sally, Mr. Ralph,' Swan introduced them.

'Drinks everybody? Sally, what can I get you?

'Double brandy and Coca-Cola,' she replied demurely.

Drinks arrived and Shaw returned to the dance floor. The Englishman fancied himself both a lady's man *and* a dancer. Shaw was easy company simply because he so seldom stuck around to chat, preferring to prowl the dance floor or vanish upstairs.

'Where are you from Sally?' asked Swan.

'Shanghai. My father is from Russia and my mother is from Korea. But Bolsheviks are in Russia and Japanese in Korea. So I'm Shanghai person. You are American?'

Swan nodded.

'Sally teaches dancing,' said Flood smugly, taking a long swig before leading her back to the dance floor, winking as he left. 'She's giving me lessons.'

Swan made his way to the toilet, an evil smelling hole in the ground. Shanghai was a small town and news travelled fast, he thought. The information about the King and Simpson was in the papers back home so it was hardly surprising the news had reached Shanghai, considering the extent of modern communications, particularly those of the U.S. fleet.

But what to make of Simpson working as a prostitute? There was a great deal Swan didn't know about the British Royal family but he imagined they cavorted with duchesses and people like that. Not Shanghai prostitutes, anyway. His head swam, muddled a bit by the whiskey and the excitement of a good story. The rapidity of events made it obvious to him that he'd have to track down some officers from the *Omaha* to try to confirm this.

On his way back to the bar he spied a pretty woman, possibly Russian, momentarily adrift among swaying couples. He redirected himself in her direction and was soon dancing a Foxtrot.

Swan noticed a row of Chinese girls tittering and looked around for Shaw. Sure enough, his dance partner had her forefinger aloft. Shaw was once again oblivious to the sign language, a happy look on his face. Shaw wasn't a bad guy really, thought Swan, a good reporter and easy to work with, unlike some of the snootier Brits.

One of the things about dancing with a ticket girl was that conversation was strictly optional, giving a man time to think should he care to. Swan had arrived in Shanghai with two left feet but regular practice had turned him into a serviceable dancer. The feel of soft silk and the alluring whiff of perfume soon had him thinking of things apart from kings and ships.

Flood noticed Shaw heading back upstairs and marvelled at his voracious sexual appetite, thinking that sex for Shaw was the same as someone else smoking a cigarette or scratching a mosquito bite...Catching the eye of Swan, he tilted his head in the direction of the bar.

'What do you girls say to the French Club?' said Flood. Swan went off to pay for the drinks, dances and girls and to thank Yen for giving him the information about Mrs. Simpson. Tipping him generously, he asked him to keep his ears open for more good stuff.

The foursome piled into a taxi for the short trip across the French Concession. The second floor cabaret at the stately *Cercle Francais* was reached by a marble staircase and overlooked a large garden surrounded by tennis courts. The oval dance floor was matched in shape a high domed ceiling. The building had once been the German Club but had been commandeered by the French after the Great War. While perhaps not the most deluxe place in town—the Majestic and Cathay Hotels were the fanciest—it was stylish and comfortable and always had good food and music.

By the time they reached the club Swan had concluded that his date, Olga, wasn't much of a conversationalist. He wondered briefly if perhaps he might have been better off on his own. Attuned to the quixotic attentions of men, Olga rewarded him with a dazzling smile and a little squeeze of his arm in an attempt to recapture his interest.

Tables five rows deep ran around the dance floor. Adjusting his eyes to the dim light, Swan made out a large group of American naval officers surrounding a single female. With hopes for some background on Simpson, he approached their table only to find the female was none other than his sometime colleague, Emily Hahn. He was glad his date was good looking.

'Evening boys,' drawled Hahn, a drink in hand and a small cigar in the other, her pet gibbon eyeing them malevolently from her shoulder. 'Grab some chairs and let me introduce you to the pride of our Asiatic fleet.'

As the sailors got to their feet, Swan wondered just what it was about Hahn that had enabled her to cast a spell over half the men in town.

Her brown bobbed hair framed an attractive face set with big dark eyes and a strong mouth that softened when she smiled which admittedly was often. She said outrageous things but always tempered with humour. Despite her mannish suit she was feminine and sexy. But it was her husky voice and sense of humour that stuck most in his mind.

Swan realised that her gibbon, Mr. Mills, had disappeared and quickly checked around his legs to make sure the animal wasn't anywhere near. An outraged cry from a young officer indicated that Mr. Mills had chosen to urinate elsewhere. Although obviously tempted to kick the beast, the young officer restrained himself, much to the amusement of his colleagues.

'Naughty Mr. Mills,' admonished Hahn sternly, bestowing upon the victim a sympathetic smile as he attempted to clean his shoes.

'Quite all right,' he replied, getting up to visit the toilet. All of the other sailors were now carefully keeping at least one eye on their white shoes.

'These gentlemen were just telling me the latest gossip about the King and Wallis Simpson *nee* Spencer,' said Hahn archly, turning back to the officers. 'Mr. Swan here is also a journalist. He mainly concentrates on dog shows and who gets on and off the passenger ships.'

Against his better judgement, Swan found himself revealing all of the information he had picked up from Yen earlier, including the business about the brothels that was quickly confirmed by one of the officers. Sally and Olga were chatting together, largely oblivious to the main conversation.

'We in the navy think she has taken a downward path ever since she dumped poor old Win Spencer,' one of the officers chipped in heartily.

Hahn looked at him blankly then turned to Swan. 'Perhaps we could work together on this?'

'Sure,' he replied eagerly. Hahn was a real journalist, a foreign correspondent, and a writer of books. Flood and Sally had hit the dance floor and Olga was off powdering her nose. He felt Hahn's hand on his thigh and a jolt of something very much like electricity shot to his brain.

'Do you mean write something together? To his alarm, his voice hit a high note on the *together*.

Hahn smiled warmly, the opium she had smoked half an hour before coursing through her bloodstream, making her mind alive to mischief.

'Well, not exactly,' she said. 'I need help finding some negatives. The negatives are of Mrs. Simpson posing in the nude. Find them and I'll buy you a new car.'

A car! Swan could barely hide his excitement. He'd get Flood to help him on this.

'But how do I know what she looks like,' he asked.

'Don't worry—I'll get you some photographs,' she whispered.

One of the naval officers interrupted their chat, asking Swan whether he could dance with his date. Swan said he didn't mind. He glanced over and saw that Olga obviously didn't mind either, although she flashed him a quick look of spite.

'Don't want to get those Russian girls mad,' said Hahn, breaking the spell. 'You're liable to get a knife in the ribs.'

He looked on as the couple went to the dance floor where he saw Swan clowning and waving at him from the crowd. When he turned back to Hahn, she and her gibbon had left the cabaret.

Chapter 4

Big Ears Tu was angry, accustomed as he was to issuing orders and having them instantly obeyed. His lieutenant and one-time mentor, Pockmarked Huang, stood before him with his eyes to the ground. Huang, Chief of Detectives in the French Concession, had come up empty-handed.

His henchmen had marched into all the racier commercial photography shops in Shanghai and told the shopkeepers they were under arrest for distributing pornography. This was a little brazen, even for the Green Gang, as it was their boss who profited most from that particular industry, having forced the photography shops to pay him protection money.

Huang's men confiscated all the dirty negatives they had found—a huge amount—and taken the owner of the last shop, a terrified Frenchman, into custody so that he could comb through them to find the ones that matched the Simpson photos. He had come up with nothing.

Like Fu Manchu, Sax Rohmer's fictional Lord of the Chinese underworld, Big Ears Tu was tall and gaunt, much of his flesh having wasted away after years of opium use. Apart from his oversized ears, his eyes were his most prominent feature. With pinpoints for pupils, they were frightening even in repose and more so when he was angry. He could summon infinite malice in a second. Tu was no longer an opium user, having cured his addiction by the copious but strictly medicinal use of heroin tablets, produced at his drug factory in Pootung, just across the river from the Bund.

With Chiang Kai-shek's blessing, Big Ears was the titular head of the sanctified Opium Suppression Bureau, the largest and best run department within the Nationalist government. The Green Gang supplied all the opium for the government agency's regulated opium distribution centres. The Gissimo himself had pushed the notion that the only way to battle the opium menace was to regulate its distribution, hence the government-run shops. It was only human nature that someone should make money from opium.

Pure grade heroin was being successfully used to cure opium addiction, a method first introduced by American missionaries during the previous century. The supply of morphine and heroin mostly came from Pootung, a sleepy village across the Whangpoo River from Shanghai, where the year before Big Ears had built a large and well-equipped laboratory, disguised as a temple in honour of his ancestors.

The building had been officially blessed by the Gissimo, who had presented Big Ears with a huge personally inscribed scroll extolling his virtues as a philanthropist and civic leader. Pootung was Big Ear's native village and the shrine was by far the largest of its type built in the area for many years. The moment the guests all departed the temple had been turned into a drug factory, albeit a picturesque one.

While Chiang Kai-shek vociferously blamed the Japanese for subverting China by smothering it in cheap opium and heroin, it was actually he and the Green Gang who were the biggest suppliers of illicit drugs in the country. Having made the product cheap enough for even the poorest coolie to afford, they were now turning their energies to selling the drugs abroad. When the French protested that their concession had become the headquarters for the trade and threatened to shut him down, Big Ears invited a leading French official over for dinner and poisoned him. With his death the French authorities had overnight decided not to bother Big Ears in the future.

Chiang Kai-shek was known worldwide as the President of the Chinese Republic but few people knew that it was to Tu's tune the Generalissimo really danced. When Chiang married Soong May-ling in 1927, she had persuaded her husband that since he was the leader of China it was beneath his dignity to pay protection money to Big Ears. After all, she pointed out, hadn't he been to the wedding and weren't they neighbours up in the mountain community of Mokanshan?

A couple of days later Madame Chiang disappeared, having jumped into a nice large black car purportedly sent for her by her husband. Panic had promptly ensued at the Chiang's presidential household in the capital of Nanking. Communists! Bandits! Japanese!

Within an hour, Big Ears had called the Gissimo to tell him his precious wife was safe and sound. He would return her home, he had assured him, once certain business matters had been taken care of. Chiang had promptly made arrangements for protection money to be paid again and his wife had been delivered home safely. The kidnapping hadn't resulted in any bad blood between Big Ears and the Chiang household and the Madame had even persuaded Tu to convert to Christianity soon afterwards. Her spiritual advisor, the American Reverend Bradford Armstrong, had personally taken charge of the conversion himself.

Tu was perhaps the most strangely attired Methodist in the world. His Chinese fortune-teller had predicted he would live a long and prosperous life provided he always wore a traditional long Chinese gown with dried monkey heads attached to the hems. His English tailor, John Jarrod, formerly of Savile Row, had made special trips to Singapore to personally collect the heads.

Big Ears kept Huang waiting, despite the fact that Huang ranked second only to him in the Green Gang hierarchy. Big Ears had forever proven who was boss of Shanghai back in 1927 when the Generalissimo had marched north with his army from Canton in the south, causing the foreign powers to mobilise their little army to protect Shanghai. At that time the communists were allied with Chiang's *Kuomintang* movement and, thinking Chiang meant to expel the foreigners, had paralysed Shanghai with a series of massive strikes.

The communists had been prepared to try to take Shanghai when Big Ears and his underworld army, after lowering the communist guard, slaughtered upwards of five thousand of them and sent countless numbers of their women to work as slaves in brothels. Shanghai went back to normal with the foreigners beside themselves with gratitude for good old Big Ears. Tu was duly honoured by Chiang Kai-shek who had bestowed upon him the Order of the Brilliant Jade, as well as the Order of the Celestial Flag and Sacred Tripod.

Big Ears beckoned Huang to look at him directly.

'These photographs are very important to little brother,' he said softly to Pockmarked Huang, referring to the Generalissimo, called 'little brother' because he weighed in at an elfin-like hundred and ten pounds. Chiang Kai-shek was definitely a member of the lightweight class among warlords, many of who were huge men.

'With these he can exert pressure on the British and cause them to lose great face in China,' he continued sinuously. 'I do not understand how this could be so but this is what little brother and his wife say and they understand better than I the ways of the foreigners. And because Shanghai is my city I too will lose face if we don't find them. Tell your men to continue their search and to use more forceful methods to find these things.'

'Is there anything you wish to say, Pockmarked Huang?' he continued softly.

It was the middle of the night and Pockmarked Huang was tired. Big Ears had started a rumour about himself that he never slept and liked to call meetings at irregular hours to prove the point. Huang knew it was the heroin that kept him awake and feared that it was also the heroin that was dictating the strange demands that were now being made of him.

Visiting Big Ear's walled compound in the French Quarter was always unsettling. Tu had received permission from the authorities to mount machine guns above the walls of his little fortress and armed guards were everywhere.

'Only this,' said Pockmarked Huang carefully. 'The negatives may be lost or destroyed. Many foreigners leave Shanghai and the pictures may have gone with them. Perhaps the foreign police have them.'

'If the pictures are in Shanghai they must be found,' replied Big Ears. 'Little brother says the pictures are of a woman who will marry the King of England and that whoever holds the pictures will have power over this King. That is all you need to know.'

'Thank you and forgive me for doubting your wisdom.'

Big Ears motioned for him to go. He was tired and his old bones ached. Perhaps some medicine would ease his discomfort.

Chapter 5

Saturday in Shanghai had once again dawned hot and humid. Sally had slipped out from Flood's bedroom before dawn while Swan slepton alone, visions of large new cars filling his dreams.

Chen prepared an early breakfast and knocked on Swan's bedroom door. Swan and Flood were playing golf that morning, courtesy of a rich hotelier about whose establishment Swan had written a flattering article in the weekly *North China Herald*, the older sibling to the *Daily News.*

Two Chinese friends, Hiram Shue and Percy Chan, were making up the foursome and had offered to pick them up for an eight o' clock tee-off. Upon arriving in Shanghai, Flood and Swan had left no stone unturned when it came to meeting people. Although not exactly graduates of the University of Michigan, they had been welcomed with open arms by the predominately Chinese men who made up the local alumni association.

Apart from being reasonably good fellows, Shue and Chan were both from rich local families and Flood had decided to invite them along to see whether they could be of any assistance in restarting his business career.

Bleary-eyed and slightly truculent after a late night, Swan repeated what he had told Flood the night before about the importance of finding the Simpson negatives. Swan mumbled his willingness to begin looking for them around town.

'How many times have you ever played golf,' asked Flood, whose hero, Bing Crosby, had inspired in him visions of the good life to be had as a sportsman. To him, being able to brag about a handicap was synonymous with arriving in high society.

'Well, my mother's brother had an old set and we used to fool around on his farm sometimes until all the heads came off the clubs. I've never played at a real course. How about you?'

The depression back home had made golf about as accessible to Swan and Flood as wintering in Palm Springs or playing the stock market for fun.

'I caddied for some friends of my dad sometimes and they let me take the odd shot but I've never really played either.'

There was a tap on the door and Chen ushered in two young Chinese men, dressed in huge, baggy plus fours and chequered caps. Both were grinning hugely and working hard to appear as American as possible.

Soon the foursome were whizzing along Bubbling Well Road in a Packard driven by a uniformed White Russian chauffeur. In the front seat was another Russian, obviously another bodyguard. The golfers sat facing one another in the cavernous back seats, talking about the upcoming Olympics, golf and other sports. Although it wasn't discussed, there was a taboo in effect which prevented Swan and Flood from referring in any way to the fact that Shue and Chan were anything but a couple of red-blooded Americans. To have referred to them otherwise would have spoiled the fun they were obviously having, reliving their days as students in America.

'We've got a bit of a confession to make,' said Swan, smiling ruefully. 'We haven't played much golf before so you'll have to be patient with us. Are we dressed all right?

Shue and Chan said they would be happy to help the two Americans.

'We'll take some practice shots beforehand,' said Shue. 'I'll have a talk with the guys at the club and get them to set our tee time a bit later so we can warm up a little. You guys will do just fine.'

The big car rattled along the road, rural China coming up surprisingly quickly once the outskirts of the city were broached. Foreigners and wealthy Chinese lived along the main roads that emanated from the foreign settlements like spokes from a hub. The roads they lived on were unofficially considered to be a part of the foreign enclaves and rate-paying households enjoyed municipal services such as electricity and police protection.

The Japanese had also extended their reach, having built a huge military encampment north of their Hongkew settlement. They now had the largest non-Chinese population in Shanghai.

The Hongjao Golf Club had opened to cater to wealthy Chinese and others who were unwelcome at the private clubs. The Jewish hotelier who had invited them to play had been instrumental in arranging funding for the club. He too had been unable to enjoy a game of golf in Shanghai until now.

All of this was left unsaid but understood implicitly as the big car approached the gates to the club, causing a slight overabundance of *bonhomie*. Not for the first time, Swan wondered if he would be so welcoming if the situation were reversed and foreigners had staked claim to a piece of the United States, only begrudgingly letting in Americans as second-class citizens while they sucked the country dry.

But Americans wouldn't *let* anyone else do that he thought, repeating in his mind the puzzling arguments for and against a place like Shanghai. Oh well, he thought, I didn't invent Shanghai. I'm just here to have a good time.

The chauffeur unloaded the golf bags while Shue went off to reschedule the tee-off time and Swan sought out the management to borrow some clubs.

'You don't mind if the bodyguards come with us do you? Chan asked Flood. 'Our fathers get pretty nervous about kidnappers when we're out here in the country without protection.'

'No that's fine,' replied Swan. 'Just promise me they won't laugh at my efforts.'

'Oh, they would never do that,' said Chan seriously.

'Why do you have *two* bodyguards?'

'Well, one is mine and the other is Hiram's. Our dads figure that two is better than one because they can keep an eye on each other as well as us. It took some getting used to after we got back from the States but there's no getting around it. I've had two cousins kidnapped here—one never came back.'

'Are the guards usually Russians?'

'Not always but they're the only ones who aren't tied by their families to triad organisations. Plus they're pretty fearless guys and scare most people half to death just by looking at them.'

Flood thought how strange it was that some Chinese like Hiram and Percy seemed American but some whites, like the big Russians, were more like common Chinese in the scheme of things.

They regrouped at a makeshift practice area where golfers could warm up by firing balls into large nets a few yards away. The caddies, old Chinese men with large conical hats, stood ready with the golf bags. The bodyguards stood back from the group and looked slowly around, the position of their hands and the bulges under their jackets making it obvious they were both armed.

The caddies placed balls on tees then stepped back. Shue and Chen wiggled and waggled before hitting almost professional looking shots. Both were obviously good at the game. Swan took a deep breath, swung mightily and failed to make contact. Flood's slightly more successful attempt skittered sharply off to the left.

'Don't try to hit the ball too hard,' offered Shue gently. 'And don't jerk your head up before you've made contact.' Embarrassed at their efforts, Swan and Flood tried hard to relax. Soon they were able to hit balls more often than not in approximately the right direction.

'We'll just learn as we go,' said a mildly flustered Flood, touchy about his athletic abilities and slightly sore at his inability to do something which looked so easy—particularly in front of people he didn't know very well. They would have no idea he was actually quite a good athlete. 'We don't want to keep you guys waiting too long,' he added.

Off marched the little army of players, caddies and bodyguards to the first tee. Shanghai and its environs were as flat as a pancake, having come into existence by the millions upon millions of tons of sand and gravel that had swept down the Yangtze River since the beginning of time. Until recently, the course had been farmland and still looked like it. Scores of workers were scattered all over the course, down on their knees planting grass, all wearing conical headgear. Some burial mounds provided the only relief from the flat land, apart from the odd water buffalo.

'If your ball lands on or beside a grave you can move it away six feet or so,' explained Chan. 'And if a buffalo steps on your ball or eats it you aren't penalised—same goes if it lands in a hoof print.'

Even though it was scarcely nine o' clock the thermometer was approaching a hundred degrees, made worse by the humidity and lack of wind. The heat had kept all other golfers away, which suited Flood and Swan just fine. A coolie stood by each tee, dispensing distilled water from porcelain containers. By freely sweating so much and replenishing it with fresh water, Swan and Flood soon lost their hangovers and began enjoying themselves. The foursome broke up into two separate competitions, Chan versus Shue and Flood against Swan.

Flood was already proving himself a better player than his flat-mate although more apt to hit his ball out of bounds. Swan was more cautious and less apt to suffer penalty strokes. After nine holes they were tied as the foursome stopped for a breather under the shade of a rough roof set on four poles.

'How's work going for you guys?' said Swan, wiping his brow.

'Well, it's pretty different than it would be in the States,' said Shue. 'First there's the political situation—the Nanking government is bleeding local businesses dry trying to pay for the war.'

'And our fathers don't seem to understand modern business the way we learned it in the States,' added Chan. 'Sometimes we wonder why they sent us there at all. To them the old ways are always the best.'

'So we're thinking about doing something on our own,' chipped in Chan.

At this piece of information Swan snatched a quick look at Flood, a keen devotee of Dale Carnegie's book on winning friends and influencing people. The liar book, Swan called it.

'I know how you fellows feel,' said Flood ingratiatingly. 'My Dad is just the same...'

'What line of work is he in?' asked Chan.

'Oh, well, he's, um, in broadcasting back home,' stuttered Flood, briefly losing his composure. Quickly regrouping, he looked at the two Chinese earnestly.

'I don't know if I should be talking about this but I think I can trust you guys,' continued Flood conspiratorially, as if the caddies might steal his plans. 'And I'm sure my partner wouldn't mind. We're setting up a business up in Mokanshan to make split bamboo fly rods. You see the bamboo up there is quite special on account of the way the wind conditions are and as a result of the richness of the soil,' said Flood, warming to his theme.

'The local craftsmen are expert in manufacturing products from bamboo and we've got them started making split bamboo fly rods for the North American market. You know split bamboo makes the best fly rods? If we can keep quality high and prices low we reckon we're on to a good thing. Would you be interested in being a part of it?'

Chan and Shue looked at each other, slightly overwhelmed by the force of Flood's salesmanship. Too polite to turn Flood down flat, both hemmed and hawed a little before Shue finally spoke.

'Well I don't know really—not quite what we had in mind I don't think....

'Of course, of course...

'But we might be able to introduce you to some other people who might be interested. I can't promise anything, of course...

'No, no 'course not. But if you think these people might be interested I'd sure love to talk with them. I'd appreciate your help. Now shall we play some golf?'

Back to the sweltering plain they trudged. As usual, Swan had Flood lagged behind the two other golfers and their shadow-like bodyguards.

'The *broadcasting* business? Your dad's a Methodist preacher,' laughed Swan.

'Hey relax, will you? This is Shanghai and this is golf and this is how business gets done...

'And what about your *partner*! That old guy in Mokanshan doesn't even know you exist.

'Not yet, but when he finds out I represent significant investors from Shanghai he'll be delighted,' replied Flood. I'm probably just what he dreams about when he turns out the lights at night.'

'And blathering on about the craftsmanship of the local Chinese. What a load of...'

'Keep it down will you? These guys might introduce me to their friends. This could be the big time.'

'Just remember. I want no part of this,' warned Swan.

The possibility of actually meeting investors seemed to galvanise Flood's golf game. Swan, on the other hand, was wilting under the glare of the harsh Chinese sun. Flood finished half a dozen strokes ahead of his friend, although well behind the two young Chinese.

They ordered Ewo beer and sandwiches from the bar and sat in the shade on the verandah to eat lunch. Swan and Flood promptly drained their beers and ordered two more while Chan and Shue sipped at theirs more decorously.

Swan, mellowed by the beer and the promise of a couple more, decided to forgive his friend's behaviour. He was a grown man, after all, and perhaps knew what he was doing. Besides, it was kind of funny in a strange way.

'How *is* your dad's broadcasting business going, Luther?' he asked innocently.

Flood shot him a tight-lipped look. 'What, oh fine, fine.'

'What kind of business is it?' asked Shue.

'Well, it's radio,' replied Flood shortly. 'With a religious flavour. Actually he's mostly retired from business. He's a Methodist preacher now,' he added, steering back towards the truth and hoping that a little bit of his father's religious credentials might rub off on him.

'Here's my card,' said Shue, as the others reached for their billfolds and business cards.

'I must have left mine at home,' said Flood, doing a pantomime to prove that all his pockets were cardless. 'I'll get one to you the next time we play and call you in the meantime for those contacts you mentioned.'

Swan and Chan exchanged their cards, Swan taking care not to hand out any with Witherspoon's name on them. The sandwiches arrived and they devoured them. More beer arrived and the conversation returned to golf.

'How did you fellows get so good?' asked Flood in his Dale Carnegie mode.

Chan laughed. 'When we went to the States we got there a few months early so we could practice our English. We got tired of sitting inside taking lessons so Hiram got the notion of finding a couple of teachers who wouldn't mind playing golf—actually the two teachers made more money working as caddies—so we spent nearly four months playing golf almost every day.

'It was wonderful,' added Shue. 'Then we joined the golf club at school and got to know people that way. Other students thought we were just regular guys when they learned how much we liked to play golf.'

'Well, I don't know which is better—your golf or your English,' said Swan, warming to the two young men. 'Maybe we should take the same approach to learning Chinese.'

'Sure,' laughed Shue. 'Maybe go dancing with Chinese girls every night.'

'Right now, Luther is concentrating on Russian and Korean lessons,' joked Swan

The good mood continued as they finished their drinks and settled their bill. The chauffeur returned to the Packard while the golfers washed up in the changing room. The driver returned with two suitcases and the two Chinese quickly changed into clean clothes. It hadn't occurred to the Americans to bring a change of clothing.

To foil any would-be kidnappers the chauffeur chose a different route back to the city. On the outskirts of Shanghai they came upon a pack of gaunt dogs, rough yellowish beasts with curled up Chow tails. The dogs were savagely ripping at a bundle of rags which, as they drew alongside, they realised was the lifeless body of a child.

The rest of the trip home was quiet.

Chapter 6

It was hard to say who was the bigger clothes-horse, Generalissimo Chiang Kai-chek or his fancy pants wife, Soong May-ling. Henry Luce, the communist-hating and Chiang-loving publisher of *Time* magazine, had dubbed them the 'Gissimo' and the 'Missimo' in gushing articles he had commissioned about the pair in his magazine.

At the moment, the Gissimo and Missimo were having one of their prolonged fights; this one caused by the Missimo having learned that one of the Gissimo's three former wives was back in circulation.

At the moment, he was being fitted for new uniforms in his bedroom at the Presidential Residence in Nanking, the new capital of China, just over two hundred miles up the Yangtze River from Shanghai.

In a distant wing of the palace, Madame Chiang was entertaining a group of American ladies from Wellesley College, her *alma mater* in Massachusetts. Emily Hahn was there, gathering notes for an article on the Soong sisters for the *New Yorker*. Earlier, Madame Chiang Kai-shek had asked about the missing Simpson pictures. She had people searching, Hahn had answered. Now the Missimo was sipping tea and explaining her heroic struggle against the Godless communists while inside her well-coiffed head she was silently fuming about her husband's extra-marital dalliances.

When she felt she would finally burst with anger she smiled sweetly and excused herself.

'My husband is writing a very important speech and insists that I visit him from time to time to pep him up,' she sighed. 'He just never seems to stop working. I won't be a moment,' she cooed to her circle of admirers.

The Gissimo was standing on a pedestal, semi-dressed, daydreaming of military glory while his trusted tailor, John Jarrod, formerly of Savile Row, hemmed, clucked and measured his diminutive client. At ease with the tailor, Chiang had removed his ill-fitting false teeth, a move that incensed the Missimo because it rendered him incommunicado. He could hear the stamp of her angry little heels coming down the hallway. He braced himself as she flung open the door.

'Get her out of the country now!' she shrieked at him in Chinese. 'And put your teeth back in! I would like to hear what you have to say! Put them in your mouth!'

The Gissimo frowned slightly then waved one hand in a vague and dismissive gesture.

The Missimo, eyes flashing with fury, switched to English, even though it was inferior to Chinese when it came to cursing. Her husband spoke no English and she liked to remind him of this fact when arguing. It made him mad.

'Gissimo,' she barked out contemptuously. Recognising his nickname, her husband's dark black eyes narrowed.

'Did you know the Americans call you Peanut Head? Ha! They call you Peanut because your silly shaved head is shaped like one and because you have the brains of a peanut! You are not a man! You are a peanut!'

The tailor Jarrod tried to make himself as inconspicuous as possible, endlessly repinning one trouser cuff. He could scarcely believe his ears. My word, he thought, Peanut head!

'You are a toothless tiger,' she hissed in Chinese, turning to leave the room. 'You always wear your teeth when you are with her! Don't you?' she snarled.

The Gissimo's bedroom was eerily quiet once she left, like the calm that follows the passing of a typhoon. He redirected his mind to more important things, vital things such as military matters. Things that women would never understand.

One of the problems with being a hundred-and-ten-pound generalissimo was that there was hardly any room on his chest to display his many medals, mainly awarded by himself. Oh, for a chest like Mussolini's! He had gone for a look which borrowed a little from each of his heroes. The shaved Mussolinian head and the small moustache which gave him a certain Hitlerian look. Unfortunately, neither was able to compensate for lack of a bigger chest on which to display more decorations.

One way to make himself look bigger, suggested by Jarrod, was to make his medals smaller. On some occasions, he could get away with just wearing the little cloth squares that hinted at his decorations. Jarrod had also suggested wearing a high campaign hat and had diplomatically inserted lifts into his boots, perhaps a little too diplomatically since it turned out as the Gissimo had shrieked in alarm when his dainty feet came into contact with them, thinking they might be bombs or pads of poison.

A sharply tucked waist emphasised the relative breadth of his shoulders, particularly since they were heavily padded. An earlier tailor, since dismissed, had built the shoulders in such a way that sometimes, when the Gissimo turned his body, his shoulders didn't move, giving him the appearance of a turtle.

The Missimo, meanwhile, was sneaking a cigarette before returning to her tea party. The 'New Life Movement', largely concocted by her, criticised smoking as being harmful to the country's aspirations of building a new society. But safely out of sight of the public she was addicted to English mentholated cigarettes.

Finishing her smoke, she swept back into the enclosed air-conditioned verandah and smiled demurely at the well-dressed assemblage.

'Oh that man will be the life of me yet,' she tinkled merrily. 'All he does is work, work, work! I get so worried about him sometimes.'

'Now, where was I?'

'At night, at the front,' prompted Hahn, who was under no illusions that the Missimo's tale was anything but pure moonshine.

'We heard hundreds of shots from a nearby hill, aimed in our direction,' continued the Missimo without a pause. 'We had been beating the communists so badly they were like cornered wolves—trapped but still capable of one last savage act before being vanquished.'

'My husband had sent almost all of our bodyguards to the front—he's like that—completely fearless—so we were practically undefended. My husband believes that to be too concerned with our safety saps the men's morale,' she paused breathlessly. 'He thrust a revolver into my hand—such a look passed between us—I was ready to die by my own hand rather than surrender—what better way to go than to die fighting for one's country!

She paused to sip some tea.

'Oh the indignities they would have taken! Thankfully, my husband rallied what men we had and led a counterattack. I was so worried—he's so brave!' She blushed, momentarily choked up. In reality, she was overcome by her husband's spineless perfidy with that cursed cow of a first wife.

'There, there,' clucked voices of sympathy, most of the women near tears themselves.

'There I sat in the dark, clutching my revolver,' the Missimo continued, her rage back under control.

'I found myself thinking of the afternoon we had spent together that day, walking in the nearby woods.'

More sipping.

'We had found a beautiful white plum blossom bush and my husband had picked a few flowers. Later he had them put in a bamboo container and presented them to me, saying they symbolised not only our future but also the future of our beloved country. He's like that—he has the mind of a statesman *and* a poet.'

The ladies burst into spontaneous applause at the Missimo's brave performance. Those shocking communists! That brave little Generalissimo! Hahn joined in the clapping, indeed had started the clapping.

Wow, she thought to herself. This woman belongs on the stage.

'Now if you'll excuse me for just a moment,' said the Missimo rising. My husband is struggling with a difficult passage in his speech.'

The Gissimo was daydreaming about leading a victory parade back to Nanking, himself on a white horse at the head of his army, the heads of communists stuck on poles as far back as the eye could see. At this moment his wife burst back into the room.

'Where would you be without me,' she screamed. 'I'm working for you day and night while you are out making love to that low-bred cow of a first wife!

'Speak to me!' she shrilled.

The Gissimo snapped his fingers and instantly a servant came running with a small case. The Gissimo extracted a set of teeth and placed them in his mouth.

'Shut up'.

He then returned his teeth to the servant.

CHAPTER 7

After arriving home, Flood began trying to call the fishing brigadier in Mokanshan. This was not without difficulties as the Shanghai telephone system only really worked well within the confines of the city.

To get through he had to ask the local operator to contact another operator responsible for the region of Mokanshan. The Mokanshan operator then had to try to find out where Brigadier Swan lived and what his telephone number was. Once all the missing pieces were in place a line would then have to be patched through from Shanghai to the brigadier, assuming that is, that he had a phone or was even in Mokanshan.

Flood sat down to wait.

'So all we have to do is find these negatives and Hahn will buy us a car?

'So she says. How do you reckon we can find them?

'Find out who sells that kind of stuff, maybe talk to some photographers I guess. How about Mike Nenchew at your paper?

'I'll talk to him tomorrow.'

'I'm thinking that if the pictures are worth a car to Hahn then they might be worth a lot more to whoever she's selling them to,' said Flood. 'It stands to reason. And so does the fact that there's probably more people than us looking for them.'

The phone rang and Flood leapt to his feet.

It was Hahn. Flood gave her their address and confirmed that someone would be at home in an hour to receive a package. Only when he had done this did she ask who had answered the telephone. Flood said his name and asked whether she'd like to talk with Swan. She said no. Just be sure, she said, that someone was home to collect the parcel.

'That was the monkey lady,' said Flood, who had been hoping for the brigadier. 'She's sending some guy around with the pictures this afternoon. I'm going to sign up with the volunteers—they're having a shooting competition at the racetrack later on.'

Both grabbed a magazine and settled down to wait.

Finally, the phone rang again.

'Hello? Operator? Yes. Please connect me.'

'Mokanshan! Yes? Hello? Yes, I can hear you. Brigadier Western? Good afternoon sir. My name is Luther Flood...yes sir, funny name...well, I saw your picture in a magazine...and I'm a keen fisherman. I was wondering if I might visit; talk about what you're doing up there...maybe do some business together...'

Flood was talking slowly and extremely clearly. Swan wondered if it was because the line was poor or because he thought the old gentleman might be a bit simple-minded.

'This weekend or next week if that's OK with you sir...right, excuse me while I grab a pencil...right, that's...that's wonderful. I'll see you then. Good bye sir.'

He hung up the phone with a flourish. 'Ha! Now I just have to organise some financing and persuade this old boy that he needs me as a partner.'

Flood's judgement was usually wrong or else right but for the wrong reasons. Swan thought about his attempts to raise money and decided perhaps he'd been too hard on him. This *was* Shanghai and a fellow couldn't wait around for opportunities to land in their laps.

'Care to come along to the shooting range? Afterwards we're going out for dinner at the Marine barracks. See some of the guys from the baseball team. Talk about tomorrow's game...'

'Sure. Wait. I have to be here when those pictures arrive....'

'Chen will be here...

'No, no, I'll come along later. You'll be busy anyway.'

Flood acquiesced and collected his things. Swan decided to go up to his room and tackle a chapter or two of Edgar Wallace's 'The Yellow Snake', a book with a lurid cover which he had bought thinking it would be about China. Mostly it had taken place in England and involved three sisters, one of which must marry a millionaire. The only Chinese thing about it so far was the bad guy, the yellow snake of the title, a gang leader who went by the very un-Chinese name of Grahame St. Clay.

The book had a picture on the cover of a huge snake coiled about a house. Swan thought it was funny how the evil St. Clay killed people by snakebite. Only in books like this did the baddies go to all the trouble of bringing snakes all the way from China when a gun would do. It was that kind of book.

The novel was soon put aside for a snooze—he'd formed the habit of an afternoon nap since taking the newspaper job and keeping irregular hours. He awoke to an urgent rapping on the door.

Opening it, Swan found Chen in a state of panic, her face pale and her eyes bright. She pointed down the staircase towards the front door.

Swan descended, half expecting Fu Manchu himself. He said hello to the nondescript man, obviously Hahn's messenger as he held an envelope in his hand. 'Mr. Swan?' asked the messenger.

Swan nodded and took the package, wondering what it was about this man that had so terrified his maid. Was he a 'Yellow Snake'? A minion of some real-life Fu Manch? It dawned on him that maybe this wasn't so farfetched after all. Chen was not usually so easily rattled.

Who exactly was Hahn dealing with?

Swan tore open the envelope and removed a single photograph and a small card. It was, as he had expected, a photograph taken of a postcard, the risqué kind found all over Shanghai, particularly in the French Concession.

It showed a heavily made-up woman with dark hair under a sailor's hat, with a feather boa around her neck while straddling a heavy looking chair, smiling somewhat haughtily. Nearby were some bits of rope and a lifesaver, adding to the vaguely nautical air. She was certainly naked although different from the usual models in that she wasn't plump. Sort of on the scrawny side actually.

The card read:

'Dear Eli,

Mrs. Simpson in the flesh! Is she your type? Find the original negatives of this card and a new car is yours.

My tel. is 6-279.

Emily

Swan looked at the photograph again, searching for clues. The picture seemed devoid of anything unusual, although it looked like it was probably shot in a studio. A velvety drape provided a background. The photo was presumably the work of a professional.

Chen was in her little bedroom off the kitchen. What the devil had gotten into her?

He tucked the photo and card into his wallet and left to find Flood.

The shooting range had been organised by the American company of the Shanghai Volunteer Corps and was located in the middle of the racetrack on Thibet Road, near the baseball diamond where Swan and Flood would be playing the next morning with the Marines. As regular players were often sidelined by duty or punishment fatigues, Swan and Flood filled in when they could.

The shooting range resembled an amusement park rather than a military camp. The regulars had already taken their practice and were gathered around, making wisecracks, as a group of young men lined up to shoot. To Swan, it seemed more like trying out for the football team than joining the army, even if the army was only the Shanghai volunteers. He spotted Flood standing at the end of the line, talking with Sergeant Jack Riley, the manager of the baseball team.

The Marines gave support to the American infantry company in the Shanghai Volunteer Force, a two thousand strong part-time army composed of companies drawn from the polyglot nationalities that formed Shanghai's international population. The Americans also provided a mounted troop. Although the British formed the backbone of the little army, it was a cosmopolitan affair with White Russian, Eurasian and Scottish companies, as well as one drawn from Shanghai's Jewish population. Each community financed their own men and all contributed towards the cost of armoured cars and artillery.

In one form or another Shanghai had financed and manned a little army of Europeans since the Battle of Muddy Flat in 1854 during the Taiping Rebellion when the Chinese had tried to kick the cursed foreign devils out of their country. They had failed and the date of this failure was celebrated with an annual parade followed by a bang-up dinner and a ball every year to mark the anniversary.

Some of the higher ranking officers were actually professional soliers, including the head of artillery and the commanding officer, a regular serving officer with the British army. The head of the Shanghai Municipal Council served as the commander-in-chief. The French had their own military force based in Shanghai, predominately Annamese from Indo-China but officered by Frenchmen. Although the two forces were separate it was understood they would work in tandem should Shanghai ever be attacked.

The toy army, dubbed Shaforce, had last been mobilized for battle in 1927 when Chiang Kai-chek's southern army had camped threateningly outside Shanghai while the communists paralysed the city and occupied a handful of nearby treaty ports. This had also marked the last time the Kuomintang. Or Nationalists, and the communists had been allies.

After the Green Gang thugs had murdered thousands of communists, mostly unarmed students and workers, General Chiang Kai-shek had ended up inviting most of the senior

Shaforce officers to his wedding with Soong May-ling. This suited the volunteers, as they were the kind of soldiers who performed better on a dance-floor than on a battlefield anyway. When it rained the British held their tank practices indoors as if war would only arrive on sunny days. The army's best manoeuvre was simply to buy train tickets for vagabond Chinese armies so they would leave for their home provinces peacefully.

There was even a Japanese company, famous for its goose-stepping, although the Imperial Japanese Army was now officially in favour of disbanding Shaforce. Many of the Sunday soldiers thought the Japanese might provide the next big threat. Some army or other always seemed to have Shanghai in its sights.

The Americans had uniforms, which, unfortunately, looked as though they were stolen from one of Sir Robert Baden-Powell's Boy Scout troops, complete as they were with the large, flat brimmed hats and baggy shorts.

The participants in the shooting competition were allowed to sight their rifles beforehand and Flood had taken great care with the job. He was now paying close attention to the men who were shooting before him but so far the shooting had been more miss than hit. At stake was a small cup he fully intended to win.

'How come you're not having a turn Eli?' asked the portly sergeant.

'Well, I'd probably be expected to cover anything that ever happened for the newspaper. It would be hard to march about with this outfit and do that too.'

Flood stepped into the firing enclosure and drilled six shots in a close pattern, all well within the centre. It was obvious he had outshot the rest of the field.

'Welcome to the army,' Riley said good-naturedly.

While the official results were being tallied by the officer-in-charge, Swan took Flood by the elbow and showed him the photograph of Wallis Simpson in the buff. Flood took his time committing her face to memory.

'Kind of a rangy looking chicken ain't she?'

Swan was telling him about how Chen had reacted when the messenger had dropped off the photograph when the officer announced that Flood had won the little cup.

Flood walked up to accept the trophy, still clutching the photograph in one hand. Swan looked on in amusement as Flood accepted the prize with the other hand, while offering the one holding the naughty photo to the officer. He jumped about acting flustered before hastily shoving the picture into his pocket and shaking the officer's hand.

To some scattered applause, he marched back to where Swan was standing.

'I don't know if you'll be able to find an egg small enough to put in this little thing,' joked Swan.

'Ha,' laughed Flood. 'I've got to go sign some papers and collect my uniform. I won't be more than a few minutes.

It was late afternoon and Hahn was hanging out a bedroom window at the Chiang's official presidential residence in Nanking, trying to light her opium pipe while remaining hidden from the soldiers who guarded the compound.

She had placed a rolled up towel at the bottom of the bedroom door to block the opium smoke from leaking into the rest of the house. Hahn had been invited for the weekend to do some interviews for an article she was planning to write, having left her pet gibbon at home with her housekeeper.

There would be no interviews this afternoon as things were obviously a bit strained between her host and hostess. People were often imperiously summoned by the Chiangs to their home then promptly forgotten about, though Hahn, inhaling deeply. She was not bothered in the least by the Missimo's abrupt dinner cancellation. The longer she was here the more snooping she could do. Some people, and Hahn was certainly one of them, thrive on intrigue. She slowly released the smoke from her lungs.

There was, of course, the added advantage of being involved in this Simpson imbroglio. Much more fascinating were the hints Madame Chiang had been dropping about how the opium supplied to Simpson in England originated in Shanghai. Wouldn't it be interesting to share a pipe with that woman, thought Hahn dreamily.

With regards to the negatives, Hahn hadn't done much for the Missimo yet except try to enlist the help of some naval officers, as well as that silly Swan from the newspaper. She realised the Chiangs probably had Shanghai's underworld involved in the search. They were presumably the ones who had delivered the photos of Simpson to Swan and the naval officers.

Her job now was to endure the whims of the Missimo while fawning over her every word. Hahn was nothing if not resourceful and the Missimo was an easy book to read. It was the Gissimo who was the difficult one to read, seeming as he did so remote and otherworldly.

Hahn had successfully insinuated herself into their circle by writing a story about the couple in the *New Yorker* magazine. She had also ghost-written a few pieces for other magazines. The Missimo loved publicity and went to alarming lengths to ensure their regime in China maintained a good image in the United States.

Hahn lay back on her bed and let the opium take control, expanding her mind in all directions. Had she been rash to offer Swan a car? After all, he was a reporter—albeit a complete nonentity in the world that Hahn inhabited. She reckoned she could keep him sweet pretty easily. She wasn't sure about his room-mate, but evidently the two were partners so Swan would have to keep him in check. Swan and his housemate were so depressingly similar to all the other American boys back home. There were millions of them and they all seemed to be cut with the same old cookie cutter.

Much more interesting was her current beau, the wealthy poet and man-about-town Sinmay Zau. Although he was a married man with children this had posed few difficulties to their relationship so far. His wife appeared delighted that Hahn was her husband's new mistress and seemed genuinely fond of her. She had even suggested that Hahn and her husband formally tie the knot so Hahn could officially become part of the household and she was seriously tempted. It would be a great help in learning the language and it was the best opportunity she could possibly have for immersing herself in a real Chinese family.

She gazed around the room. It was furnished in a strange mix of ornate Chinese and imitation colonial-era American furniture. She opened drawers and poked around. Returning to the window, she looked down on the grounds below. Along with Chungking and Wuhan, Nanking was known as one of the three furnaces of China on account of its brutally hot summers. The evening heat remained oppressive and what she could see of Nanking looked as though it had indeed been left to bake in a giant furnace.

She lay down on the bed and thought about the saying in Chinese that referred to the famous Soong sisters: One of them loved money; that was Mrs. Kung; one of them loved power, that was her hostess, May-ling; and one who loved China, Madame Sun Yat-sen, born Soong Ching-ling. Well, give me power every time, Hahn thought, bouncing back out of bed.

Although not in the least bit hungry she decided to visit the kitchen. It was approaching dinnertime and she had presumably been left to fend for herself. Moving quietly in her crepe-soled shoes she opened the door of her bedroom and crept down the hall towards the main entrance of the house.

The house was jammed with treasure. Hahn stopped to admire a beautiful carving of a fish made from ancient jade. In a house like this would anyone ever notice it was missing? Although the Missimo sometimes seemed a bit scatter-brained, Hahn knew she was usually as sharp as a tack. Hahn imagined her hostess kept track of all the valuables in the house and probably knew exactly how much they were worth. She put the carving back.

Hearing a slight commotion near the front door, she pressed her back against the wall and peered down into the front hall. A military aide had answered the door and let in a small group of men. The Chiangs greeted them and ushered them into a large drawing room.

Hahn realized the visitors were Japanese, remembering that the Gissimo had undergone military training in Japan early in his career. Word had it he had made a pact with them, giving them Peking and Manchuria. She had heard from some friends in high places that he still harboured hopes that the Japanese would take care of the communists for hi, leaving him firmly in control of southern China...

What was going on downstairs? From where she stood she could see the boots of a guard posted outside the door to the meeting room, ruling out a frontal approach. She'd have to outflank him but the only way to do this would be to try to eavesdrop from a window outside the house.

She descended the staircase nonchalantly, flashing a coquettish smile at the heavily armed soldier. The guard's eyes scarcely moved as she passed him. She soon reached the front door. Obviously, as a foreigner and a woman, she posed no threat to the Generalissimo. Little did he know, thought Hahn, as she gave another smile to another guard posted at the front door.

She wandered around to the side of the house where the meeting was being held. Sure enough, some of the windows were open to let in a breeze. Pausing every few seconds to smell some flowers, she advanced towards the open window from which angry voices could be heard.

Squeezing between the wall of the house and a shrub, she got as close as possible to the open window. An argument was clearly taking place but one with long pauses as the interpreters translated from Japanese to Chinese and back again.

Inwardly cursing her inability to fully understand what was going on, she resolved to become Sinmay's second wife, if only to better her Chinese. What she could make out, however, was that the Japanese were saying things that the Gissimo clearly didn't like. She reckoned they were threatening him or else giving him some kind of ultimatum.

What that threat or ultimatum was she couldn't figure out. She would have to find out by other means, she thought, as she crept back around to the front of the house and was admitted inside by the unsuspecting guard...

CHAPTER 8

Shanghai in 1936 was likely the most crime-ridden city on earth. A few years earlier an exchange had been organised between the Shanghai Municipal Police and their Chicago counterparts, thought to be the toughest police in America. The Shanghai police, mostly British and Irish, had enjoyed their time in America, regarding the trip as something of a paid holiday. The legendary Chicago cops, on the other hand, had mostly fled Shanghai in droves after a few weeks, unable to stomach the city's grim realities.

At some of the city's better hotels, heroin and children were obtainable simply by calling room service. Thousands of young girls, some no more than five years old, were sold into prostitution each year. Early in the morning beggars would search vacant lots looking for the corpses of babies—preferably female—as they proved useful when begging for coins.

In Shanghai every vice known to man was cheaply and effortlessly provided while pulpits around the world echoed to sermons comparing the city to a modern day Sodom and Gomorrah.

Nonetheless, the flip side to Shanghai was pure enchantment for those who could afford to revel in its *laissez-faire* morality. The city was already an anachronism, but one that made all other cities in the world seem tame and bland by comparison.

People, who back in their own countries would be struggling to put food on the table, were often magically transported to a world of luxury and privilege that obscured the terrible realities of a city known for such wild extremes in wealth and grinding poverty.

And for all its horrors, Shanghai was a haven of relative calm compared to the rest of China, where rapacious warlords, supported by the sale of illicit drugs and their own personal armies, were absolute rulers. The Japanese had invaded the country from the north and were steadily conquering vast tracts of territory. In addition, scarcely a day went by without a skirmish between Nationalist and communist troops. The China Sea was equally lawless with almost daily acts of piracy along the thinly guarded China coast. It was said the British Navy, policeman of the world's oceans, was lucky to stop one in every five acts of piracy.

Shanghai hummed with excitement and energy. The city had grown like no other place in history. From its relatively humble beginnings it had been transformed, in less than a hundred years, into the fifth-largest city on earth and the world's third busiest port. It had long since left behind, in terms of importance, its sister cities Hong Kong and Singapore. Shanghai had captured the imagination of the world.

No world cruise was complete without a stopover in Shanghai. Few celebrities could resist its reputation for glamour and fun and they, in turn, helped fuel a round-the-clock sense of excitement. The social season, although it varied throughout the year, never really ended. Of course, many of the foreign visitors to the city were of more serious mien, spiritually aroused by the sheer numbers of potential converts to Christianity.

Shanghai was somehow both ugly and beautiful, a mix of fantastic wealth and starving beggars. God and gold. Western technology and organisation flourishing in an environment of political chaos and mayhem. Sensuality vying with a puritanical Western missionary mindset. Scorchingly hot and damp in the summers and cruelly cold and damp in the winters.

Refugees and adventurers were the dominant strain among the foreign population, their rough edges soon glossed over by quick success and the kind of polish only big money can buy. The city had been threatened and invaded so often, as recently as 1932, that these dangers were thought tobe inevitable, and almost as meaningless, as bad weather. Shanghai always seemed to bounce back more prosperous and vibrant than ever.

Apart from the International Settlement and the smaller French one, there were two Chinese pockets inside Shanghai, Nantao and Chapei, the latter the main focus of Japanese aggression in 1932. The areas beyond Shanghai proper were called the 'Badlands' and were rapidly being colonised by Japanese criminals backed by th Imperial army. When the Japanese army finally defeated the Chinese troops in 1932, most of the retreating Chinese soldiers had been forced to sell their Mauser rifles to obtain food. The sudden appearance of thousands of weapons in and about Shanghai had led to a massive crime wave.

Yet the city also featured municipal concerts, churches, free hospitals, orphanages with revolving indoor-outdoor 'receptacles' for struggling parents to drop off their unwanted children, prestigious universities, countless newspapers and various international schools for foreign children. The city abounded in sports clubs and large social functions were all the rage as foreign powers and splashy millionaires vied to outdo all others. If a white man failed in Shanghai his compatriots would usually chip in to buy him a passage home. Unless, of course, he was a White Russian.

The Russian revolution and later, the Japanese invasion of northern China, had driven into the city a huge stateless army of desperate White Russians, the first large group of impoverished foreigners the Chinese had ever seen.

The League of Nations, shocked by the ramifications this might have on the world's colonised peoples, commissioned a study which concluded that thousands of Russian women were prostitutes, many of whom sold their services to Chinese men. Their male counterparts, often formerly army officers, begged on the streets, pulled rickshaws, worked as bodyguards and did jobs only non-whites had ever been seen to do.

Beautiful Russian women, some former dancers and some even vaguely aristocratic, shattered dozens of marriages in the city's European residential areas. When wives and children escaped the hot Shanghai summers, the men were often left at home then captivated by some beautiful young Russian woman eager to obtain the security of a foreign passport or some financial security.

With the Russians came their passion for music which, coinciding with the spread of jazz, brought Shanghai roaring into the Jazz Age. Young Chinese were equally captivated by the music and dancing became their dominant social pastime. Older Chinese called dance halls 'bamboo shoots in the spring rain' because by the mid-1930's they were springing up everywhere.

Despite recent outbursts of Chinese nationalism and the subsequent granting of a few more rights to the Chinese residents of Shanghai, the city was still firmly under the control of the foreign treaty powers, British, American, French, Italian and increasingly, Japanese.

The Whangpoo River swam with traffic, everything from men-of-war to innumerable sampans, sailing junks, fishing trawlers, bamboo rafts and ocean liners. The sampans often flocked around large ships to collect scraps of food thrown from the galleys.

The Bund was equally fascinating with coolies pushing wheelbarrows of silver ingots towards the vaults of the Hong Kong and Shanghai Bank, virtually unguarded except by a huge Sikh wielding a long bamboo *lathi*. At other times the streets came alive with elaborate funeral processions, featuring brass bands whose favourite tune was often 'Hot Time in the Old Town Tonight'.

Although at night, Shanghai's streets reeked from the sweet smell of burning opium, the real money lay in China's hinterland up the Yangtze River Valley where opium addicts in the tens of millions all relied on Shanghai's warehouses for their daily pipes.

It was opium that had built Shanghai and it was opium that remained the city's most important commodity. Without it, and the six million U.S. dollars its sale raised each month, Chiang Kai-shek and his Nationalist army would be virtually bankrupt.

Opium was the glue that held Shanghai together.

CHAPTER 9

Flood was on a roll. After scoring a clutch double in Sunday's baseball game he had emerged later in the week from a meeting with a group of Chinese investors clutching, miraculously, a line of credit. Flood had been jubilant but nevertheless slightly evasive when Swan enquired into the details of how this loan had been arranged as they sat together in the kitchen figuring out some plans.

All Flood had said in answer to Swan's questions was that Percy Chan, their golfing friend, had given his family's chop as a guarantee for the loan. The line of credit was significant, amounting to twenty thousand Shanghai dollars, the equivalent of almost seven thousand American. The money could be withdrawn from the Commercial Bank of China, which conveniently had a small branch office in Mokanshan.

Swan had negotiated with his boss to take a week's holiday and planned to spend it with Flood in Mokanshan, starting with the wedding on Sunday. He had also arranged with some other Americans to rent a houseboat for a trip along some canals to the base of Mokanshan where local transport would carry them up to the resort.

Hahn had phoned to say she too would be in Mokanshan as a guest of the Generalissimo and his wife. Their Methodist preacher, the Reverend Bradford Armstrong, was officiating at the wedding and there was even talk that China's most famous couple might drop by to give the bride and groom their blessing.

Both Swan and Flood had made some attempts to track down the missing negatives. Swan had talked to the Russian photographer at his paper and asked him to make enquiries among other photographers around town. Flood had visited a couple of photography shops where his questions had been met with frozen silence. He learned there were others looking for the negatives, others who inspired fear in the small shops they visited before him.

Flood had initially been dismissive that Shanghai's underworld could also be after the pictures of Wallis Simpson but Swan had been warned on countless occasions by his more experienced colleagues not to have anything to do with Chinese gangs. He quickly put his friend in the picture.

'So what if you're bigger than the average Chinese crook, they play real dirty and there's thousands of them,' he said…The moment we even catch a whiff that we have upset them in any way is the moment that we drop this thing like a hot brick, car or no car.

'There have been a few journalists here and up in Peking who have tangled with gangs and they've all ended up dead,' he continued. 'I'm serious about this Luther.' The rare use of his friend's first name testifying to his sincerity.

'All right, all right, I get the picture,' replied Flood. 'I don't imagine we'll unearth the pictures up in Mokanshan anyway and that's where I'll be relocating if this fly rod business gets going.'

'If he doesn't want you to join his company then you'll return that money you borrowed won't you?' asked Swan. 'What sort of interest rate did you get?'

'You don't want to hear about it. I'll return the money if that happens even if it costs me. I've got a feeling that the fellas I borrowed it from might play a little rough too.'

'What have you gotten yourself into?'

'Nothing I can't handle—like I said I'll get out fast if things look dicey. I promise.'

'It would be a fine thing if we had to go back to the States on account of you getting into trouble with moneylenders or gangs,' said Swan, fearful at the thought of going home.

'Don't worry; say do you want to go to the Great World tonight? We haven't been back since we first got here. What do you think?'

The Great World was a six-storey building that housed all the fun, both innocent and otherwise, that Shanghai had to offer. They had gone there shortly after arriving in Shanghai and had the time of their lives. They had been talking about going back ever since.

'I may be in Mokanshan for a while,' said Flood. 'This will be our last chance to have some fun; meet some Chinese girls; whoop it up a little.'

Swan, as usual, responded eagerly to Flood's enthusiasm. Who could resist such an extravagant place? 'I'm going to grab a nap before work. Why don't you call me later at the paper and we can meet up there. What are you doing till then?'

'See what the municipal library has got on bamboo fishing rods, maybe drop by that Jap fishing store in Hongkew to see what I can learn about bamboo rods—the Japs are supposed to make good ones. Check out prices,;see what's selling. Research.'

Swan had been working at the paper for a few hours when he received a phone call from his friend.

'You won't believe what I saw tonight,' he said. 'Jesus Murphy. It's a totally different city north of the Soochow Creek.'

'What happened?'

'The Japs bayoneted a Chinese man in front of my eyes. I saw it happen.'

'Look, we'll be wrapping up soon. It wouldn't make the paper now anyway as it might upset them but why don't you come over and tell us about it?'

Flood was slightly calmer when he got to the *North China Daily News*. Hoste, Witherspoon and Shaw were there, putting the finishing touches on the next morning's paper.

Swan looked up.

'So what was that about a man being bayoneted?'

The eyes of the newshounds turned to Flood.

'That's right. Just across the bridge where they have a post. The Chinese guy was yelling a bit and waving his arms then *phsst!* Just like that. One of the guards just stuck him with his bayonet then acted like it was no fuss at all. Just left his body right there in the ditch, his wife screaming her head off.'

'What time was it,' said Hoste.

'Around ten.'

'Which of you chaps can do the Jap news briefing tomorrow morning?'

The daily Japanese press conferences at the Broadway Mansion, just across Soochow Creek, were generally a waste of time and most reporters didn't like going for fear of giving face to the Japanese military, as if the Japanese army might conclude that reporters actually swallowed their whoppers.

'What about you Swan? You're taking next week off. Get the details from your friend.'

The newsmen all went back to work, except for Swan.

Swan thanked Flood for adding to his workload.

'Eli, it was just terrible. Terrible. The man was having some problem with his papers. That's all. No big deal. Then whoosh,' he mimicked the bayonet thrust a second time. 'He murdered him in cold blood. They even laughed a bit about it after…

'I was yelling at them but they didn't pay any attention to me,' he added.

Swan had never seen Flood so worked up about anything. Half an hour later Hoste announced he was happy with the proofreading and wandered over to Flood, whose head was deep in a sporting magazine. He had quietly ripped out a few more pages on local fishing information.

'I wonder if that killing didn't have some larger significance,' Hoste said. 'Usually Japanese soldiers don't act without permission.' Hoste, formerly a British officer, was the paper's military authority.

He turned to Swan. 'Try to dig around a bit tomorrow at that press conference and see if there might have been a spat recently between the Japs and the Generalissimo. That goes for you fellows as well,' he said to the two other reporters.

'Maybe the Japs are sending him one of their little messages, delivered on the end of a bayonet,' he continued with dramatic hyperbole. Hoste was also a leading light in one of the local drama societies.

'Do you still want to go to the Great World?' asked Swan.

'What? Yeah, I could do with a couple of drinks first.'

'Do you chaps fancy a quick one at the Club?' asked Hoste.

The Shanghai Club, located at Number Three, the Bund, was by far the city's most exclusive and elegant watering hole. Neither Swan nor Flood had ever been there, although it was just a short walk from the newspaper along the waterfront Bund. Within five minutes of arriving in Shanghai, visitors were usually told how the club had the longest bar in the world, something that many Shanghailanders were proud of.

'Chaps in most armies would get shot for doing what they did, even if it was just a Chinese beggar,' said Hoste as they walked along the Bund, as humid and busy as ever. 'Could you tell if the same guards were back on duty tomorrow night?'

Flood said he didn't think he could. That was the trouble with uniforms, he added.

They entered the club. The inside of its expansive foyer was all polished mahogany and brass, as was the main bar. One's standing in society determined their place along the main bar. Hoste stood about half way along. It had been a slow journey.

Over whiskies Hoste continued with his theme as Swan and Flood took in the sights of the club in all its colonial splendour. Even the whiskey tasted better thought Swan, before realising that this was probably because it *was* better whiskey.

'Certain friends in the know have told me that things aren't well between Brother Chiang and the Sons of Nippon,' Hoste said expansively. Hoste was the kind of Briton who would cheerfully sacrifice a finger to be asked to do something hush-hush for the government to make up for the fact he'd missed most of the fighting in the last war by serving in Mesopotamia.

'Things are getting a bit feverish up north so it wouldn't surprise me if the Japs are planning something. Then, of course, there's the argument that the only way to do business with the Chinese is at the point of a bayonet. Stiffens them up a bit. Were there many people around?'

'The usual amount I guess,' replied Flood. 'I'd been at the Heiwayoko toy store where they sell fishing stuff, and had just crossed the bridge when I heard the noise and turned around. The funny thing is that the guards had looked at me really carefully before they let me cross. I don't know why.'

'Perhaps they wanted a foreigner to witness the killing,' said Hoste. 'That might help to ensure that it got Mr. Chiang's attention. The death of a Chinese beggar doesn't mean much around here unless the message gets home. Another drink?'

They declined, not wanting to overstay their welcome and eager now to get to the Great World. Things had taken rather a sombre turn but now it was time to relax and have some fun. They didn't live in Shanghai to feel sombre.

The Great World, or House of Multiple Joys as it was known in Chinese, was located at the corner of Avenue Edward VII and Thibet Road. A six-storey building with a wedding cake roof, it was slightly dangerous, definitely low-brow and probably the most eye-popping place in Shanghai, famous for being a combined brothel-dancehall-circus-restaurant-theatre-gambling joint-beauty parlour side-show of fun.

They entered the front doors, both clutching their billfolds tightly in the front pockets of their trousers. Taken for tourists, both were besieged instantly by pimps, moneychangers and pickpockets, the latter repulsed roughly, accompanied by some rough words in pidgin. Swan and Flood had first visited the previous summer when Flood had been expertly relieved of his wallet. Swan had said that Flood might as well as been wearing a sign saying: 'I'm new in town! Free money!'

The crowded first floor was a maze of gambling tables, singsong girls, magicians and acrobats all vying for attention. There were no other foreigners around at this late hour and the two Americans, much taller than the others, stood out like a lonely pair of pine trees. The sounds of slot machines and fireworks prevailed, accompanied by the smell of burning ginger. They quickly went upstairs. All the girls wore cheongsams and the higher the floor, the higher were the revealing slits on the sides of their dresses.

The next floor was dominated by restaurants and small food stalls, Swan and Flood grabbed cold beers and were again besieged, this time more enjoyably, by a group of Chinese singsong girls. Each restaurant had its own form of entertainment, either groups of actors putting on plays or bands, some playing Chinese music and others cranking out a hybrid form of jazz. Pimps abounded, many with slick George Raft-style haircuts and suits with exaggerated shoulders. Barbers, ear wax extractors and dentists were all doing a brisk business. Still the two Americans continued climbing, clutching their beers and wallets.

The third floor, where cheongsams were split up to the lower thigh, featured acupuncture specialists and more gambling, as well as ice cream parlours and photographers. The two exchanged looks and shrugged their shoulders, the busy throng making small talk difficult.

Flood approached astall selling postcards.

'Girlie photos?'

The man behind the counter reached below and brought up two large boxes crammed with hundreds of postcards. Flood took the boxes to a nearby table and ordered two more beers. Swan pulled out his wallet and extracted the photo of Simpson.

'You got?" said Flood.

The photographer bemusedly pointed to the boxes of postcards.

'Can do missy that side? Catchee me missy? Savvy?' said Swan.

The man took the photo and looked at it closely. Slowly he shook his head, shrugging his shoulders. He pointed back at the boxes. Flood was already thumbing through them.

'What do you think?' said Swan, sitting down.

'Some of these girls look pretty good...right, um, let's get started.'

Swan indicated the vendor. 'He doesn't seem to recognise our photo.'

'Well, the chances of finding *that* photo won't be that great anywhere,' mused Flood, looking at one card after another. 'But if we look for other stuff, like the lifesaver or the chair in our photo then we might get somewhere. They went to work, soon attracting the attention of a group of laughing girls.

'Wanchee all same that', pointed a tall girl with bobbed hair at a card showing a naked couple entwined on a divan. The rest all giggled merrily at her audacity while Swan and Flood studied the cards closely, periodically comparing them with the Simpson photo.

'You what side?' asked another girl.

'USA', answered Flood, looking up at the girl. The postcards were having their effect on him and the nearby girls were much prettier than the ones featured on the postcards. 'Shall we take a break?' he said hopefully.

'Look at this,' replied Swan, pushing over a card. The photograph card showed a girl dressed in a sailor's hat. Among the nautical odds and ends was a lifesaver ring. 'Could be something.'

Flood sat back down and grabbed more cards. He looked up and smiled at the outspoken girl with the bobbed hair, hoping to encourage her to hang around.

Swan was also getting a little hot under the collar.

'This may be something,' said Flood. 'This chair has got the same curly legs as ours.'

Swan examined the photo. Sure enough, the chair was the same kind, popular around the turn of the century. He put this picture with the other one and went back to work.

'This velvety backdrop could be the same,' said Flood a half hour or so later, putting another card on the pile.

'What we'll have to do is get a good magnifying glass and really look at them closely.' No sooner had they finished the two boxes than another postcard vendor arrived, having heard about the two foreign pornography enthusiasts.

'Take a break?' asked Swan, paying for the small stack they had collected.

'Sure,' replied Flood who turned to the pretty Chinese girl who had spoken to him earlier 'Go topside? Bang, bang?' He mimicked the shooting of a gun. There was a shooting range on the next floor.

'Um, Go topside. Lookee,' said Swan to the postcard seller, pointing to the box of postcards. 'This side bime by, catchee girly um.' His pidgin failed him. 'Bime by', he repeated, turning to a willowy Chinese girl in a tight cheongsam. He took her elbow and followed Flood and his girl upstairs.

Flood went to the shooting range where he put down a few coins and was handed a toy rifle. The girl with the bobbed hair clapped her hands as he potted away at moving targets. The area was smoky from incense burning at a nearby makeshift temple, complete with statues of dragons and altars surrounded by decaying fruit, mostly oranges.

Beyond the temple was a huge stuffed whale. Evidently it had been shellacked with preservative but still smelled pretty fishy. A line of girls dressed in billowing Arab-style pantaloons and vests danced to music from a huge phonograph. All wore veils and kept well away from a tightly meshed cage containing large, pale green snakes. Nearby was a row of small massage parlours and some stuffed animals. Beyond that were large aquariums with brightly coloured fish for sale.

Swan pointed up and the girl shook her head in agreement.

'Topside number one,' she said smiling. Swan called over to Flood, still blazing away, to tell him they were going up to the roof to get some air.

The air was much fresher outside, despite the whiff of gunpowder from fireworks. Tightrope walkers, silhouetted against the night sky, were crossing wires above a small crowd. In the distance bright lights flooded the Bund and all around the rooftop electric signboards advertised whiskey and tires. Unlike the lower floors, there was only one band, which played a light waltz to which shadowy figures were dancing slowly. Swan and the girl began moving to the music and when fireworks exploded nearby she pretended to be frightened, pressing closer to Swan. He held her tightly, smelling a trace of jasmine in her hair and wondering if she was holding a forefinger aloft behind his back.

After several dances they sat down at a nearby table. Feeling expansive, Swan ordered a bottle of champagne. The girl's name was Kuling and she was very pretty, her makeup not too heavy and her smile sweet.

Swan was negotiating prices when they were joined by Flood and his dance partner.

Twenty dollars, she said, pointing to the other two.

'Same, same.'

'Sounds fair to me,' said a smiling Flood. 'Ho! Champagne!'

Clinking glasses, they toasted each other and the city around them.

Later Swan and Flood flipped through a couple of more boxes of postcards like madmen, much to the amusement of the Chinese girls. They bought a few more then raced down to the street below to catch a taxi home.

CHAPTER 10

Patrick Givens sat at his desk studying a calendar, silently counting the days and weeks until his next home leave.

With 478 days, divided by seven that meant another 68-and-a-half weeks to go.

Lord Christ, he thought, I'll never make it with my sanity intact.

What had been bad the week before had only gotten worse. Half the city now seemed to be searching for the Simpson negatives, and for all he knew someone may well have tracked them down by now.

A couple of police reports had come in regarding the terrorising of photography shops by gangsters. This meant that not only was the Green Gang now in the game, but that in all likelihood all of the photography shops in the city had by now been visited by their thugs.

Givens was trying to cut back on the buttermilk, his size having ballooned since his rugby playing days. To his embarrassmenty, he'd been unable to find a bullet-proof vest large enough to fit him the last time he'd needed one.

The latest report had, of all people, the bloody Germans joining the search. Lord knows why the Nazi party would be interested in such matters but there it was. They were now clumsily following in the tracks of the Green Gang, Emily Hahn and the other American amateurs she had recruited.

Givens had assigned a couple of good Chinese men to tail Hahn and put Ralph Bookbinder, another American, in charge of overall surveillance. That particular trail had led to Nanking and the hearth of the little Generalissimo and his scary wife. What's more, his men had stumbled across what appeared to be a fairly high level meeting between Chiang and some high ranking Japanese soldiers. This had become important a couple of days later when word came in reporting the cold-blooded assassination of a Chinese national at the Soochow Creek Bridge for no apparent reason.

One thing about the Japs, he thought, was that there were usually reasons behind whatever they did. Givens hoped to God that if they got stroppy again like they did back in '32 they would leave Shanghai alone and turn their attentions to the new capital in Nanking or somewhere else.

One thing about the battles back then had been the unexpected mettle shown by the Chinese troops. That sissy Chiang had been completely uninvolved, of course. Instead, a vagabond Chinese army had happened to be visiting Shanghai from somewhere down in Southern China near Hong Kong, the heroic Nineteenth Route Army under a tough and cagey warlord named Cai Ting-kai.

Expecting his army to get whipped by the Japs, Chiang Kai-shek had almost completely disassociated himself from them, dismissing them as little more than a gang of bandits. Ironically, the wayward army of southerners had already been paid off by local Chinese business interests and were about to entrain home when they were attacked by a brigade of Japanese marines.

What had followed had seemed totally unreal to Givens. The foreign nightclub crowd, champagne glasses in hand, had popped over to Chapei, the Chinese section of the city across Soochow Creek, as if they were going to the dog races or a cricket game.

It was as if a little war had broken out as a form of entertainment on their comfortable doorstep. Sentiment had been very much in favour of the Japanese then. After all, weren't they a part of the Shanghai Volunteer Force?

Old Cai may have been a bandit and a warlord but he and his men certainly knew how to fight, digging in and resisting Japanese warplanes, naval bombardments and the cream of the Imperial armed forces. Chapei had been levelled and thousands killed, marking the first time that Shanghai had been the scene of modern warfare. The bayoneting yesterday, in all its familiarity, recalled brought the whole horrible period.

Givens despised the Generalissimo and back in '32 had secretly hoped that the Nineteenth Route Army, composed of young peasants, might teach both he and the Jap a lesson. Get the little bugger's wind up a little. The local Chinese population had thrown in their lot completely with the young soldiers,sending them supplies and food and even joining their ragtag army.

Givens had little time for newspapers such as the *North China Daily News* which, much to no one's surprise, had come down heavily on the side of the Japanese. That pusillanimous poltroon of a generalissimo, jealous of their fighting spirit, had later conspired to send the Nineteenth Army off to the northwest to chase phantom communists.

Now it looked like it might all be coming back to haunt them. And him out wasting his time looking for pictures of some naked adventuress. He had, of course, seen the picture of Simpson in the buff so every time he thought of her this was the image that sprung to mind. A tart in a dirty picture.

Givens had arranged for the British Consul to have a quiet word with Stuart Fessenden, the amiable but empty-headed American who headed up the Shanghai Municipal Council. That had gone nowhere fast, he thought ruefully.

Hahn's current chumminess with the Chiang Kai-sheks meant that she was pretty much beyond his control. The only way to lean on her would be to lean on her Chinese boyfriend, whatever his name was. The opium addict. But what real purpose would that serve? An angry Emily Hahn, backed by the Chiangs and in all likelihood, the Green Gang, would be biting off far more than he could chew.

And now the Germans were getting involved. The cables from London had been growing more frequent of late. The Nazis had taken a real shine to old Edward, thought Givens, and Britain's band of Nazis were, according to the consul, now among the King's strongest supporters now that word had begun to leak out about his affair. Hitler had even held a funeral in Berlin recently in honour of George VI, whose passing had resulted in Edward being crowned king.

One thing they had been able to verify was the fact that Wallis Simpson continued to be an enthusiastic user of opium and although it was a somewhat muddy trail, it was possible that her source of the drug was none other than Big Ears Tu.

Christ, thought Givens, next he'll be forced to address the old scoundrel as Sir Big Ears, purveyor of goods to the Royal family. Like everyone else in Shanghai, Givens had a healthy dose of fear when it came to the leader of the Green Gang. To those he meant to kill, Big Ears first delivered a coffin to their home, as if stating in advance that no matter what you did or where you went, you were as good as dead already.

Givens felt he had a few pieces of the puzzle but not enough to know what the final picture might be or what dimensions it might assume. It's like being blindfolded and told to find a needle in a bloody haystack, he thought bitterly.

And no respite at all for sixty-eight-and-a-half weeks! Unless the Japanese started something big enough to make everyone else forget the beastly pictures.

Just not here in Shanghai, he prayed.

CHAPTER 11

Swan and Flood were eating lunch at Jimmy's Kitchen, a recently opened American-style diner that had quickly become their favourite restaurant...Swan was describing the Japanese press conference he had attended that morning at Broadway Mansions, a skyscraper that overlooked the Soochow Creek, as well as the scene of the killing.

'The Japanese colonel in charge said it was self defence, plain and simple, end of discussion and move onto the next topic.'

'You know that wasn't self-defence!' said an angry Flood...

'I told him that there were witnesses to the whole thing and......'

'What did he say?'

'...he said through his translator, that Japanese American guy named Bob something, that all any witnesses would have seen was a Japanese soldier defending himself against an attack from a Chinese criminal.'

'Those little bastards. I'd like to show them a thing or two about a fair fight,' Flood glared belligerently at his friend. 'Is there anything we can do about what I saw at the bridge?'

'I don't think so. Remember what Hoste said about the Japanese wanting to send a message to Chiang Kai-shek? They probably aren't bothered at all by the fact you saw the killing.'

They continued eating their hot beef sandwiches. To get off the subject and on to something less disturbing, Swan asked about his research into bamboo fly rods the day before.

'Well, first off bamboo isn't a kind of tree like I thought but a grass; the largest grass in the world. And of course there's different kinds of bamboo, actually hundreds of different kinds,' added Flood, his anger forgotten.

'The split rod was invented by an American named Philipps back in 1846 using bamboo that had been brought as a curiosity from China," said Flood. 'Philips was a violin maker in Pennsylvania and he was the first to glue triangular pieces of split bamboo together, laminating them and making a tapered rod.' He paused for breath.

'The best bamboo is supposed to come from three places—here in China, Calcutta in India—I think the article said the brigadier is from India. And a place called Tonkin which is in Indochina—both those places are much further south than Mokanshan which is interesting.

'That I got from the library,' he continued, pushing away his plate. 'I had more luck talking to the Japanese guy who owns the fishing shop in Hongkew; he told me about prices and what to look for in a rod. He said he'd be happy to have a look at the Mokanshan ones and maybe even sell them.

'He also said the best line for fly rods is made from Chinese silk but that it's mostly spun in the States and England—so I'm thinking why not spin the line right here where the costs are less and where you have the best supplies? We could maybe even do that in Mokanshan too.

'A fellow generally only buys one split bamboo fly rod in his life but chances are he'll buy lots of fishing line. If you're going to make the rods why not make the line too? It makes sense don't you think?'

'Sure it does,' said Swan, smiling. 'You sound like you actually know what you're talking about.'

'The Japanese guy at the fishing store was really nice,' said Flood. 'When I left that shop I thought wasn't it great how the Japanese appreciated fishing the same way we do…and then came that business at the bridge.'

'I don't think the Japs even think the Chinese are humans the way they treat them,' said Swan. 'I've heard some stories at the paper about what they did five years ago here and it didn't sound like human behaviour at all; more like animals than people.'

'Any luck looking at those postcards this morning?' he continued, again steering the conversation away from the killing.

'I almost forgot about that I was so wrapped up in everything else,' answered Flood. 'I compared the original with the ones we bought and this one,' he pulled out a post card. 'It looks like it was maybe shot in the same place. See this light on the wall in the corner? Same as ours. The floorboards look the same and so does that bit of curtain.

Swan squinted at the picture. There was a resemblance all right.

'And if you turn the card over you can see where it was printed, Rue…

'Rue Marcel Tillot, a place called "Imprinterie Rivet". Can you check it out before we go up to Mokanshan?'

'I was going to head over there after this and have a look.'

'Hey that's great. Maybe we'll be able to drive ourselves up to Mokanshan.'

'We'll see,' said Flood. 'It could be nothing or the store may have moved or whatever. Worth a try though. I may not get a chance to do much else on this for a while if everything goes OK up in Mokanshan. I really feel like getting out of Shanghai for a while.

'For the first time since we got here I'm a little sick of the place,' he added.

'Probably because of what happened last night,' suggested Swan.

'Yeah, probably.'

'I know what you mean though, all I've been thinking about recently is getting away for a while, getting some fresh air in the countryside,' said Swan. 'I wonder what it's like up there. It's so flat around here it will be nice…'

'And cool,' interjected Flood.

'…to get somewhere high up with a view. They say there's a huge swimming pool there dug out of a mountainside, horseback riding, dances.'

'It's run by religious folks though right?' asked Flood.

'I guess so but it shouldn't stop us having fun,' replied Swan. 'We should bring some whiskey though.'

'Do you think you'll ever get married,' asked Flood, completely out of the blue.

The waitress approached with some blueberry pie, providing Swan with an easy answer.

'Not while I can have my pie and eat it too.'

'I can't see ever getting married here,' said Flood seriously. 'It seems like something that you'd do back home.'

'You're thinking about Bert and Dot getting married this weekend up in Mokanshan?'

'I guess so. But they pretty much act here the same way they would back home,' answered Flood. 'Here they're doing missionary work and back home they would be doing pretty much the same sort of thing. I can't see Bert carrying on with Chinese girls the way we do.'

'That's for sure. But I don't think he misses it do you?'

'Probably not. It's just I can't see myself going back to the States now and settling down,' continued Flood. 'Things are just so easy here. Easy *and* exciting. When I think about back home everything seems so slow.'

'Maybe we'll grow out of it and want things to be that way.'

'Maybe,' reflected Flood. 'But I sure hope that doesn't happen for a while yet. Are you getting Bert and Dot something for a present?'

'I saw a cuckoo clock at a shop on Bubbling Well Road a few days ago,' said Swan. 'I thought I might pick that up this afternoon then go home and start packing. Why don't you come with me then we'll go to that printing shop together?'

'Sure, but why don't you let me pay for half the clock? I feel kind of bad that I said I wasn't going to go to the wedding now that I'm going to be up there after all.'

'Oh I would imagine they'll probably find a way to squeeze you in. But that's fine, we can get them a bigger one.'

To their dismay, Rue Marcel Tillot was a short street dominated by a large Catholic Church. There were a number of smaller Church-like buildings, including what appeared to be a printing shop.

Swan stood at the door, the cuckoo clock in a package under his arm.

'I can't imagine a bunch of naked ladies cavorting about this place can you?'

'Looks can be deceiving but no I can't,' agreed Flood.

'May as well have a look inside'.

Swan knocked on the door. Their hearts sank when it was answered by a man dressed in the robes of a priest.

'Bonjour messieurs,' said the man.

They bonjoured back and stood there awkwardly. Finally, Flood broke the silence.

'We're Americans, he's a journalist,' he shot his thumb at Swan as the priest looked on with amusement.

'And we're looking for something rather unusual,' continued Swan, handing the man a business card. 'Something that might have been printed here a few years ago.'

'Not a bible?'

'No, not a bible. A, um, picture of a woman without many clothes on.'

'A woman who is very close to us,' broke in Flood, improvising quickly. 'We need to find the negatives of this photograph so we can protect this lady.'

The priest looked at them sceptically. 'And for this you brought us a present?'

Swan and Flood both said yes.

'Well, if it is to protect the honour of a lady perhaps I can help,' he said. 'We had with us a few years ago a priest who became involved with some bad people, who did some things here which were not so good—A Father Jean—but he was sent away and never came back.

'He left some things behind but I do not know what they are, probably not the sort of things which belong in a church so….' He left the sentence unfinished. 'I will ask one of our people if they know where they are.'

The two Americans looked at each other in amazement. 'I hope you like cuckoo clocks,' said Swan, handing it over.

A Chinese man led them to an outbuilding used for storage. He unlocked a giant padlock and opened the double doors. The priest indicated some boxes in the corner, one of which was stamped BOUCHARD.

'Those are his things. You may look if you promise me that this will not go against the wishes of God.'

They promised him it wouldn't, although both wondered to themselves how God would feel about their new car.

Inside the boxes were some books, a few clothes and some cheap local knick-knacks. There were also some boxes of photographs and some envelopes containing what appeared to be negatives. The photographs were of a variety of subjects, none of them remotely pornographic.

'We're going to need more light,' said Flood. 'I'll take this envelope and you start on this one.'

They moved closer to the doorway and began examining the negatives against the light.

'This looks more like it,' said Swan, excitement creeping into his voice as they feverishly rifled through the contents of the box.

'I've found her,' said Flood, waving a strip of negatives in the air. He let loose a second, more subdued whoop.

Swan grabbed the strip from his hands. 'There's more than one of her. This is a whole roll. Some of the negatives were more forthcoming than the copy they already had.

They went and thanked the priest.

Still not believing their luck, they celebrated with champagne while packing their bags for the trip the next morning. They would be taking a convoy of cars organised by some other Americans, driving west some fifty miles to the Grand Canal where they would board a rented houseboat for the trip south to the mountains of Mokanshan. The Grand Canal was an ancient waterway which flowed from Peking all the way south to Hangchow, a distance of more than a thousand miles.

Swan had asked Chen to arrange for two rickshaws to come pick them up at five thirty a.m. so as to make the rendezvous with the other travellers at the race-track. Flood regretted he hadn't time to pick up a small shotgun for the trip when Swan mentioned he'd heard there was plenty of waterfowl to be found along the banks of the Grand Canal.

Swan had to put in a late shift at the newspaper, his last for a week. For once they planned a relatively early night so they would be ready for their early departure. They had debated whether they should try getting hold of Hahn before leaving but thought it was probably easier just to give her the negatives when they met in Mokanshan.

To celebrate their good fortune after leaving the Rue Tissot, they had bought the largest cuckoo clock in the shop as a present for Wattie and Porter. Neither of them realised that in China, the giving of a clock as a present is bad manners and worse luck.

CHAPTER 12

King Edward VIII accepted a large white pill from his paramour, the now notorious Wallis Warfield Spencer Simpson. They were celebrating the end of the official mourning period for his departed father, as well as his decision to tell the Prime Minister, Stanley Baldwin, that as the most popular king in recent history, he planned to make the twice-divorced Simpson his Queen.

'What blasted supper,' he muttered absently with regard to a polite letter from the Foreign Secretary's requesting that he meet the King of Greece while cruising the Dalmatian coast with Simpson aboard the '*Nahlin*', a luxurious fourteen hundred-ton ship. Curiously, for an Englishman who nominally ruled one-third the globe, he spoke the language with a bit of a mid-Atlantic accent, perhaps having absorbed some of Simpson's Baltimore accent.

He was also keen to get back out on the golf links and try for his third hole-in-one in three outings although confounded protocol demanded his presence at various ceremonies of state. He would have gladly chucked them all had Simpson, her eyes on the prize, not taken care that he performed all his duties. The King had already attracted comment in various ports by flashing about in a very small pair of shorts and no shirt.

Wallis had introduced him to opium, albeit circuitously, through the use of her so-called 'pep' pills. When he enquired once what they were made from she had replied, utterly seriously, that they were derived from a chemical called 'pep'.

The King, a believer in miracles, thought the warm glow of confidence he had recently acquired was due to his love for her. In truth, the opium had played a starring role in their romance and in other areas of his life as well.

The King now considered himself a crack golfer and the pep pills played a part here too. Twice he had golfed in the past six weeks and twice he had scored a hole-in-one, a feat unheard of in history, he imagined.

Drugged to his royal gills, he hadn't noticed that on each occasion one of Simpson's small gaggle of servants, a man serving as a forecaddie or 'spotter', had popped the golf ball in the hole before hiding in the woods. The first shot had been particularly miraculous, having zinged out of the King's sight then off a tree near the startled spotter. The king had marched away from the hole to look for his ball, embossed with his insignia, a three-feathered cluster. He'd been shocked when told he'd 'potted a holer'.

The following week a good shot had been transformed into a perfect one by a similarly deft hand, in effect, one representing the long-fingered Wallis Simpson. The hole-in-one balls had been cleverly dipped in silver and transformed into small trophies by her, much to the delight of her lover. Opium had been remarkably helpful to Simpson, since she now controlled most of the things he did and even some of the things he said.

He'd been blithely calm when he'd been the target of a weird assassination attempt a few weeks earlier, lost as he was in a happy opium-induced trance concerning a theory that his prowess at golf could almost certainly be duplicated with a nearby cannon. He was imagining how he'd become the first person in the world to score a hole-in-one with an artillery piece when the bomb was tossed in his direction. His first reaction had been to try getting down off his horse to inspect it more closely. Fortunately, his tight trousers had ruled this out.

His renewed vigour also transformed his everyday royal performance, although the only audience who counted these days was a former Shanghai adventuress who'd struck the mother lode. The cruise had provided her with a perfect opportunity to get rid of a couple of his loyal retainers, as well as sniff the rarefied air of an English king on holiday. He was still miffed the government had poured cold water on his suggestion that he attend the Olympic Games as a guest of Hitler, a leader who had impressed him deeply.

Already dubbed by some in London as the 'Good Ship Swastika', the *Nahlin* had been the perfect antidote to all the nonsense back home. The pair had basked in the Mediterranean sunshine, playing the part of young sun-kissed lovers as though their passion, by itself, was of sufficient brilliance to convince the 'old men' in England not to make any trouble by challenging their lovely plans.

Simpson had discovered opium in Shanghai and been thrilled by how it not only relaxed her but helped her maintain a strict diet as well. Her tiny waist was the result of her aversion to food after taking a pep pill. Ernest Simpson, her latest husband, had connections in the shipping industry which made it easy for him to get his hands on the opium pellets. In return for not raising a fuss about being cuckolded by Edward, the king was keeping Simpson's business afloat.

She hadn't an inkling that British Secret Service had traced the drugs all the way back to Shanghai and had gotten the goods on her latest lover, the divine Guy Trundle—or 'Trundle Bed, as she often called him. Simpson had convinced herself there was nothing illegal about the pills, and the King of course, hadn't a clue that he was now an enthusiastic devotee of opium—or that the was being two-timed. The pills had even reduced his daily intake of alcohol and he felt as though ten years had been lifted off his slight frame, not much larger than the weedy Generalissimo who had taken such an interest in Wallis Simnpson.

'David,' drawled Simpson in *her* strange accent, half Virginia and half Belgravia. 'Be a darling and fetch me my wrap.' The King hurried to obey her wishes. 'And while you're up perhaps you'd be so kind as to get my book. It's over there somewhere.'

The king mumbled something unintelligible. At once, Wallis became concerned about his incoherence and wondered whether some of the pills might be stronger than others. Usually they didn't have quite this effect on him.

'Come lie with me here, darling,' she said caressingly, making room for him on her divan. Christ he'll be drooling next, she thought. Soon he was in a sleep-like state, his blonde head resting on her hip, hard as a wooden Chinese pillow.

The opium had occasionally surprising side effects. Sometimes he was a jibbering wreck while at other times he acted as if he'd just pulled a sword from a stone.

Just that day he had gotten it into his head that there was a beautiful golf course in Turkey, the next stop on their trip. Mustafa Ataturk, once a sworn enemy of England, had invited them for dinner and had offered the use of his private railway car to transport them to Constantinople. Perhaps the King would revive if given a couple of bracing martinis later that afternoon, thought Simpson. He would be upset if he missed seeing the approaching Dardanelles, as well as the graves of thousands of Australians and Kiwis.

The Dardanelles. An American friend of hers had taken a European cruise the previous spring. When asked afterwords by a reporter in America what she had thought of the Dardanelles, she had confidingly replied: 'Loved him, hated her.'

The King stirred, a shaft of sunlight lighting up his golden head.

'Splendid body of men what eh Fruity,' he mumbled, as Simpson shifted the weight of his head onto a nearby pillow and extricated herself.

She cut one of the pills in half before washing it down and returning the bottle to her purse. No telling what kind of a fuss the King's personal physician might make if he knew what was going on.

Things had taken a strange turn recently. The King had insisted upon trying out a Turkish bath at a palace a few days earlier and had found himself sitting naked in a steam room, alone but for his six bodyguards, equally naked, all clutching their revolvers and keeping their eyes discreetly to themselves.

Simpson caught a glimpse of herself in a nearby mirror.

Wallis, Queen of England, she thought happily.

CHAPTER 13

The air was still cool when two rickshaws arrived at dawn to collect the Americans and their copious amounts of luggage. Possession of the negatives and the prospect of a week in the mountains had both of them in high spirits, even at this ungodly hour.

They had clothes for parties, tennis, hiking, riding, swimming, as well as suits for the wedding, although Flood was still hoping to avoid the ceremony. They had eagerly unearthed two matching pith helmets, solar *topees*, cork lined and canvas covered. These had been bought in Hawaii under the assumption that their use was *de rigeur* in Shanghai. They had been mildly disappointed to discover upon their arrival that pith helmets weren't worn in the city but were reserved for outdoor pursuits. Their excitement was now palpable as this would mark the first time they would be worn, signifying their coming of age as *bona fide* colonial adventurers.

The large cuckoo clock was protected inside a stout wooden box. Flood had already checked with Swan twice to ensure that the negatives were safely stored for the trip.

Reaching Avenue Joffre, they caught the delicious smell of fresh baked bread from a Russian-owned bakery nearby. Swan shouted for his rickshaw puller to stop and ran inside, returning with two fresh loaves of bread for breakfast.

Shanghai's bustle never ceased although the municipal authorities kept the residential areas relatively quiet overnight. The last of the night soil collectors were making their way down to the river with their barrels of recently gathered human waste. Once there, the stuff would be shipped by sampan to nearby Tsung-ming Island, Shanghai's main source of vegetables, where it would be used as crop fertilizer. Even the lowliest workers, such as the night-soil men, owed their allegiance to the ubiquitous Green Gang, whose long tentacles reached everywhere.

Most waste was worth something in Shanghai. Spoiled food and kitchen slop was used to feed pigs and even humans, while rancid grease was used to make cheap soap. Rags would be used to stuff mattresses and old newspapers were transformed into firecrackers. The city at this hour seemed a peaceful place.

Vast temporary food markets had materialised in alleys where household servants bought fresh food for the day's meals. Not a trace of these markets would remain after seven o'clock, by which time streets sweepers with long straw brooms would have erased all signs of their presence. A steady stream of carts pulled by wiry men arrived from the countryside with goods needed to keep the city fed and functioning.

There was little automobile traffic and the rickshaw pullers ran swiftly down the empty streets, tireless and strong from the effects of their first twist of cheap opium smoked soon after waking up. While they worked, other coolies had taken their places to snatch some sleep.

North down Thibet Road their bare feet steadily slapped the warming pavement, past sleek racehorses being exercised by *mafoos*, or trainers, at the city's main racetrack. They reached the rendezvous where three large Fords stood ready to transport them west to the Grand Canal.

The coolies loaded their bags onto the cars, taking special care with the clock, before receiving their paltry reward. The iceman arrived with his wagon and fresh supplies as Swan and Flood said hello to the only other American there. Harvey Middleton was a manager with Shanghai's YMCA, built in 1925 at a cost of $280,000 Shanghai dollars.

'Morning fellas,' he said. 'Looks like we may get lucky and avoid the rain.' The tail end of a typhoon had recently lashed Shanghai. Middleton was a round-faced and likeable man, though devoutly Christian. Like many Americans in the religion business he spoke Mandarin well, something wildly beyond the twenty-odd words of pidgin spoken by Swan and Flood, to whom proper Chinese was regarded as outlandish gibberish. Most of the religious people were also university educated, some quite extensively.

'I've been talking to the drivers and they say it's crazy going by boat to Mokanshan—they say it would have been faster, cheaper and smarter just to drive us there by car.'

'So why aren't we doing that?' asked Swan.

'The romance of it all I guess,' he replied.

As six o'clock rolled around, other holiday makers arrived by rickshaw and private car. All were American and all, save Flood, were going to Mokanshan to celebrate the marriage of their friends in the clear mountain air.

The chaperone, a Mrs. Munro, arrived last with her pretty daughter, Daisy, a girl headed for a life of few bumps, judging by her spectacles and bluestocking air.

The others, all young and unmarried, were obviously the wedding's 'fast' element. Two couples were themselves engaged and thus allowed to hold hands, provided the situation allowed for such licentious behaviour. Flood suspected a singsong was in the offing. Given his upbringing, he could smell one from a mile away before it even started. Introductions were made all round and seating arranged for the journey. Not a bible was in sight and all appeared determined to have some fun.

Soon the small convoy, laden with food and luggage packed up on the tops of cars, was heading westward. The city quickly gave way to farmland, flat and steaming in the heat. All that remained of Shanghai was a slight smudge of coal smoke adrift over the farmland. Swan and Flood were travelling in the lead car with Middleton, who sat in the front conversing with the driver about the recently constructed road to Soochow, which had been built by the soldiers of

Chiang Kai-shek's army. Before long the three Americans had been lulled to sleep by the heat and the rocking motions made by the big car.

Three hours later they arrived at the Grand Canal, just south of the ancient city of Soochow. The surrounding area was prosperous looking with neat farms facing both sides of the waterway.

Their boat was basically a flat-bottomed barge, about seventy-five feet long and fifteen wide, with a second covered deck on top. It featured a narrow verandah around the top floor, as well as a kitchen and small dining room on the deck level where the crew stored the baggage.

A wizened boat boy, whose age could have been anywhere from forty to sixty, slipped the mooring ropes and off chugged the little craft of Christians into the melee of small boats that clogged up that section of the canal. The trip was an entirely novel experience for all the passengers. Brownie cameras were unpacked and the passengers began excitedly recording the start to the journey.

In the vain hope of catching a breeze, Swan and Flood found some chairs near the stern of the boat on the upper verandah. Most of the other boats on the canal were heaped with cargo. Though most were propelled by engines and steered by long oars in the stern, bits of brown sail, accordion-like in appearance, could be spotted in the distance.

They were joined by a thin young man wearing a straw boater and dragging a chair along behind him. He introduced himself as Herbert Armitage.

'You've captured the coolest part of the boat,' he said in a friendly way.

Swan and Flood made room for him to join them.

'The scenery around here hasn't changed much in the past 4,000 years,' Armitage said conversationally. 'I teach history at St. John's University and to me this is like travelling in one of H.G. Well's time machines—you work at the *North China Daily News* don't you?' he asked Swan who nodded.

'This Grand Canal that we're on,' said Flood. 'I was reading that it's kind of like the pyramids except that it's a lot more useful and, of course, not as interesting looking.'

'That's one way of putting it,' laughed Armitage. 'Except that the pyramids don't really capture the scale of this canal—on some sections more than five million people were press ganged into working on it and altogether millions died while building it.

'And all, according to legend, so that the Emperor in Peking could get his lichee nuts fresh from Canton. It plays second fiddle to the Great Wall but is really much more impressive.'

Others had joined in the impromptu history lesson, enjoying the novelty of hearing about Chinese history while travelling through it. Swan broke in.

'If the canal runs all the way from Peking, which is near the sea, all the way to Canton, which is *on* the sea, then why did they have to go by canal when they could have just sailed there on the ocean instead?'

'Pirates, then as now,' replied Armitage, 'But the Grand Canal really only goes from Peking to Hangchow—after that you have to follow various rivers to get to Canton.'

'Do you think there might be any pirates around here?' asked Swan hopefully.

'I doubt it,' said Armitage. 'But I brought along a couple of guns just in case the ducks start acting up.'

Soon he and Flood were discussing guns, shooting, fishing and Flood's plans of getting into the bamboo fly rod business.

Although the area had been ravaged by war less than five years before it was once again fully under cultivation with huge fields of mulberry trees, now stripped of the leaves that would be used to spin silk. Further along was cotton, fields of sugar cane, grain and surprisingly, flowers, mainly chrysanthemums used to flavour tea. Every hundred yards or so was a pond with a thatched bamboo building nearby, usually housing ducks being fattened up for the Shanghai market.

Everywhere in the fields were stooped figures crouching under the shade of large conical hats, their children not far away. The sounds of the city had completely vanished.

Miss Munro approached Swan.

'You're one of the wayward YMCA boys aren't you? The ones who jumped ship in Shanghai. I've heard all about you. My name is Daisy.'

For a religious type she was pretty bold, thought Swan.

'It's not the kind of work you can do if your heart's not in it I guess. What do you do?'

There was a sudden commotion up near the bow. At the prospect of some action the sportsmen, Flood and Armitage, practically vaulted through the cabin onto the small front deck where Daisy's mother had been enjoying a late-morning nap.

Some fishing cormorants had been spotted. A fisherman in a flat bottomed rowboat with two pointed ends was working eight of the large fishing birds, long necked and dirty black in colour, one pair at a time...The birds were well-trained and free to work without the neck rings used to prevent them from swallowing their prey whole.

As the houseboat passed alongside, the captain haggled briefly with the fisherman, who with effortless agility, proffered two fish in a basket at the end of a long bamboo pole. Satisfied, the captain tossed some coins into the same container. Cameras clicked furiously at the exchange.

'I go to college in Virginia,' responded Munro finally. 'Or at least I did until I decided to accompany mother on this trip to China. My father passed away this winter and my sisters and I, I'm the youngest, thought it would be good for her to get away for a while.

'Hey, look at that boat on the shore!' she added, interrupting herself. Another fisherman was bringing his pointy boat down to the riverbank on a set of wheels. Inside the boat sat six cormorants delicately preening themselves. More cameras clicked.

'I love China,' she said. Swan realised it had been some time since he had spoken with a girl who wasn't a prostitute, servant or adventurer. He found himself telling her about his work at the paper, exaggerating his role a little but giving her a good idea of how his job gave him the opportunity to see parts of Shanghai that few Westerners ever saw.

In places where the ground rose on the sides of the canal parts of the waterway had walls that reared up sixty feet high. In the partial shade on the top deck, the group broke open large hampers containing fruit, sandwiches and bottles of soda pop, all packed in ice.

'What time do you figure we'll get to Mokanshan?' Flood asked Armitage.

'It's quite a ways yet,' he replied. 'I think we'll be lucky to get there tonight by midnight, barring anything unforeseen.

Several of the group had pulled out books and magazines and were settling in for a leisurely afternoon of reading.

Daisy asked Armitage whether he was working on research of his own.

'Well, not really much; so far just a few articles. The latest one was about how Westerners and Chinese looked at each other way back in the old days. She smiled, encouraging him to continue.

'In the absence of any real knowledge they had some pretty funny ideas—early explorers from Europe wrote of a tribe of people who were hunted down for their blood which the Chinese were said to use as a special ink. All hogwash of course.'

'The Chinese for their part described gifts of pillows given to emperors by foreigners which, when used for sleeping, enabled the sleeper to travel around the world. I guess that's what had me thinking about time travel earlier,' he said to Swan and Flood.

'More recently,' he continued. 'Before Chinese people took up dancing the way they have, their newspapers regularly reported how foreigners in their dance clubs usually danced together without clothing on...'

Swan and Flood exchanged looks of amusement.

'You see, because Chinese people weren't allowed in the dancehalls, except perhaps as workers, the average Chinese person greatly enhanced what went on inside them—the same is true with people everywhere.'

'Care to try some fishing?' Flood asked Armitage. 'I've got some line and a couple of hooks in my bag somewhere.'

The canal at this point was between sixty and a hundred yards wide with stone facings on each side. Elegant rounded bridges, designed to let boats pass underneath, periodically crossed smaller offshoots of the main canal. The traffic was steady in both directions, small sampans keeping out of the way of immensely long barges carrying grain, silk, coal and cotton. Sometimes these were pulled along the shore by large groups of trackers using ropes. Whole families in Sampans would cheerily wave at the ungainly pleasure boat as it putt-putted south at about four knots per hour.

Every couple of miles stood reinforced blockhouses, bristling with machine guns and manned by soldiers of Chiang Kai-shek's army. Both Japanese and Kuomintang warplanes flew overhead, contrasting sharply with the utter peacefulness of the surrounding farms and sluggish riverboat traffic.

A few scattered raindrops began falling, much to the relief of those suffering from the high humidity and hundred-degree temperature. The two fishermen gave up their lines and stripped off their shirts for an *al fresco* shower. Swan descended to join them, as did Daisy before she was intercepted by her mother.

'Perhaps the gentlemen should bathe at the back of the boat and the ladies at the front,' she suggested reasonably. Before long the entire boat all the passengers were enjoying a shower.

The rain then began beating down furiously, reducing the visibility to a few feet. The bathers all sought shelter in the small dining area where they laughingly used odd bits of clothes to dry themselves. The effect was erotic with clinging wet dresses and everyone jostling about. Mrs. Munro soon sorted the different sexes to various upstairs rooms where they could change as the boat boy prepared the kettle to make everyone hot cups of tea.

The inside of the cabin was festooned with wet clothes as the party gathered. Flood winked at Armitage and the three separately nipped upstairs to discreetly add a dollop of whiskey from a hip flask provided by Flood.

'Wouldn't do to let the others know there was whiskey on board,' murmured the professor. 'We'd soon find ourselves walking to Mokanshan.'

'Mrs. Munro is sitting right beside a few bottles of the finest,' whispered Swan.

They sipped in companionable silence, the beating of the rain on the roof making conversation difficult. Soon they were joined by Middleton.

'Did any of you fellows bring any guns or rifles along on this trip?' he asked. 'The captain says that sometimes bandits use the rain to sneak up and rob boats when it's like this.'

Armitage took his pipe from his mouth with alacrity.

'I've got a shotgun and a rifle.'

'I'm with the Shanghai Volunteer Force,' enjoined Flood.

'Right,' replied Armitage, squaring his shoulders. 'You take the .410.'

Middleton, realizing he would be without a gun, slumped his shoulders in disappointment.

Swan elected to stay upstairs sipping whiskey while the other two made ready to repel the pirates. Soon he was joined by Daisy, her mother and another couple, Alice Marsh and Nick Brown.

All the lights on board had been turned off to help the captain's vision and to present less of a target to any thieves who might be watching from the banks of the canal.

'Someone mentioned field of fire so I though I'd be safer up here,' giggled Daisy.

'If we aren't attacked then Luther will sulk for a week,' whispered Swan, remembering the outline of Daisy's body in her wet dress.

Soon every sound heard through the noise of the rain was fraught with menace. Except for the crew and perhaps Mrs. Munro, everyone was thoroughly enjoying themselves.

'I have a cuckoo clock in a box downstairs,' said Swan softly. 'Perhaps we should unleash that on the pirates.'

'Maybe a dose of Christian fellowhood might set them straight,' she whispered back.

Swan realised he had read her all wrong. He wondered whether she might even like some whiskey.

'Are you all right out there Daisy?' asked Mrs. Munro from the upstairs cabin where she'd gone for a rest.

'I'm fine mother,' she replied. 'Mr. Swan and I are just keeping an eye out back for the pirates.'

'Fine dear, I'm just going to have a bit of a nap. Let me know if they climb on board.'

Swan and the girl sat face-to-face, knees touching as the light began to fade. Soon the rain lessened.

'Say Daisy, would you mind if I had a drink?' he whispered. 'We've got a bottle hidden away downstairs.'

'Go right ahead,' she replied. 'I don't toe the line.'

Swan crept downstairs. Flood and Armitage were passing the flask back and forth, their weapons wedged between their legs. The captain also held a small glass of whiskey.

'The captain says that three boats have been attacked in the past two months,' said Armitage, obviously enjoying himself immensely. 'They usually sneak on board then go after the captain, hold a gun to his head.'

'They particularly like these boats,' added Flood in a whisper. 'They know there's often rich foreigners on board. So we might get lucky.'

Swan held out his cup to be filled.

'Good luck,' he said. 'I'll keep an eye out the back.'

He crept back upstairs, taking the opportunity to move his chair closer to Daisy.

'Want to try some?'

She took a sip. Outside the sky had been perceptibly getting lighter as the rain slowly diminished and the setting sun shot in under the clouds.

'How long are you going to be in China?' he asked.

"Our ship sails in two weeks for Hong Kong, on a Thursday I think,' she replied. 'I wish we were staying longer. Where do you come from back home?' she asked.

'Outside a little town called Hastings in Michigan,' he answered. 'My Dad owns a fox ranch there but things have been pretty slow since the Depression started. What about you?'

'We're from Norfolk, Virginia. Is that where you know Luther from?'

'We met at the university there a couple of years ago. We spent more time away from school just having fun and finally we just packed it in. There didn't seem much sense wasting money on college when neither of us was that interested. Then his dad got us the jobs with the YMCA. That's how we ended up over here last summer.'

'All the way from a fox farm to Shanghai,' she said. 'I don't blame you for wanting to try something else, especially something like newspaper work. Do you know Emily Hahn? I've read some of her stories in the *New Yorker* and I've been dying to meet her.'

Swan smiled and nodded that he did, recalling that Emily Hahn would soon be giving him a car. Then he remembered that Hahn was only expecting a few negatives at most. He and Flood had almost twenty.

Why not sell some then sell some of the others separately? This *was* China and he had nothing against getting rich.

'Um, Emily, she's a friend of mine,' said Swan.

A shotgun blast filled the air.

The boat rang with screams and shouting. Much to Swan's delight, Daisy flung herself at him.

'Got him,' yelled Armitage from below.

The houseboat cut its engines as the upstairs passengers gathered, the smell of burnt powder rising up the staircase.

Swan took the opportunity of grabbing Daisy securely around the waist.

Flood's face popped into sight.

'Hi there! A flock of ducks set in and we couldn't help it—the prof here just knocked one down! Sorry to wake you all up!'

Swan's arms remained around Daisy as she laid her head on his shoulder, laughing softly. Checking around to see her mother wasn't anywhere, he gave her a quick kiss on the lips. She enthusiastically kissed him back. Swan, forgetting for a moment he wasn't dancing with a prostitute, put his hands on her buttocks and pulled her close.

She broke away, readjusting her glasses, as her mother hove into sight, eyeing them suspiciously from the doorway of the cabin, their bodies silhouetted against the sunset.

"Hehem, perhaps it's time we ate our dinner,' she said, grabbing the railing and turning to face the stairs.

The rest of the night passed quietly, with people talking in low tones. Swan and Daisy sat next to each other. Although the others were now impatient to reach the Mokanshan landing, Swan and Daisy were in no big rush to be anywhere.

A couple of hours south of the farming town of Kashing the awkward barge finally reached its destination, a well-constructed boathouse on firm stone pilings set on the western side of the canal.

Immediately a gang of coolies swarmed into the dining room, upending the luggage and shouldering it onto the wharf. The Americans stood aside, gathering odds and ends and checking for missing objects before stepping onto dry land.

Flood and Armitage were keeping to the side of the pier, leaning slightly unsteadily against one another and laughing.

It had become apparent that the coolies meant to carry them up the mountain in sedan chairs.

'I don't think we even made arrangements at a hotel,' said Flood.

"That's OK, said Armitage. 'You can sleep in my room and get settled in the morning.'

Swan helped Daisy's mother onto a sedan chair then Daisy herself, giving her hand a squeeze. Already the other coolies had begun the climb up the mountain.

They were about to arrive in Mokanshan.

From the *North-China Daily News*:

GUERILLA TACTICS AGAINST THE REDS

Generalissimo's Difficulties In Chasing Fugitives

Kweiyang, Apr.13

Pursuing communists is no joke for the Generalissimo or any of those whose serious business it is to cope with the menace. In themselves the communists are not altogether fools when it comes to trekking across country evading the Government troops; and aiding them is the very nature of the country itself. The more one travels through it, and looks at it, and thinks about it, the more one is convinced that only a miracle, or the exhibition of crass stupidity, can corner them. Miracles are not likely to happen, and the communists, who have their lives to save, are not likely to commit any act of stupidity. The hundreds of square miles of conical mountains, the consistent cloudiness of the sky and the lowness of the ceiling for flying, help them against infantry and aeroplanes. It is only on odd days that any observation or bombing can be done from the air, and the exceptional mobility of the communist hordes over the ground soon gets them out of range of the troops. The communists have no supply columns to harass them in their marching. Each man looks after his own stomach, and they all feed off the country. They have their ammunition to carry and a few cooking pots, and that is all. They travel by night by pressing the country people to guide them, and the darker and rainier it is the better they like it. But they are in a land far from flowing with milk and honey, and for 10,000 of them to get food is a tremendous problem. Some say that there are more of them, but that is a large mouth to feed while running willy-nilly about the country. Now they have Mao Chao-tung, a boon companion of Chu Teh to depend on but he is no military man. He is a politician and a theorist, native of Hunan. Once he was a schoolmaster. He used to be one of the original members of the Central Political Committee in Canton after Dr. Sun Yat-sen's death. Under Russian influence he threw himself and his dreams in with the communists, and he has been in the field since the advent of the so-called communist movement.

CHAPTER 14

Word had travelled north to Mao Tse-tung that his arch enemy, Chiang Kai-shek, might soon be visiting the capitalist retreat of Mokanshan. The information came from none other than Chiang Kai-shek's sister-in-law, Soong Ching-ling. Sun Yat-sen's widow had also defied Chiang Kai-shek's censorship ban by arranging a meeting between Mao and Edgar Snow, an American journalist who lived in Shanghai. Further tugging the toothless tiger's tail, Ching-ling had also been shipping revolvers and ammunition to the communists through a German dentist working in Xian.

Mao and his men were living in caves in Baijiaping in the mountains of north-west Shanshi Province, just south of the Yellow River. The ragged army were hiding in a maze of four thousand *loess* cliffs in the Bao An region. Everywhere was fine yellow sand, sculpted by the wind into a surreal landscape.

The guerrilla leader sat on his haunches and ran his hand through what was left of his hair, he and his men having shorn their heads in an attempt to cut down on body lice. Mao idly picked at his back teeth in a futile attempt to stop a nagging toothache. He pondered what to do with the information that Chiang might be vulnerable in Mokanshan.

Having recently survived the Long March with the remnants of his tattered force, Mao had managed to strengthen his position in the Chinese Communist Party and, against long odds, turned the wayward journey into a propaganda victory. To have avoided complete annihilation at this stage of the war was, he thought ruefully, an achievement of sorts. Nevertheless, it had been a near run thing.

In reality, the trek had been a headlong, usually directionless, flight in which most of his army had died or deserted and no territory gained. In fact, all of the CCP's southern and eastern bases, both rural and urban, had virtually ceased to exist.

To most of the soldiers—poor, young, uneducated farmers from the southern provinces—the whole exercise had been one long nightmare of starvation, ambush and aimless wanderings through huge swamps and over bitterly cold mountain ranges, some like the aptly named Snow Mountains, fifteen thousand feet high. During one disastrous river crossing in Tibet five hundred men had been drowned. Twice Mao had been reported dead and indeed two of his children had been left to die. He'd succumbed to malaria and had to be carried over some of the mountains in a litter, a blow to his prickly pride.

Yet his leadership was now widely acknowledged. How long this continued depended on whether he could orchestrate some kind of victory and rejuvenate the tired communist movement. Mere survival was no longer enough. The current situation favoured only the Japanese, masters of divide and conquer, attracted to China the way flies are attracted to a rotting corpse.

It had become painfully obvious that the communists must form a pact of some sort with the Nationalists to get the pusillanimous Chiang Kai-shek to take on the Japanese. With even a fraction of the Nationalist's arms and gold the communist guerrillas could achieve miracles.

'The enemy of your enemy is your friend,' he thought absently to himself. The problem was that Chiang, who at the moment was about as mobile as a hog on ice, was paralysed by Japanese power. His instruments of organisation and government were easy targets for their warplanes and clearly Chiang didn't relish being a leader on the run.

Since landing in the remote fastness of Shansi Province, however, Mao's emissaries had made contact with the forces of the Young Marshal in Xian, a northern warlord under no illusions concerning the ambitions of the Japanese. He understood that it was just a matter of time before the invaders turned their eyes, not to mention their guns, to the rest of the country, particularly the coastal regions in the south.

The Young Marshall, Chang Shu Liang, although nominally a serving officer in the KMT army, was proving to be the most farsighted ally the communists had found. Even Mao's Moscow advisors were supportive of a pact, their view being simply that allies of all stripes were needed to fight the fascists. To this end Moscow had sent feelers to Chiang in Nanking.

The Russians had enjoyed mixed success trying to import their revolution to China, thought Mao. One gang of happy-go-lucky Bolsheviks had arrived in Shanghai ten years before with a large stash of Moscow gold. They had promptly embraced capitalist excess, buying convertibles, smart suits and champagne and setting off a small economic boom amongst the city's prostitutes.

Mao turned his thoughts back to Chiang Kai-shek. The Young Marshall, who had cured his opium addiction in Shanghai and travelled widely in Europe, was now demanding the creation of a common Chinese front by bringing together the Nationalist and Communist armies.

Ironically, the Young Marshall was a fascist of sorts, having been heartily impressed with Germany and Italy during his Grand Tour. But he was nevertheless a patriotic Chinese and had clashed many times with the Japanese. They had killed his father, the Old Marshall, when they bombed his train in nineteen twenty-eight. The Japanese had driven the son's army out of Manchuria three years later.

The Young Marshall had gone on, in accordance with the wishes of the little generalissimo, to destroy the communists in Anhwei Province in nineteen thirty-four. Still, he was no lover of Chiang Kai-shek, who had trained at a military school in Japan early in his career and seemed content to let Japan conquer China piecemeal. Mao suspected that Chiang had even signed some kind of secret pact with the Japanese. Even old Cai Ting-kai, the warlord hero of the battles in Shanghai in 'thirty-two and another KMT general, had been itching to have another crack at the Imperial army.

Perhaps he should try to arrange a meeting with Chiang while he was in Mokanshan, a forest covered mountain range where his men could manoeuvre without attracting attention. But how to arrange a meeting without risking his own neck? The Generalissimo had put a bounty on Mao's head worth a cool quarter million Chinese dollars. If Chiang Kai-shek walked into this cave, he thought, I'd put a bullet in his neck.

The image put him in a better humour, momentarily vanquishing his toothache. Like an earlier revolutionary, George Washington, he had a head filled with rotten teeth. With Chiang out of the way, the Nationalist army would welcome the opportunity to stop chasing his ragged-assed army and try for the Japanese, especially if Chiang could be coerced into publicly supporting him.

Some of Chiang's leading warlord generals in southern China had already begun marching north, demanding to be allowed to fight the Japanese. It made sense to have them join the armies of the Young Marshall. With Chiang dead, or at least a prisoner, there would be nothing to prevent them then joining what Mao had grandly named the United National Defence Government, with himself, naturally, as the head of the tribe.

Assassinate him? This might risk the ire of the Nationalists and force them into seeking revenge for the murder of their leader. That left kidnapping him to keep him out of the clutches of the Japanese.

The only problem was Mao's scouts had reported that Chiang's retreat in Mokanshan was a heavily armed fortress, bristling with machine guns and guarded, when he was there anyway, by members of his elite forces. But Mao had spies almost everywhere.

There was a woman in Mokanshan who worked in the kitchen at the little general's compound. She had recently sent word that they were stocking Soong May-ling's favourite delicacies. She'd also reported an advance guard of troops. Despite his efforts to portray himself as a man who loved danger and roughing it, Chiang rarely went anywhere without lots of food and protection.

This was the new problem.

He stepped outside his cave to get some air, wrapping a padded jacket around himself as protection against the cold. Shensi Province, to the north of Inner Mongolia, was as cold as Mao's native Hunan Province was warm and humid.

The camp was hidden from the air. From the cockpit of a plane it was just another peak in a sea of mountains. The safety of the camp was offset, however, by the great distances necessary to reach virtually anywhere. He had sent six men down to Mokanshan to scout the village and the environs of Chiang's little castle. He had been told the fortress contained a little Christian church that could be converted into a firing position to the west of the valley.

He had a half column of men not far from Mokanshan, all ready to move once they'd received the signal from Michael Lindsay, his British radio operator.

Attack his headquarters in force? Appeal to the better instincts of Chiang's soldiers, many of whom might be patriotic Chinese wanting nothing more than a chance to defend their country? Poison him? Trick him into leaving his soldiers behind? Would poisoning be possible? He had, after all, a spy in his kitchen who prepared food for the Nationalist soldiers.

Perhaps it would be easier to drug the food of the guards? Then his men could sneak in and pluck the little chicken from his roost.

Mao sat down and wrote out an order to be radioed to his men, telling them to quietly make for Mokanshan and to await there for further orders. On no account were they to make their presence known to the Nationalists.

The time had come for action.

Chapter 15

Swan was the first to awake, having slept awkwardly in two easy chairs facing one other while Flood and Armitage slept head-to-toe in the room's only bed, an iron framed rack with a lumpy mattress. Flood had ended up using a mosquito net as a blanket and his head was now nestled in snugly alongside Armitage's feet.

Three full glasses of whiskey were placed about the room, which overlooked a valley of lustrous yellow and green bamboo. All three travellers had slept in the sedan chairs on the way up the mountain then gamely attempted to continue the party in the hotel room. Weariness had quickly overtaken them, however, and they had no sooner had a couple of sips before all had fallen asleep.

A waste of fine whiskey though, thought Swan, as he poured the dregs down the sink in the corner of the room. Back home the unfinished alcohol would have been carefully saved. Lots more where that came from though, he thought.

The day promised to be a fine one for the wedding of Bert Porter and Dot Wattie. The sky was postcard blue and there was a chlorophyll-laden tang to the air that Swan had forgotten even existed. Mokanshan's mountains were lent a certain grandeur by their contrast to the flat plains below and their kinship to the distant Himalayas.

Elated by the prospect of a week in this perfect little mountain village, Swan began rustling about the room in an attempt to wake the other two for breakfast and a swim in the village's spring-fed swimming pool.

He threw open the windows and looked down upon the village square. He breathed deeply while surveying the bamboo-laden mountain range, gently swaying like the grass skirt of a Hootchie Kootchie girl. Although the mountain top was a touch under two thousand feet in height, the altitude was sufficient to cut the temperature and freshen the breeze. There were few sounds apart from birdcalls and the odd clang from villagers getting ready for a day of work.

There was some stirring on the single bed. Flood was extricating himself from the tangled netting and looking distastefully at Armitage's feet mere inches from his head.

'A wonder I survived the night,' grumbled Flood.

'You've woken up alongside worst sights, I'd imagine.'

Flood re-examined the recumbent form of Armitage, twitching lightly. The professor grunted and shook his head. 'How does this place look?' he asked.

'Perfect. Not at all like Shanghai and not much like China either,' replied Swan, whose knowledge of the country was confined to Shanghai, a tiny speck on the map of China.

'Those negatives…how are we going to get them to the monkey lady?', asked Flood groggily.

Armitage raised his head painfully.

'Agghh…not used to drinking that much…head hurts.' He looked over grimly at Flood's socks, now wagging beside him on the narrow bed.

'She's supposed to be staying with Chiang Kai-shek so I thought I'd leave a note over at his house telling her where we are,' said Swan. 'And then I guess meet her wherever she wants.'

'How do we know she'll come through with the car?'

'We don't I guess but I think we should deliver all the goods,' replied Swan. 'How about we get our own room while we eat some breakfast? It's a beautiful. You up for a swim Herbert?' Swan turned back to Flood.

'When do you think you'll go see the brigadier?', Swan asked Flood.

'I'll give him a call after breakfast and try to set something up. What time's the wedding?'

'Three o'clock this afternoon.'

The trio opened their suitcases and began rummaging around looking for shorts and swimming costumes. Away from the domestic help they took for granted the room soon looked like it had been ransacked. Swan hastily repacked and moved his bags over to the door, suggesting that he go ahead to try to arrange a room.

'Thanks for putting us up last night,' he said to Armitage, still moaning.

'My pleasure,' he replied painfully.

Swan went to the hall to descend the stairs to the lobby of the Mokanshan Hotel, the biggest and oldest in the area, dating back to the turn of the century. The clerk, a White Russian, soon found them a room down the hall from Armitage. Swan entered the small dining room where among some of the other fellow travellers sat Daisy and her mother.

He joined them, making small talk about the trip and the village. But Daisy had reverted to her bluestocking mode, no longer the playful girl of the night before. They were joined by Flood and Armitage just as Daisy and her mother were finishing up. Swan invited Daisy for a swim but she declined, saying she and her mother were moving after breakfast to a rented house. She said she might drop by after that if they were planning to be there for a while.

He said they probably would although they might take a walk at some point. As Flood and Armitage wolfed down their eggs and bacon, Swan went to find an envelope and some paper to write a message to Emily Hahn saying that they had the negatives and were staying at the Mokanshan Hotel.

Swan next asked the Russian if the hotel had a strongbox. Being told they did, he went upstairs to get the precious package of negatives, still wondering if they should give Hahn all of them or keep a few for themselves.

Soon the negatives were safely stored away and the three Americans heading in the direction of the enormous swimming pool, restricted to members of the Mokanshan Summer Resort Association, mostly Americans, hotel guests and a few Chinese families.

Carved from the mountainside, the little village was almost entirely made from granite. All the houses covering the nearby hills had large verandahs and were of a variety of styles ranging from Indian hill station to Dutch colonial, all of grey dressed stone. A group of foreign children sang a song as they cheerfully descended an amazingly long series of stone steps under the supervision of older versions of themselves.

'Raise a cheer for Mokanshan!
Shout 'til the hilltops ring!
Stand and lift your voice again!
Let everybody sing!

For the birds, for the bees!
For their feathers and their knees!
For the boys and the girls!
For the beauty of the trees!

Raise a cheer for Mokanshan!
Sing for the happy days!
Sing for dear old Mokanshan!
Our heart's delight always!'

'I liked the bit about the birds and bees,' said Armitage. 'Quite progressive. Yesterday it felt like we were in the middle ages and now it seems we've woken up in a different country altogether. It takes a bit of getting used to.'

'I like it,' said Flood with the air of a man who had already decided to move in, settle down and run for mayor. 'I can't wait to meet the brigadier and get things going with the fly rods,' he added, gazing around at the bamboo that might earn him a living or at least enable him to frolic with intent in the mountains for a few weeks.

'Have you called him yet?' asked Swan.

'I tried after breakfast but there was no answer—I'll try him again after a while.'

The pool was literally perched on the mountainside, just at the edge of the village below the big church that loomed down from the largest hill nearby. The pool had to be fifty yards long, Swan estimated, as they paid the few cents admission. The shallow end hugged the hillside and the deep end overlooked a streambed below. The pool even sported a mahogany diving board. Almost everywhere in Mokanshan there was the sound of cascading water.

Adirondack-style chairs stood alongside the shower rooms where the three quickly changed from their clothes. The expectant looks from the children in the pool meant they had little choice but to launch themselves from the diving board.

All three looked liked farmers on holiday with their darkly tanned faces and forearms contrasting vividly with their white bodies. The scorching heat and high humidity of Shanghai didn't lend itself much to sunbathing.

'Do you think you'll be able to just walk up the to the General's house and drop off that note for Hahn?' asked Flood, lying prone in the sun.

'It's easier than trying to call her I think,' responded a similarly incumbent Swan. 'I still think we should give her all the negatives. It's a good deal and I don't want to get tangled up with any gangsters or whatever.'

'Seems a waste of a good opportunity.'

'What are you guys talking about? That fly rod business?', asked Armitage.

Flood looked at Swan who nodded that it was OK to tell him about the Simpson negatives. Flood explained how they had come to possess them and how much Emily Hahn was willing to pay for them.

'Could I take a look at them later on? A fellow doesn't get this kind of opportunity every day,' said Armitage. 'They're really quite historic.'

'Well they're locked up in the hotel safe at the moment,' said Swan. 'But I'm sure we could let you have a peak later on—she's not much to look at.'

'The whole thing is fascinating,' said Armitage. I'm sure the King of England has always had a mistress or two tucked away somewhere or other. Usually they don't marry them.

'Maybe he doesn't believe in being king and is just looking for a way of chucking the whole thing away and trying to live a normal life,' he continued.

'The chances of him just living a normal life are about as high as me taking over his job,' laughed Flood. 'I can't see him out mowing the lawn or taking out the garbage or anything.'

'Well no, I guess not', agreed Armitage. 'It all seems part and parcel of all the awful things happening in Europe. They seem to be heading for war. Look at Spain, Germany and Italy. Spain is already fighting, Mussolini is trying to recreate the Roman Empire and Hitler is the strongest and scariest of the bunch.

'And everyone in England is getting their knickers in a knot over two people who just want to get married.'

Nearby a white boy repeatedly dunked a Chinese boy in the pool. Rich Chinese Christians had recently been allowed to use the pool. Though smaller, the white boy was a much better swimmer and seemed to delight in plunging the larger boy's head under water.

Armitage, watching the boys absently, continued. 'People like the King think fascism is OK because it's the only thing strong enough to beat communism; that's what really has them worried—communism.'

'Do you think the United States will get involved?' asked Swan, turning over on his stomach.

'I don't see it happening.'

Swan and Armitage decided to have another quick dip before trying to find the Generalissimo's house. Flood went off to try to telephone the brigadier from the hotel.

The two swimmers splashed around a bit then hung from the sides at the shallow end.

'What's going to happen here in China?' asked Swan.

'I really don't know but I guess the country will get carved up into different pieces,' replied the professor. 'If push comes to shove between the Japs and the Gissimo I wouldn't put my money on him. As for the communists they'll get taken care of only after the other issues are resolved.'

'Did Luther tell you he saw that killing down at the bridge a couple of days ago?'

'He mentioned it on the boat—pretty terrible.'

Flood returned, having failed again to contact the Brigadier. They changed and left their swimming clothes and towels in the office then asked directions from a man who had dropped by to visit his two deeply tanned and tow-headed little girls.

There was a squawk from the pool. Everyone looked down where the Chinese boy swam slowly away from his victim, who held his hands to his eyes and shrieked painfully.

'What the heck got into him?' said the man, turning his back on the boy. 'As the crow flies it's just directly behind the church up on that hill but a bit over towards the west—you boys going to the wedding later?' They nodded.

'But to walk there you have to follow this path here down to the Andrew Field place, its got blue gables, then up and away from the main road and down for about a quarter-mile. Then you just go back up and over the side of the second hill there…then down to the road that faces the far valley beyond. His place is on a bit of land which sticks out over the valley.'

All three nodded knowingly, counting on the others to have the directions memorised. There seemed no end to the profusion of granite paths that criss-crossed the mountainside. They followed what appeared to be a main one, hugging a level grade around the side of the hill.

Five minutes later they were lost. Each break in the bamboo offered a startlingly different perspective as the trails curved around the main hill of Mokanshan. There were more than a dozen small peaks within a mile or so from the village. Again they asked a foreigner for directions, this time from a woman who more ably steered them back on course. Soon they were atop another hill looking down over another lush valley of bamboo.

In the distance was a compound of buildings, which resembled a cross between a deluxe hunting lodge and a walled seminary, built on a point of land hanging above the valley on three sides. There was a heavily guarded blockhouse at the only visible entrance. A road buzzing with soldiers and vehicles led down from the entrance.

Realising this could only belong to the Generalissimo, they followed another winding path down towards the collection of stone buildings, most topped by two chimneys and girthed with verandahs. Despite its air of an armed camp the Gissimo's compound was remarkably pretty.

'From what I could see the buildings looked a bit like a university campus back home,' said Armitage. 'Sort of New England style but a bit more warlike. Maybe we should get out some white flags.'

Swan had thought there would be a house, perhaps a biggish one, but one he could nonetheless walk up to and ring the doorbell. He hadn't expected a small castle.

Gravity taking over, they descended the path quickly, almost running into a soldier with a bayonet. He barked out what Swan and Flood could only assume was an order to stop dead in their tracks. Armitage, his ability to speak Chinese thrusting him to the fore, bowed his head and explained their mission.

The soldier barked out another order then spoke quickly to a second soldier who had materialised from the undergrowth. He then escorted them down to the road by the entrance to the compound. Above them on the top of a small incline was a machine gun post. Reaching the gatehouse, yet another soldier ran off to the main house beyond. Soon an officer, immaculate in jodhpurs and carrying a Malacca cane, came out to see what the fuss was about. In his wake trailed a half a dozen more soldiers, all armed to the teeth.

Once again, Armitage explained the situation. The officer spit out a command and one of his men took the envelope. The officer turned on his heel and returned to the large building.

Deciding not to go back the same way, the small group began walking down the paved road looking for an easier way back to the hotel. They walked slowly past pickets of armed soldiers guarding the various approaches to the compound from whatever threats might lurk in the valley below. The road, sided by a four-foot wall, was designed to provide cover. The soldiers on picket duty looked at them carefully with the arrogance that all soldiers reserve for unarmed men their age.

In the lee of the mountain the midday sun was quite hot. Swan looked at this watch, while removing his pith helmet to wipe his brow.

'We've got time for a quick swim and a quicker lunch if we're going to make that wedding at three,' he said.

I don't think I'm on the guest list,' said Flood. 'I didn't confirm I'd be coming.'

'I imagine you'd be made real welcome,' said Armitage.

Swan, hoping to get back to the pool in case Daisy was there, suggested a short cut up the mountain then down to the church. All the trails, he explained, were flat and meandering so if they wanted to make time they should go for a more direct, uphill route.

Briefly out of sight of the soldiers, they slipped into the undergrowth then up the hill, following the course of a dried-out stream. The hill was steep and the footing uncertain. Sweating profusely, they bypassed a trail on level ground and continued to make for the top of the hill. Getting into their stride, they hoped that by getting as high as possible they would be able to spot a landmark such as the church or the village.

It worked. From high atop the main mountain they could survey most of the area around them, including the far slope dotted with holiday homes around the village of Mokanshan. They now gazed down on the turreted church that occupied the hill directly above the village. The view was breathtaking, a toytown obscured in green and yellow.

They paused to catch their breath. Thankfully, there was a breeze at the summit.

'Why do you think these negatives are so important?' asked the professor.

Both Swan and Flood looked over at him carefully. Finally Swan spoke.

'Because they might be embarrassing to the King?'

Armitage, in the manner of all professors, prepared to answer his own question.

'Well, maybe', he said. 'But I think it's two things really. The first is the Chinese love of plots and secrets—their history, like ours, is full of stories about how love either conquered all or brought everything crashing down—sort of like Romeo and Juliet.

'Secondly, and this is more important, the Chinese government—that is the Chiangs—see something really big happening on the other side of the world and their sense of self importance is such that they long to be involved in the drama. Sort of importance by association.'

'Then the negatives aren't really that important?'

'Oh they might be for a while but I reckon it'll all be hushed up somehow.'

Choosing the most promising looking descent they aimed for the village below, soon finding a path leading to the swimming pool. Approaching it, they saw Daisy step up onto the diving board, bounce a bit then flex her legs and arms confidently.

Her figure was silhouetted against the sun as the three young men stopped to watch. Her calves tightened as one foot sprung slightly before the other. Her figure was peerless, legs and hips perfectly in proportion.

All three exhaled simultaneously after she dove, popping up close to them at the pool's shallow end.

'Where have you been?' she asked, her personality having transformed again since breakfast. 'This water is heavenly.'

After their hill climbing exertions, the water felt even better than it had earlier. The sun was warmer and their hangovers had been left behind on the hillside. Amazingly, Daisy seemed as friendly to Swan as she had been the day before. Whispering to him, she apologised for her behaviour at breakfast, explaining that she had been trying to dampen any suspicions about them her mother may have been harbouring.

Still in the water while Daisy pulled herself up the ladder, Swan found his throat constricting and his heart beating faster. He followed her out of the pool, trying to keep his wits about him.

'Would you like to sit with us at the wedding?' she asked. As if on cue, the church's organ emitted a few exploratory notes from atop the hill.

'I guess I should be getting back to our house—it's a wonderful big place on the back side of the hill—the views are breathtaking.'

After drying and changing, the four made their way back towards the hotel. Before they reached it Daisy gave Swan a smile and a squeeze on the arm, said goodbye to the other two, then took one of the many paths which branched off from the main road.

Armitage and Flood ribbed Swan about Daisy, much to his enjoyment. As Armitage had predicted, an invitation to attend the wedding was waiting for Flood back at the hotel. Caught up in the tribe-like enthusiasm of the place, he was now glad to be going.

The lobby of the hotel was filled with Americans dressed for church. Some couples with children had obviously lunched at the hotel, the men in white linen suits while the women wore floppy hats and sleeveless silk dresses. Many of the fathers wore pith helmets as did their sons. The girls were topped with floppy straw hats, smaller versions of their mothers.

All of the gifts, including the cuckoo clock, had been taken by bearers to the tennis club where everyone would assemble after the wedding. Flood had wound the clock before wrapping it, joking that it might be taken for a bomb.

In small groups they began the ten-minute climb up to the church, organ music accompanying them on their way. As they grew nearer, the music was augmented by bells, giving the valley a pure and alpine flavour. Waving their riding crops jauntily at passing friends, some of the guests headed for nearby stables on horseback.

To reach the Protestant church, the procession passed through the grounds of a small flint Catholic chapel, more Welsh Methodist in style than Church of Rome. The path up the hill, from which the three tennis courts of the club could be seen in the distance, was steep and everywhere small clusters of celebrants paused to catch their breath in the shade of the bamboo groves.

Daisy and her mother stood chatting with the Reverend Bradford Armstrong, leader of the local Baptist flock, as well as spiritual advisor to Chiang Kai-shek and Big Ears. Armstrong was an established conduit to influential religious groups back in the United States, possibly explaining his importance to the Generalissimo.

The church was the centre of American life in Mokanshan. It boasted a reading library stocked with more than two thousand books; a kindergarten and the office of the Mokanshan Summer Resident's Association. The local boy scouts and girl guides met here, separately of course, while the auditorium was used for concerts and amateur dramatics. There were more than two hundred private houses in Mokanshan, slightly more than half occupied by Americans who had taken the lead in raising the money for the new church, built in nineteen twenty-three to replace an earlier one hit by lightning.

The community had turned out in force for the wedding. Neighbours, visitors and other friends were introduced and re-introduced. The Munroes, Flood, Swan and Armitage entered the church together and sat together near the back. After the bright sunshine it was dark and cool inside. As Mrs. Munro introduced herself to the people beside her on the pew, Daisy whispered to Swan.

'Sorry again about this morning,' she smiled conspiratorially. Before she could continue the organist began the wedding march and everyone rose. She gave Swan's hand a squeeze and his heart gave another small lurch.

The pastor, his voice taking on the measured cadences of his calling, began his sermon. Although Flood and Swan weren't particularly close to Bert and Dot, they had gotten to know them fairly well on the trip over to China the previous summer. The two young missionaries faced each other near the pulpit as Armstrong read the service.

As a son of the manse Flood was an able judge of sermons. What set this one apart was the exotic setting, although the words and music gradually overcame the surroundings.

Swan's thoughts were solely on Daisy. His mind dwelled on erotic images of her, with and without her swimming costume on. Remembering he was in a church he struggled manfully to think more suitable thoughts, failing completely.

Armitage was considering what an amazing streak of coincidences had put the racy negatives into the hands of Swan and Flood, two likeable but terribly naive fellows caught in an unlikely web of international intrigue.

Tuning into the sermon he listened to the reverend allude to the Boxer Rebellion of nineteen hundred in terms of a religious catharsis. Emotion catching in his throat, the pastor entreated his flock to consider how that terrible uprising ultimately served as a rite of passage for Christianity in China. That's a bit of a stretch, thought Armitage. There's still an awful lot of heathens out there.

Daisy was considering taking things with Swan a step further. Soon she and her mother would be leaving for the United States and she'd yet to have an affair to tell her friends about back home.

The couple at the front exchanged rings and, blessed, were joined in holy matrimony. The groom appeared bathed in perspiration, no doubt in anticipation of some really serious praying, thought Swan. The organ music burst back into life and the congregation into song as the newlyweds trooped down the aisle.

Outside the church a horse and buggy was waiting for the happy couple. The guests hip-hip-hoorayed and showered them in rice as they led the way back down the hill to the tennis courts to celebrate.

CHAPTER 16

Mr. Mills, Emily Hahn's pet gibbon, thought he was human and acted accordingly. He had been getting a bit aggressive recently, thought Hahn, probably as a result of her frequent absences.

Hahn was packing for another *tête-à-tête* with the Chiangs. At any moment, she was expecting to be picked up by one of their chauffer-driven cars. Mr. Mills seemed fully aware of this and shifted fitfully in his diaper.

Gibbons are defined as any small ape of the genus *Hylobates*, native to South-East Asia and characterised by slender bodies and long arms. Shortly after arriving in Shanghai, Hahn had spotted Mr. Mills wailing horribly in a small cage at a local market. Outraged, she'd promptly paid a tidy sum of Shanghai dollars and secured his emancipation. While at first a model pet, he was getting to be more and more of a handful every day.

Although in Gibbon terms he was now considered middle-aged, the diapers were a necessary precaution and help for dealing with his angst-ridden urinations when vexed. Hahn's *ayi*, or maid, was terrified of the beast, who was entirely indulged by the animal-loving Hahn.

Mr. Mills, as his name indicated, was male and the possessor of a hearty fondness for masturbation, preferably whilst rubbing up against a human leg. The *ayi*, Fung, had been forced to fight off his aggressions on several occasions. He was careful to control himself with Hahn, however. She didn't tolerate any monkey business.

Things had been very interesting in Nanking, she thought, stuffing clothes into a suitcase. Fung stood by, periodically offering to take over the packing duties from Hahn while keeping one eye fixed on Mr. Mills. Changing the diaper of a frisky Mr. Mills tested the maid's sanity while bathing him was even worse.

Hahn spoke Chinese fairly well for someone who had only been in China for a year. She explained to Fung she would be away in the mountains for at least a week. Fung busily computed the cost of hiring someone to help her keep the beast under control.

Hahn packed some stout shoes for exploring wherever it was they were going. From what she had heard it was a small mountain village recreated as a fairy-tale type of place for foreigners and their children. She was slightly wistful about children these days, having spent some time a few days before with a friend and her newborn baby boy. Mr. Mills was not, she reflected, a good substitute for a real baby.

Something was stirring with the Generalissimo and his clan, she thought, racking her mind to the possibilities of what might happen next in this amazingly Machiavellian country. Recently talk had swirled around a KMT alliance with the communists and the possibility of what she considered to be some long overdue resistance against the Japanese. Several nationalist warlords had developed restive notions of late, notions that Chiang had previously squashed. Then, of course, there was the matter of the recent slaying at the bridge.

Rumours had it the Japanese were taking a hard line against the Nationalist government and were threatening to attack his forces in the Yangtze River delta. The bayoneting at the bridge lent support to this theory. Hahn was astute enough to realise there might be something in Mokanshan which was drawing the Gissimo there. She had heard his neighbour there was Big Ears Tu. In all likelihood, he would be needing the triad boss's help in facing whatever calamities were in store. But why not do it in Shanghai or Nanking?

Of course, there was the small but influential American community in Mokanshan. Even Big Ear's money shrunk in significance to what the American government could provide. Was the Gissimo meeting with Big Ears and the Missimo with the Americans?

Hahn had failed to find the negatives of the Simpson postcards although there was now no shortage of stories about Simpson's escapades in Shanghai. While some were true and others fabricated, Simpson's chequered history in Shanghai had become the hottest gossip in the city.

The Italian community was proving to be the most fertile source of stories. Simpson had enjoyed affairs with at least two leading fascists, one in Shanghai and the other in Beijing, having spent considerable amounts of time in the two cities.

Hahn's good friend and admirer, Sir Victor Sassoon, had told her that a few months previously a few voyeurs, including a visiting Charlie Chaplin, had passed the postcards around at a private party hosted by a visitor from Hollywood. Sassoon couldn't remember the man's name or much else about him except that he had been travelling with Chaplin. Back then, Simpson was only rumoured to be an acquaintance of Edward, then just Prince of Wales.

Hahn mentally ticked off all the opium paraphernalia she would need for her journey. At least a week's supply of the drug and her collection of pipes, parts of which were cleverly concealed in a teapot. She wondered if she should snatch a smoke now before the trip began. She suspected they might be travelling by train, in which case smoking was no problem. Cars and boats were much less convenient. She decided to light up.

She went into her bedroom and closed the door behind her. After filling her bowl she switched on a large fan behind her and opened the window to clear the fumes from the room.

Big Ears had accompanied the Chiangs to Mokanshan for their honeymoon, she remembered, hauling on the pipe. They were practically inseparable. She let the smoke drift out the window. Hahn was quite careful when smoking the drug. She had seen men executed for doing what she now did at least half-a-dozen times daily.

There was a knock on the front door of her house. A car was waiting for her outside.

Big Ears and Pockmarked Huang were meeting in Big Ear's Frenchtown headquarters. Huang had news to report concerning the missing negatives. By going through government records and combing them for all references to shops and organisations that had ever printed photographs, Tu's men had heard about the French priest and his secret hobby.

Two of Huang's detectives had visited the printing shop and spoken to a man there who had witnessed the two Americans going through Bouchard's belongings. On the detective's orders, the man had searched the priest's room and found one of their name cards.

He was a newspaperman, Huang told his boss. His name was Redvers Witherspoon and he worked at the *North China Daily News*.

'Get the priest's pictures from this man, this reporter, as quickly as possible,' said Tu quietly. 'I would like to give them to little brother when we meet. Do whatever it takes to get them.'

CHAPTER 17

A lone communist scout, surnamed Wu, peered down at the wedding party on the tennis courts from his hideout on a nearby hillock. While the Generalissimo was nowhere to be seen, Wu was nevertheless transfixed by what strange creatures these foreigners were.

The men had nice hats though, he conceded, remembering sun-baked marches or night watches in which the rain had teemed down on him like endless buckets being emptied over his head.

The presence of the foreign *Kwai Loh* caused him to reflect bitterly on the fate of his poor country, an ancient civilisation that seemed so very easy for foreign barbarians to pluck clean. Most people he knew struggled merely to survive. He was made angrier by the tantalising smell of cooking food—whole pigs on spits and flocks of frying chickens lined up in neat rows. Chinese pigs! Chinese chickens!

The white people seemed to have very poor balance for they were all crammed onto ground which was perfectly flat, amazingly so in this country of hills and valleys. The grass had presumably been nibbled short by animals. White lines were painted everywhere, presumably to keep the foreigners from straying beyond the safety the flat ground provided.

Strangely, this fear of uneven ground did not seem to affect the young foreign devils that scampered as easily as Chinese children over the rocks which surrounded the level patch of ground. Perhaps, he said to himself, the older people were affected by the clothes and shoes they wore, making it necessary for them to stand on ground as flat as the face of a compass.

They seemed a jolly bunch and certainly well fed. Some of the people were the biggest he had ever seen, both males and females. That they were all rich he had no doubt for they were not only big but richly dressed as well. He could hear music but couldn't see any musicians. He strained his eyes to see if the music came from one of those machines that could make sounds. Some of the men in camp were familiar with them. Come the revolution everyone would own one. Not just rich capitalists.

The music began to slow down and the scout focussed intently to see if he could trace the source of the dying sounds. A Chinese man, a servant most likely, replaced a flat, black disk and began winding up a box on which a huge flower-like horn was placed. Different music began playing and the mystery was solved. The scout got more comfortable, the sun warming him nicely as he lay down his rifle.

He remembered bitterly cold nights during the Long March when he had tried to sleep while standing up, the ground too wet to lie on. His sunny little lookout made a comfortable roost. And it was exciting to see up close what life would be like after the revolution.

In a bold tip to modernity and as a courtesy to those guests who weren't Methodists or Baptists, some light and sedate dancing was to be allowed. Swan and the others, including Daisy, had already eaten some cake and were idling slowly, punch glasses in hand, towards a quiet spot at the corner of the tennis courts, the nets of which had been removed for the party. Mrs. Munro had been keeping an eye on her daughter but had been diverted by a new-found friend from Charleston, her girlhood home.

The foursome was discussing the writer Pearl Buck, a reliably hot topic of conversation amongst Americans that summer in China. Her divorce the previous year had mortified the young missionaries sailing with Swan and Flood, both of whom had grown to loathe the mention of her name.

'I just mentioned the *Good Earth* and the woman I was talking to reacted like I'd blasphemed,' said Daisy to Armitage. 'It's just a book about poor people in China for Heaven's sakes.'

Flood was discreetly pouring whiskey into their punch. 'I think everyone is jealous of her,' he said. 'Did you know Hollywood paid her fifty thousand, the most ever, to make that book into a movie?'

'A lot of the people here have crossed paths with either Buck herself, her father old Absolom Sydenstriker—the only missionary in China not to have read his daughter's book—or her ex-husband, Lossing Buck,' said Armitage, who would be leaving Mokanshan the following day.

'And I think you're right Luther,' he added, sipping his drink. 'People here have been giving their life's work to spreading the gospel with little thanks for their efforts. Pearl Buck comes along; writes a book; gets a million dollars and eats at the White House. No wonder they all hate her so much.'

'So much for Christian charity,' added Daisy.

'And that's another thing,' continued Armitage. 'The only mention of Christianity in the book is a missionary who is almost comically out of touch with reality.'

Swan asked whether they had heard of all the problems the crew from Hollywood ran into while they were filming scenes of rural China for the movie. No one had.

'Well the KMT got all up in arms about how backward looking China was going to be on the silver screen so they raised a fuss. But they didn't want to interfere openly and make the Americans mad.

'Anyway, the filmmakers shot off roll after roll of Chinese countryside. It was only when they got back to Hollywood did they realise the KMT had X-rayed everything just before they left and destroyed miles of film.'

'We're southern Presbyterian, same as the Bucks and the Syden-whatsits,' Daisy turned to Armitage, returning to the topic of Buck. 'And I can tell you that generally the older you are, or the more religious you are, the more you dislike the woman. And that's another thing. It's women who buy her books and women who seem to hate her the most—try to figure that one out.'

After a while, Flood wondered off to try to make another telephone call to the brigadier. Armitage decided to join him, leaving Swan and Daisy alone for the first time.

'Would you like to live here?', asked Swan.

'It's exciting and exotic and I guess I might for a while. But I'm pretty homesick now and I'm looking forward to getting back home, seeing my friends and going back to school. I don't know really.' She paused. 'Do you think you'll be here long?'

I guess until I'm ready to settle down a bit,' he replied seriously. 'There isn't much waiting for me back home…but soon you'll be leaving China so that makes me think less of it.'

Daisy was suddenly overcome with shyness. 'Well,' she said slowly. Then she looked him straight in the eye and kissed him. He kissed her back wishing they were well away from missionaries and mothers.

'Would you like to dance?' she asked. 'I think my mother might be looking for me.'

They went off to join the other people attempting to dance on the grass. It was harder than it looked and after a while they went to get more to drink from the punch bowl. Her hand brushed against his, sending jolts of electricity up his arm.

Flood returned, a huge grin spread across his face. 'I finally got a hold of him,' he said happily. 'I'm going over to meet up with him tomorrow and talk business. He lives down in the valley, somewhere below Chiang Kai-shek's place. He's sending someone over to collect me at nine in the morning.'

Wu had fallen asleep at his post. When he awoke he was looking straight into the big, blue eyes of a very young foreign girl in a white dress and matching white hat. She put her finger to her lips.

'Don't say a word O.K?', she said to him, not realising he didn't speak English. He looked back at her blankly. 'We're playing hide-and-seek.'

She turned her attention to the scene below. Wu began sweating profusely, wondering how to extricate himself without drawing the attention of anybody else. Slowly he got to his feet, just as a young foreign boy came into sight, catching a glimpse of Wu and his rifle. The boy gulped dramatically then began climbing quickly down the hill while yelling for his parents. The little girl smiled at Wu then turned to follow the boy.

'Thanks for keeping quiet,' she whispered.

Keeping low to the ground, Wu fled for the safety of the hills.

The boy's cries had alerted his parents. Someone quickly turned off the phonograph as the boy stumbled onto the courts, breathlessly reporting his discovery of a Chinese man with a rifle up on the hill. Parents dashed off to collect their children, many of whom were still hiding in the woods. The word kidnapping was unspoken but was at the forefront of everyone's worst fears.

The little girl with the white hat came traipsing out of the bamboo, wondering what all the fuss was about, and into the arms of her relieved mother. Her father asked her if she saw anything up on the hillside.

'There was a Chinese man with a gun,' she said, delighted for once to be the centre of attention. 'He was asleep but I woke him up and told him to be quiet because we were playing hide-and-go-seek.'

The adults conferred quietly. Perhaps it had only been a hunter after something for the pot, they said. Perhaps it was one of the Gissimo's men. Looking up into the hillside, covered in gently swaying bamboo, some shivered at the thought of what the forest might be hiding.

The music was turned back on and the party was bravely resumed, parents occasionally taking quick looks at the bamboo groves, now darkening with shadows. The hillside swayed back and forth, mocking the revellers.

CHAPTER 18

Swan and Daisy were idling by the pool, sunbathing and waiting to hear how Flood's interview with the Brigadier had turned out. Nearby sat Mrs. Munro, keeping an eye on her daughter while knitting what appeared to be a large shawl or blanket.

The evening before, just when things were progressing towards what Swan had hoped might be an amorous conclusion, Mrs. Munro had swooped down like a vengeful angel and taken Daisy back to their lodgings, much to Swan's disappointment.

Although he wasn't sure, Swan suspected that perhaps Daisy's mother had discovered that Swan and Flood were not typical God-fearing, young Christian-in-China types. When it came to the American community, Shanghai was a small town indeed and the two had never taken much of an effort to conceal their habits. Until now it had been fun to flaunt it a little bit.

It was also widely known they had used the YMCA as a means of free travel to China, having jumped ship, so to speak, at the first opportunity. The only good news was that Daisy didn't seem to mind his roguish past but, instead, seemed rather attracted by it.

Swan was going slightly cross-eyed while simultaneously trying to catch glimpses of Daisy in her fetching bathing costume while ensuring that her mother didn't catch him at it.

He wished he had some dark tinted aviator's glasses, the kind which had recently become popular back home and which were often advertised in magazines. He resolved to get some at the first opportunity. In the meantime he had to make do with the occasional peak while giving full rein to his voyeurism only when she dove off the diving board.

Her blonde hair contrasted perfectly with the honey brown colour of her skin. From her nicely turned ankles upwards she was about the most perfect specimen of womanhood Swan had ever clapped eyes on. The fact that she seemed willing to go the next step had Swan in a near swoon.

Mrs. Munro, with two other equally beautiful daughters older than Daisy, was an old hand at nipping romance in the bud. She had no intention of lowering her guard for this reporter, much as her daughter seemed to like him. They were leaving for Shanghai in a week or so and from there catching a ship to Hong Kong and then California. She had no intention of letting her daughter out of her sight until they were safely aboard the ship.

If this reporter followed the typical pattern, and she reckoned he would, his next step would probably be a moonlit visit to her bedroom window late at night, particularly if he had hoisted some Dutch courage aboard.

The trouble with young people, she thought to herself, is they think they invented the world and everything in it, including romance. The wedding the day before had been nice in its way but utterly lacking in style. Mrs. Munro intended to marry off her youngest daughter to one of the many rich and eligible Virginia boys back home. It would be a proper Presbyterian affair and her daughter's virtue would be fully intact when she stepped up the aisle.

Her reveries were interrupted by Luther Flood bursting into the swimming pool area, smiling broadly while ripping off his tie. Mrs. Munro was thankful for the fact her daughter wasn't interested in *him*—he looked the type who would ride up on horseback armed with six shooters and kidnap Daisy.

'Well,' he said excitedly. 'It looks like I'm in business. The brigadier and me hit it off like a house on fire—we're partners.'

The sunbathers enthused their congratulations. Mrs. Munro dropped her knitting and asked what the fuss was about.

'Luther has just become a partner in a company which makes fishing rods, mother.'

'Harrumph,' snorted Mrs. Munro mildly. 'Sounds like a wonderful proposition.'

Flood vanished into the changing room. Swan got up on one elbow, the better to look at Daisy.

'I hope it works out O.K.,' he said quietly, jerking his thumb in the direction taken by Flood. 'He borrowed a bunch of money to get into this thing.'

'I hope so too,' replied Daisy as Flood jumped into the pool, shrieking dramatically before miming a fly fisherman hooking a big one, rocking back and forth and pulling back on the imaginary rod.

'No hope for you,' he yelped. 'You're up against a man with a Mokanshan fly rod!' Performance over, he leapt up onto the side of the pool and accepted a towel from a bathing attendant.

'I'm going back down to his house tomorrow for lunch to sign some papers and stuff. You're welcome to come along—there's a reservoir down there which he's got stocked with trout.'

'We'll see how it goes but, sure, sounds fine,' said Swan looking at Daisy.

'He's got a crew of Chinese fellers working on the rods and he thought we'd like to give them a try,' continued Flood. 'You'll like the Brigadier. For a Limey he's a pretty nice old guy although a little funny.'

'In what way?' asked Swan.

'Well, the Brits are different than us. He lived in India for a long time but retired here. He's very proper acting and everything; he has these two little Indian guys as servants and he treats them like they're his soldiers—they salute him and all and sort of click their heels—which doesn't work as they're barefoot.'

'Maybe they *were* his soldiers,' said Daisy.

'Yeah, maybe,' continued Swan. 'Anyway he gets all dressed up for lunch and dinner—it's a good thing I wore a tie at least and well, he's British, he talks funny—old boy this and old boy that.'

'What's the operation like?' asked Swan.

'Well, the Indians are supervising maybe half a dozen Chinese. They've only really begun to produce the rods; they've been experimenting a lot and all…'

'What're the rods like?' asked Swan.

'Well, there's two sizes, one ten foot and the other twelve—the only real problem they've had is fitting the various lengths together. You know, for travelling with. They looked OK, the bamboo seemed fine. Tomorrow I'll find out better when we use them to fish. You wouldn't believe his house though—he's got tiger skin rugs, spears—looks like the headquarters of the Bengal Lancers.'

'Mother, could I…'

'I'm sorry dear,' she replied without looking up. 'But we're having the Reverend Armstrong and Mr. Field over to lunch tomorrow and I'll need your help getting everything ready…

'Humph,' snorted Daisy, much like her mother had earlier. 'This is supposed to be my holiday too.' She crossed her arms.

'Well, why don't you come by for tea later tomorrow afternoon? asked Flood. 'I'm sure the brigadier won't mind if we have a little picnic there. I'll arrange it with him then organise some transportation for you.'

Daisy looked at her mother who sighed and acquiesced. 'Providing we're not imposing on the brigadier,' she said. 'Daisy's late father was a colonel in our army during the Great War, you know.'

Daisy looked over appraisingly at her mother. It was obvious to her that her mother was also taken by the notion of the mysterious brigadier. She thought to herself that perhaps this British guy could amuse her while she and Eli slipped away.

'We'll organise it for four o'clock,' said Flood brightly. There's a small waterfall and we can all try our hand at fishing—the shorter rods are designed for lady anglers and I'd like to hear what you think of them,' said Flood, already imagining selling the rods in America. Perhaps Daisy could be persuaded to take some samples home with her.

It was Tuesday morning and Emily Hahn was in a contemplative mood. Her trip had started with a huge black Packard arriving at her Kiangse Road home and whisking her off to Nanking, a backwater where, she thought, very little had ever happened until the quixotic general decided to make it his capital.

Scratch that thought, she decided. There isn't a Chinese city anywhere that hasn't had something tremendous happen at one time or another. Their history pre-dates history, she thought. No wonder all the China experts back home were so wrapped up in themselves, peering suspiciously from their exclusive intellectual towers. They wanted to keep it for themselves.

Hahn's career had coincided perfectly with a surge in sexual emancipation that had enabled her to do things back home which women had rarely been able to do—not for lack of ability but simply because of what they were. But like a lot of things, she thought, institutions included, just give 'em a push and over they fall.

Gaining access to the Chiang Kai-chek regime hadn't been too difficult although she hadn't been the first American to exploit the pro-American stance the Nanking government had taken. Fully half of the cabinet ministers in the government here had been educated in the United States.

A Canadian journalist, Thomas Mackenzie, had for a while been the Madame's favourite dancing partner. The two of them had made quite a thing of it in Shanghai's nightclubs until the Gissimo had arranged for him to be packed off home. Hahn hadn't minded seeing the back of him as he'd been altogether too successful at figuring out what was happening chez Chiang.

Hahn had soon filled the breech, providing no threat to the Generalissimo because of her sex. He wanted American aid and his wife, May-ling, had turned out to be by far China's best spokesperson in a United States that seemed increasingly fixated on China.

There were few parts of the world, Hahn reflected, that an isolationist United States was really that interested in. Europe was a rat's nest of trouble, always had been, always would be. Nevertheless, a rat's nest which ran most of the world's colonies. China was the American Raj, of sorts, similar in a way to what India was to England. The feminine ying to the masculine yang and all that rubbish.

The United States had become a very large presence in China, far outstripping the British in terms of investment. In the past twenty years the Brits had seen their net worth in China cut in half whereas the Americans, as well as the Japanese, had more than doubled their investments.

In this neck of the woods it's down to us and the Japanese, she thought.

Hahn was itching for action. After racing to Nanking, she expected the Chiang's semi-Imperial entourage would embark immediately for Mokanshan. Instead she was once again cooling her heels and waiting for Chiang Kai-shek to decide when they were leaving. It was clear that things vis-à-vis the Japanese were at a boiling point. It was no secret that certain members of the KMT high command were clamouring for a fight with them and that the Japanese were upping their ante by increasing their pressure on the Nanking government.

In the present excitement, Hahn had forgotten about the missing negatives. She had done her best to find them and failed. That had been at best a long shot anyway. What she needed to do now was find out which way Chiang was going to jump.

The Japanese were shaking the branches of the Chinese Mulberry tree and it was Hahn's intention to be the first journalist to see which way the fruit rolled once it hit the ground. Hahn wondered if the fruit might roll up to Mokanshan and why? What was in Mokanshan that would warrant a trip there by Chiang at this particular time?

There was a knock on her door. They were on the move.

Chapter 19

Redvers Witherspoon was not a pretty sight, although he was certainly a colourful one. His face was a mass of bruises standing out dramatically against his clean, white bandages. He looked as though he had been dropped off a tall building or two; bombed by a Japanese warplane then run through an industrial wringer a few times for good measure.

Or been worked over by the Green Gang.

He had finally convinced his captors that he knew absolutely nothing about the Wallis Simpson negatives. Unfortunately for him, he did this by pleading ignorance long after it would have been physically or mentally possible for anyone to do so. Just to be certain, his torturers had brought in their informant from the church. He had confirmed that the man they were working on was neither of the two men who had found the negatives the week before. Just his namecard matched.

As a warning to others who might be after the negatives, Big Ears Tu decided not to have the reporter killed but dumped off outside a hospital early on Monday morning. The police had been duly contacted and Patrick Givens had decided to investigate the incident himself.

Givens stood outside his room wondering what this could be about. Was this a crime with political implications? Had Witherspoon written something that had caused this to happen? Yet the *Daily News* rarely published anything that warranted treatment like this. Had he been poking his nose somewhere he oughtn't have? Or was it just another wanton act of Shanghai violence?

A tired looking doctor gave permission to Givens to speak with his patient for a few minutes but warned him not to tire the poor man out. It was a wonder he was conscious and able to even speak, the doctor said pointedly.

Although Witherspoon knew Givens through his work, the superintendent introduced himself anyway.

'Who did this to you lad?'

Witherspoon swallowed heroically before replying. 'I don't know except they were Chinese. They grabbed me near the newspaper office and threw me in a car.'

'Do you know why?'

'They thought I had some smutty negatives.' A tone in Witherspoon's weak voice nevertheless registered a hint of outrage at such a notion. The truth was Witherspoon, having been pumped with enough opium by the doctors to eradicate the pain completely, was rather enjoying the attention.

Wallis Simpson no doubt, thought Givens. And no doubt it was Green Gang bully boys doing the asking.

'This isn't the first time I've been mistaken for another person,' added Witherspoon in yet another heroic whisper.

'What do you mean?' prodded Givens gently.

'For the past few months I've been getting telephone calls from people.' He paused and coughed delicately before continuing. 'From people I've never met who claim we have met—I thought it might be a prank of some sort.'

Emily Hahn had enlisted the help of the American who worked with Witherspoon at the newspaper. Had the goons grabbed the wrong newsman? Did this mean that Eli Swan had the negatives?

'Do you think the men who questioned you thought you were American?'

'I don't know but it's odd you should ask—the strangers on the telephone always did.' Witherspoon closed his eyes.

'Rest up there boy. We'll get to the bottom of this yet,' said Givens confidently. 'In the meantime we've put a round-the-clock guard on your room to make sure you get a proper rest.'

Givens closed the door behind him quietly and went to the nurse's station to use their telephone. He called Dickson Hoste at the *Daily News* to give him a report on Witherspoon's condition and to arrange a chat with Swan. To his disappointment, Hoste informed him that Swan was on leave in Mokanshan until the following week.

He then called back to his office to speak with Ralph Bookbinder, the American responsible for the team of Chinese tailgaters he had assigned to keep tabs on Emily Hahn the previous week. Bookbinder said Hahn had been trailed back to Nanking where, once again, she was discreetly ensconced at the residence of the Generalissimo.

Givens told Bookbinder about what had happened to Witherspoon and added that it was possible the Green Gang had mistaken him for Swan.

'Do you think Swan has the negatives then?' asked Bookbinder, trying hard to conceal his excitement.

'Could be,' replied Givens. 'He's up in Mokanshan so there's a chance he hasn't already given them to Hahn. Did you find out whether Hahn is working for Chiang Kai-shek on this?'

'Hard to say, Chief, but that would be my guess,' replied Bookbinder. 'Do you reckon we ought to find Swan?'

Givens pondered this for a few moments. 'I suppose we should—if the pictures end up in Chiang Kai-chek's hands we can pretty much forget about them.'

'I say we get up there real fast.'

'I'm coming back to the office,' said Givens. 'I'll think about it on the way over.'

Givens descended the stairs of the hospital to the street where his car was parked. If Swan was responsible for Witherspoon's torture then he was in a world of trouble, thought Givens angrily. The boy had been quite a sight with a broken arm and collarbone, as well as bruises and burn marks all over his body.

Givens wondered if he should go to Mokanshan himself and escape, for a couple of days at least, the endless trouble brewing in Shanghai. But a trip would involve spending a few days away from the office and he'd be incommunicado if something big happened. He arrived back at the headquarters to find Bookbinder standing outside.

'Chief, we've just had word that Hahn and all the Nationalist bigwigs are headed south in a convoy from Nanking but away from Shanghai—it could be towards Mokanshan, sir.'

'Lord Suffering Jesus!' sputtered Givens. 'You'd better get moving. Grab some guns, a fast car and a couple of men and try to get between Swan and Hahn—don't kill Swan or anything but use force if you have to. And Bookbinder?

'Yes sir?'

'Get me those negatives.'

Bookbinder ran inside to make a quick telephone call. Although he held an American passport, Bookbinder had been born in Munich and also answered to the name Rolf Buchbinder, agent of Germany's Social Nationalist party.

A member of the Fascist American Bund, the pro-Nazi brotherhood in America, Buchbinder was moonlighting for the local Nazi party and had reported to their leader, Ernst von Staubel, since the day he'd signed on with the Shanghai Municipal Police. It was through Buchbinder that von Staubel had heard about Simpson's Shanghai past. In a routine wire to Berlin he had mentioned the hunt for the negatives and had been shocked when none other than the Fuhrer himself had taken a personal interest in this case.

Buchbinder reached Von Staubel at the shipping office where he passed his days. Von Staubel effusively congratulated Buchbinder on his work, already imagining how this would galvanise his own career in the Nazi organisation.

'Kill Swan if you need to but get the negatives first,' he said urgently to Buchbinder. 'Bring them to the consulate and you'll be safe. We'll get both them and you safely to Germany. Heil Hitler!'

Buchbinder hung up the phone and went to find a couple of Chinese policemen to drive him to Mokanshan and provide some help tracking down the American. He could use them to find Swan then order them out of the way. On the other hand, he realised he might have to kill them too.

Buchbinder easily reconciled being an American and a Nazi. It was the Jews who had ruined Germany during the War and it was the Jews who were now attempting to do the same to America. Buchbinder believed that by serving the Nazi cause he was working to save the United States. True Americans were Aryans—even if they themselves didn't see things quite that way yet.

He hurriedly filled out a requisition form for a revolver. Givens, coming out of his office, saw him painstakingly filling out the forms in duplicate.

'Are you still here?' he asked loudly.

'On my way, chief,' said Buchbinder, nodding at the two Chinese constables, Chang and Ming, the latter holding a map of the Mokanshan region in his hand. Buchbinder ordered Chang to find a strong electric torch.

Then off they sped for Mokanshan, eight hours hard driving away.

CHAPTER 20

Hahn rode in a car in front of another one carrying Chiang Kai-shek and the Missimo. There were a dozen vehicles in front of them to ensure that soldiers bore the brunt of any landmines planted by their enemies.

Uneasy is the head that wears this crown, thought Hahn. This was an army on the move, complete with airplanes flying overhead and machine gun-equipped, sandbagged bunkers guarding the road every few hundreds yards or so.

All rather exciting, she thought, for what is basically a trip to the cottage in a small American-run village up in the mountains. I hope we give them a bit of a fright, she mused. Little chance of that as her fellow Americans would probably be thrilled to bits at the sight of the convoy, convinced it was a show of force put on for their edification.

She pictured Chiang Kai-shek as a Mongol invader bent on rape and slaughter and Mokanshan as an unarmed Chinese village placidly going about its business. Kaboom!

Better nip these fantasies in the bud, she thought to herself, keeping in mind how opium could result in delusions of grandeur, particularly after countless pipes per day for several months. She was a journalist and this was a story. Her job was to keep her eyes open, record the facts then try to make a book out of her experiences.

The problem was she felt more drawn towards China each day and less concerned about her once prized objectivity. Agreeing to consider marrying Sinmay Zau was a big part of this. Educated in Paris and England, Zau was a very attractive man—witty, polished and wealthy. Their relationship had gone full circle, having started with Hahn thinking of herself as an adulteress in full view of his lovely wife and children to the present state of affairs in which she and his family were as compatible as she had ever been with her own family.

His wife and cousin, Zoa, had been the one to suggest that Hahn formally become part of their household. Crafty old Sinmay. He'd realised that coming from Zoa it would seem a bit churlish for her to refuse. Well, it worked, she thought. Emily Hahn, number two wife. She smiled to herself.

Things were not quite so relaxed in the Chiang household, she reflected. And what a household! The Missimo used Hahn as a sounding board for her theories, some of which she'd later float in the United States. May-ling fancied herself as something of a writer but one on a far more lofty plane than the one inhabited by more lowly journalistic types like Hahn.

The Missimo reckoned she was a bit of an *artiste*, thought Hahn ruefully. One of her zany ideas which had already found success in the United States was that China was simply a big house and that she and the Gissimo were indulging in a little spring-cleaning. Simply *tidying up* the six hundred odd million Chinese who live here, thought Hahn. Just giving them a bit of a *dusting*.

The only problem was that part of the house was on fire and it looked like the whole rambling edifice might burn to the ground before the Gissimissimos managed to get it licked into shape. If China was a building, thought Hahn, it would probably be equal parts museum, brothel, summer palace and condemned tenement. The Missismo's vision of her country reflected a serious lack of reality. Nevertheless, this China-as-a-house theory was easily understood in America, particularly among women, her natural allies. American women love a clean house.

And there was no doubting her effect when let loose upon American women in China either, particularly those who wore their Christianity prominently on their sleeves. Madame Chiang was assiduously courting middle America and why not? The Gissimo's attempts to curry favour with the Germans and Italians had fizzled out when those dictators decided to leave the field to the Japanese. The Brits, generally speaking, had their hands full elsewhere. So it's down to us Yanks to save China, she mused.

Hahn was unaccompanied in the back seat and was separated from the driver by a glass screen. The old opium clock inside her head was telling her it was time for a quick smoke. They had hours to go before they arrived in Mokanshan and nothing would speed the trip along quite so well as a quick hit from her pipe.

She glanced up at the driver and his accomplice, in all likelihood one of the Chiang's Blueshirts or bodyguards along for the ride and to keep and eye on her, as well as provide protection. Whoever he was or whatever he was meant to be doing, he was fast asleep.

Hahn figured that feigning sleep herself was probably the best course of action. First she opened the windows a bit then yawned and tucked her head into the corner of the large back seat. The driver's eyes flicked to the rear view mirror. He reached up to the dashboard and began turning a small handle. A black felt screen began lowering from the ceiling of the back compartment, completely obscuring the window between her and the front cab.

Hahn wondered for what reasons the spacious back seat was usually put to use. It was certainly spacious enough for a lot of purposes, she thought happily, deciding for the sake of decorum to postpone her smoke for a few minutes.

The opium was like treacle, thick and sticky. She used a knitting needle type instrument to pull the substance from a small jar, clamped between her tweed-trousered knees. She twirled it around like candy floss then held it over a small flat candle she'd already lit. As it became molten she placed a small blob in her pipe.

Less than a minute later she was drawing contentedly on her little pipe, watching the picturesque squalor of rural China whiz by the car. She had read somewhere that during the Great War some less than sharp military minds had initially dismissed aerial reconnaissance for the simple reason that, to a pilot travelling so fast, everything on earth would be a blur.

All they had to do was travel by fast car to realise this was about as wrong as could be, she thought, drowsily. She closed her eyes and thought of Madame Chiang Kai-shek's insistence that all meetings between them be kept strictly off the record and that Hahn must never reveal to anyone that they were on such close terms.

Perhaps May-ling had some future plans for her that made it necessary to hide the fact they had established a relationship. Hahn had been thinking about writing a book on the Soong sisters. Surely the Missimo wouldn't object too strongly to that, provided that in exchange for her cooperation, she could have a look at it before publication.

The car continued to eat up the miles. Perhaps everything would be made clear when they arrived in Mokanshan.

CHAPTER 21

Brigadier Western possessed an upright military bearing and a splendid moustache. He was stout, bluff and bullish, a walking compendium of everything commonly associated with retired Indian army officers.

Having finished tea, he was showing Mrs. Munro how to cast a fly, having already won her over with flattering small talk over scones and cucumber sandwiches. The group were taking their ease beside a large reservoir alongside Western's bungalow in a pretty valley below Chiang's Kai-shek's compound.

Due to the limited number of reels everyone was taking turns casting for the small trout that swam in the pool. The highlight of Swan's afternoon had been removing a fly from the hem of Daisy's dress. He had been reminded of the fishing cormorants on the Grand Canal and how they caught fish but couldn't eat them.

The Brigadier had a way of starting sentences with: 'When I was in…'

He would then draw upon his large repertoire of stories. Like an actor, he'd perfected the twinkling of the eye with the punch line, the dexterous patting of his moustache and the low grumble of mirth, cleverly muffled so as not to interfere with the laughter of his audience. Then on to the next story.

Mrs. Munro was acting younger than her years, basking in the attention of the gentlemanly brigadier. It was a welcome change after months of dutifully mourning her husband.

Western began a lecture about the art of fly-fishing.

'A fly rod is a much more delicate instrument than any gun, even one as fine as a Holland and Holland. A shotgun, you see, for all its delicacy and balance, still relies on an explosion in order to function effectively—so there's the unfortunate percussiveness of it all. A fly rod makes no noise, you see.'

He gently whipped the twelve-foot rod back and forth like a wand, high up over his head.

Flood was seeing dollars signs in every word he spoke. He sat and revelled in his luck at having found this wonderful old man simply by idling through a sporting magazine. The subject of his adoration turned to the subject of bamboo.

'Rather like the relationship between buffalo and your Red Indian this stuff,' he said, watching a brightly coloured fly resting on the water thirty feet away.

'John Chinaman uses bamboo to build his houses and boats, uses it to carry everything he owns, attaches it to tools and weapons; makes ladders from it and even, in the form of shoots, eats the damn stuff, pardon my French,' he said, pausing to catch his breath.

'When I was in Weihaiwei, north of Qingtao the summer before last, they'd built an enormous bamboo scaffold around an old temple in order to make repairs—it must have been six storeys high. I'll be deuced if a typhoon didn't smash the temple to bits—but left the bamboo standing.'

'The only thing the Chinaman can't do with bamboo is use if for fuel. It burns something awful—foul and smoky,' he added, toying with the fishing line with his free hand. As if on cue the rod jerked satisfactorily as a trout hit the fly. He gave an elegant flick, dooming the fish, before handing it over to Mrs. Munro with a mock bow.

She tittered appropriately while Flood helped her land the fish and put it in a wicker creel. The brigadier had invited Flood and Swan to join him for dinner and celebrate in style the expansion of the Mokanshan Fly Rod Company. There seemed no end to his hospitality. Once he learned that Mrs. Munro, or Eustace as he now called her, and Daisy couldn't join them that night he invited them all back for dinner on the weekend.

Swan had offered to escort the Munroes back to their villa while Flood and the Brigadier talked business. Flood had some papers to sign, which would make him a full partner in the enterprise while enabling Western to withdraw from the funds they had on tap. Flood's arrival could not have been more welcome as Western had, he had told them, been wondering how to arrange the necessary financing to take the company to the next stage of development.

The walk back to the Munro's villa was uneventful and pleasant. As he said farewell he scoped out their rented house with a thought to perhaps returning by moonlight if he couldn't separate Daisy and her mother for an hour or so the next day. On the spur of the moment he decided to check at the hotel to see if there was any word from Hahn.

He wondered what Western had meant when he had said they'd do a 'proper mess' that night at dinner and figured it probably meant something vaguely military. The old brigadier sure looked like he knew how to have a good time.

It seemed that Flood's harebrained scheme might actually bear fruit. He realised he'd miss him if he decided to settle down in Mokanshan. Flood had already mentioned he was going to start looking for a place to live and the genial old soldier had offered to let him stay with him until something turned up.

Mokanshan seemed almost magical, a place where anything could happen. Thinking of Daisy he gave a short prayer that some of the magic would rub off on him.

Buchbinder and his men had been forced to wait for the Generalissimo's entourage to pass them by as all roads in the region has been blockaded to ensure the Gissimo had an uneventful trip up to the mountains. Despite the fact the convoy had passed an hour earlier, the unmarked police car may as well have been rooted to the ground for all the progress they were making.

He was reluctant to show his police papers as he and his men were well out of their jurisdiction and the soldiers looked liked they meant business. Although it was difficult, Buchbinder had decided that the best way to do this job was to do it as inconspicuously as possible.

His mood had worsened with each passing minute as he imagined the negatives leaving the hands of Swan and his partner. He raged quietly and thought perhaps he would kill them even if they didn't have the film.

The thought made him feel a bit better.

Although the main village of Mokanshan was still accessible only by foot, horseback or sedan chair, a proper road had been cut into Chiang Kai-shek's retreat which stood at a lower elevation than the main village. Hahn's car passed a number of troop carriers on its way into the compound.

An aide was on hand to take her to her room, located in a building away from the Generalissimo's substantial mansion. Opening the door her eyes were drawn to an envelope on the bed. She ripped open the envelope.

I'll be damned, she thought happily, reading the note from Swan.

Her presence was required at dinner that evening although guests never knew whether affairs of state might crop up and leave them to forage for themselves. There was just time to make a quick telephone call to the Mokanshan Hotel before snatching a pre-dinner nap. By eleven o'clock that night, she figured, the negatives of a naked and vulnerable Mrs. Simpson would be in her hands.

And shortly thereafter in the hands of Madame Chiang Kai-shek. Won't it be interesting to see where they go from there, she thought.

When Swan reached his hotel the Russian clerk handed him the brief message from Hahn.

'Wonderful!' it read. 'Meet me at the front gates of the Chiang place tonight at eleven o'clock. The car is as good as yours!'

Swan grabbed a quick shower then retrieved the negatives from the safety deposit box before starting back to the brigadier's house on the other side of the mountain, his spirits sky high.

Before he was halfway there, Buchbinder and his men arrived at the village by sedan chair. The policeman hadn't reckoned on leaving the car parked at the base of the mountain. It would make leaving more cumbersome, he reckoned, but hardly impossible.

It's always faster coming down a mountain than going up.

When Swan arrived back at the reservoir, the brigadier and Flood were enjoying a swim, apparently unencumbered by bathing suits. Swan thought this was the best idea he had come across all day and immediately shucked his clothes and hopped in the water.

One of the brigadier's Indian menservants stood alongside the reservoir's cement edge tending a portable bar complete with cocktail shakers, soda siphons and ice. The sun was sinking towards the mountains and shone like speckled gold on the surface of the water.

The brigadier was explaining the intricacies of a tiger hunt. One had been terrorising some villagers to the south of Mokansan only a few days before and Western was toying with the idea of hunting the beast down. Flood floated nearby with his jaw agape, literally agog with excitement.

'I'll show you some of my guns and trophies before dinner,' said Western. 'One of my boys has aired and ironed a couple of mess jackets and trousers for you chaps; actually old ones of mine that seem to have shrunk somewhat.' He patted his upturned belly with satisfaction.

'They've removed all the insignia, of course, and might be a bit short in the leg but apart from that they ought to do rather well.'

In the fading light, Swan thought he could just make out the faintest outline of a moustache on Flood's upper lip, in embryonic imitation of his new hero no doubt.

'Where was I Luther? Oh yes. The tiger hunt. Well it might be difficult to round up any elephants in these parts so it would mean tethering up a goat and building a treetop blind.

'When I was in India, we used to choose a goat based on on how well it could bleat. We had the boys give them a whack with a *lathi* then picked the one that made the most satisfactory sounds. They don't seem to have many goats here, though. What do you reckon old boy?'

The brigadier began languidly paddling towards the bar.

'A bunch of chickens; Eli?' said Flood, smiling.

Swan swam over to Flood.

'Hahn left a message at the hotel,' he said softly. 'She's here in Mokanshan and wants us to drop the negatives off tonight—at the Chiang's place at eleven.'

'Perfect, we can meet her on the way back to the hotel after dinner. How are we going to share the car if I'm living up here? Maybe I could use my share of the car to buy a truck? We could use it to get the rods from here to Shanghai or wherever.'

'Sounds fair,' agreed Swan.

The brigadier reached up and took a whiskey soda from his manservant.

'What's all this whispering about? No secrets in the mess!'

'Nothing really, I was just talking about getting some kind of truck for the business.'

'Splendid, splendid. Now come over and have a drink.'

The brigadier climbed awkwardly out of the pond and was immediately wrapped in a large towel by his servant. Swan and Flood joined him.

'Thing about bamboo rods is they're light; easy to transport,' said the brigadier, towelling himself down, standing quite naked. The two Americans had never met anyone quite so lacking in modesty. They both studiously avoided looking at the old soldier's naked body.

'Get some chaps here to carry them down to the canal and ship them to Shanghai what? Nothing could be easier. Now in Shanghai young Flood, you may need an automobile of some sort to put on a bit of a show.' He chuckled contentedly.

'I dare say a young man needs transport in that place hey?'

They dried themselves and began walking back to the brigadier's bungalow, appropriately set in a large stand of bamboo.

'I was thinking that once we send a big enough shipment back to the States that maybe we should place an advertisement in the National Geographic or some fishing magazines,' said Flood. 'Offer one of those money back guarantees.'

'Good idea,' replied the older man, ushering them into his house.

Swan and Flood, eyes wide, took in the leopard and tiger skins, spears, brass shields and other exotica from India. Then their eyes were drawn to the huge tiger skin in front of the fireplace.

'This chap reputedly ate more than a hundred villagers,' the brigadier said proudly. 'We used four hundred people to drive him to where we had the elephants. I was the lucky one who got a clear shot at him,' he said modestly, indicating with a toe where he had drilled the beast.

'Right you chaps, off you go and get ready for dinner,' he ordered his two guests. 'You'll find the jackets in the spare bedroom. Drinks in twenty minutes sharp.'

Chapter 22

The scout Wu and close to a hundred other soldiers were concealed in a thick bamboo grove, waiting to receive orders. Rumours were rife that the hated generalissimo, Chiang Kai-shek, and his men were now in Mokanshan. Although he had seen bits of the convoy entering the compound, Wu had not been close enough to see Chiang himself. He wondered if they were going to attack them.

He hadn't told anyone about the stir his presence had caused among the foreigners two days before. After all, he had only been seen by young children and had quickly fled back to camp. He was also embarrassed to have fallen asleep on duty, something he had been doing frequently of late. The cursed sleeping sickness, he thought morosely.

Wu had very little worldly knowledge except that which had been gleaned from his boyhood experiences of working his family's fields in Anhwei Province and his adventures with the communists during the Long March. Yet he was loyal to the communist cause in a way that few of his contemporaries were to the Nationalist Army.

When he was a boy the arrival of soldiers had usually meant hardship. Poor people were forever at the mercy of roving armies and had little recourse but to submit to their demands. The communists, however, treated villagers and farmers with slightly more respect and often paid for food, an act virtually unheard of among armies throughout China's long and violent history.

There had been too many mouths to feed at home so when the call was raised for volunteers a bashful Wu had stepped forward with his family's blessing. That had been two years before and he had not heard from his family since.

His encounter with the foreign 'ghost' children had resulted in some thinking about the wider world and its inhabitants. The little girl, for example, seemed like she was from a different world altogether than the one inhabited by Wu and his rough fellow soldiers.

Yet she had ears and a mouth like everyone else, fingers and presumably toes like Chinese people, and she had given him a bright smile, much in the way of children everywhere.

But her people, in league with Chiang Kai-shek, were enslaving his people and helping the wicked Japanese conquer his country. Perhaps, like the Chinese, foreigners could be both bad and good.

Pondering this, he was caught by surprise when his group leader materialised nearby and summoned Wu and the others to gather around. They sat on their haunches, listening raptly to what he had to say.

'Comrades,' he said firmly. 'We are here to do a job which could save China. Chiang Kai-shek is in Mokanshan. We have an opportunity to capture him and make him see the error of his ways. Many generals in his army wish to join our cause and he alone is preventing this from happening.

'We must move quickly as we are many and our presence will soon be discovered—already Kuomintang patrols have begun probing the forests and some disloyal people might talk. So tonight, after his soldiers have eaten special food which will make them sleep, we will strike.'

He unfurled a rough map outlining the generalissimo's compound.

'We will begin our approach three hours after dark. A comrade with a timepiece will pass the word when it's time to begin moving. Others will go before you and take care of the guards outside the walls of the fort.

'They will show you where to attack,' he continued. 'Once you have succeeded in entering the compound you men, along with others, must take care of the soldiers on duty there. Another group will capture Chiang in his house.

'While they are taking him back to our headquarters you must cover their retreat and provide them with protection.

'Now get some rest,' he added. 'It will be a long night.'

Buchbinder sat in his room with the two Chinese detectives and pondered his next move. He wished he'd had enough time before leaving to get a better description of Swan and the man he was with, Luther Flood. All he knew was they were tall and skinny and had brown hair. They had a room down the hall he had already burgled, hoping to find the negatives or failing that, their passports or some clues to their whereabouts. But there was nothing but some clothes and toiletries to be found. Meanwhile, Chiang Kai-shek's mobile army had arrived at their fortress nearby, presumably with Hahn in tow.

His detectives had spread some money around the village and learned that a message had been left earlier that day for Swan, delivered from the summer retreat of the Generalissimo. He concluded that there was still chance that the Americans hadn't met but knew he was running out of time. The negatives would soon be beyond his reach.

Hahn was with Chiang Kai-shek but where was Swan and his partner? Buchbinder gave more money to Chang and Ming and ordered them to find out where they were. It was a small village and the amount of money he gave them was substantial.

They returned shortly with the news that both men were visiting with their friend, a retired British army officer who lived beside a reservoir in a nearby valley. Although it was now dark they were confident they could find his house.

After all, Mokanshan wasn't very big.

Hahn was sleeping the sleep of the dead, having gone for days without either proper rest or adequate food. In her sleep the opium wove dreams which alternated between visions of great clarity and ephemeral wispiness, dominated by Zou and her desire for children of her own.

In this coma-like state she was oblivious to the hammering on her door. Finally a key rattled in the lock and into the room stepped a nervous young soldier. Shaking Hahn gently, he informed her in English that she was expected for dinner in half an hour.

Groggily she got up and began preparing to meet her hosts.

Chapter 23

Swan and Flood were admiring each other in their borrowed uniforms.

'We're redcoats,' chuckled Flood. The brigadier's menservants had laid out two identical kits of short, scarlet bumfreezer jackets and black trousers with gold stripes down the sides. All evidence of rank and regiment had been carefully removed.

'Amazing what a get-up like this will do,' said Swan with amazement.

He turned to the side to admire his reflection in the mirror. 'Oh you kid.'

The only flaw was perhaps their mundane black lace—up shoes which peeped out meekly from beneath the brilliant ensemble above.

'I'm going to ask the brigadier if we can come back tomorrow when there's more daylight and get him to take our photographs,' said Swan. 'I look like Errol Flynn in *The Charge of the Light Brigade.*'

This particular film had recently played in Shanghai, reinforcing their naive understanding and strengthening their belief in the righteousness of colonialism. Although dyed-in-the-wool Republicans, both had to hide their tears at the end of the film. Along with dozens of others, the film had been a factor in Flood's decision to join the Shanghai Volunteer Force, though he had yet to actually drill with them.

The uniforms had transformed them from gauche hayseeds into English aristocrats. Flood stood transfixed, preening his nearly invisible moustache. Swan had tightened up his speech in a parody of an English gentleman.

Promptly on time, they strode manfully out to meet the brigadier. Unfortunately, the effect was ruined by their inability to march in step. In an attempt to match Swan's gait, Flood brought his left arm forward at the same time as his left leg in a sort of Frankenstein lurch. Looking over, Swan began snorting with repressed hilarity at the sight of Flood's Zombie walk.

The resplendent brigadier, with a chest full of medals, choked on his drink as Flood loped awkwardly across the floor, head well back of his body.

'Hi brigadier sir', Flood said, coming to rest, trying to remember how Flynn had pranced around in the movie. Swan wiped the tears from his eyes.

'What you chaps need is a good, stout smoke,' said the Brigadier, snapping his fingers at a manservant and barking out a string of strange words ending in *hookah.*

He proceeded to give them each a careful inspection, brushing of imaginary bits of lint and straightening their shoulders.

'You chaps make quite an entrance there, you especially Luther,' he said. 'Looked like you were trying to dislodge a lead poker from your arse without using your hands.'

'I was trying to get in step with Eli but I couldn't quite pull it off. What's that thing?'

The manservant had brought in a large device, a sort of big magic lamp with a hose attached.

'Ah ha, that's the old hubble bubble,' said the brigadier as if greeting an old friend.

'Mess night on the Northwest Frontier often started off with a smoke of *kif* to get the old juices flowing for dinner. Of course the native chaps up there often smoked it prior to battle—made them uncommonly fierce if a trifle reckless.'

He offered the business end of the two-foot high pipe to Flood.

'Care to try some?'

Such was Flood's hero worship he would have cheerfully sucked smoke from the exhaust pipe of a Shanghai bus if asked. He eagerly reached for the mouthpiece of the pipe.

'Remember,' cautioned the brigadier. 'Suck don't blow, old chap, suck don't blow.'

Flood gripped the mouthpiece, connected by a flexible hose to a large brass container of water through which the smoke was cooled. The brown substance in the bowl, attached like a short arm off the main piece, was smouldering away, having been stoked by a manservant who carefully wiped the mouthpiece before handing it to Flood.

The Indian stood alongside the pipe, a small stream of smoke slowly escaping from his nostrils. Flood exhaled mightily then began sucking away, determined to make up for his less-than-impressive entrance.

The hashish blazed.

After about ten seconds Flood exploded, expelling smoke directly back into the mouthpiece. The hashish at the other end shot from the bowl and landed squarely on the tiger skin rug a few feet away where it began burning.

Encircled by a haze of smoke, Flood clutched his neck and rolled his eyes as the brigadier shrieked and began stomping the burning tiger skin, hands held high to his chest in a fussy manner at odds with his military bearing.

'Do you know what this cost......' he stopped abruptly and rallied his thoughts. '......err, to have this mounted?......or the cost in men's lives to kill him?'

The manservant grabbed the offending ember and tossed it into the fireplace where it continued to burn. Western nodded curtly and the servant began preparing a second bowl. He started it up then passed it to the brigadier who took a good puff before handing it back to the Indian who again cleaned the mouthpiece before handing it over to Swan.

In this manner they finished the bowl and began another. Soon the second manservant appeared, dressed in the same loose blue clothing as the first servant. He was carrying some round bread and some steaming curries. Eyeing the pipe wistfully, he returned to the kitchen for more dishes as the aroma from the steaming food hit the three men simultaneously.

'What's that?' asked Swan with interest. 'It smells wonderful!'

'Indian food old man,' said a mellowed brigadier. 'Nothing like it on earth, particularly after a session with the *hubble bubble*. One of these curries is made from the trout we caught earlier.'

He beckoned to the manservant to pour some wine. The brigadier clearly intended to celebrate the evening in style. Swan and Flood began tucking into the food, obviously finding it much to their liking. The brigadier joined them at the table, watching with satisfaction as the two dunderheads wolfed down the food. He glanced at his wristwatch, wondering how long it would take for the chilli peppers to hit. Swan was the first.

His eyes bulged slightly as his fork stopped in mid-flight.

'To the King,' proposed Western, raising his glass to the stricken Swan, who mumbled incoherently before draining his glass of wine. Flood began choking alongside his friend. The two began emptying everything in sight as the manservant hurried to replenish their glasses. The drinks did little to extinguish the fires that raged in their bellies.

The brigadier chucked. 'Try some of this bread. It's the only stuff that will help. I must apologise for not warning you but I couldn't resist. Rather a tradition that a chap's first mess night should be a memorable one.'

The faces of Swan and Flood matched their scarlet dinner jackets. Sweat had broken out on their brows and their eyes watered copiously as their sensory capacities switched into high gear.

'Perhaps some fresh air would do you good,' added the brigadier consolingly, as they slowly began coming around. They dutifully followed him outside, the fresh air doing its bit to cool down their digestive systems.

'Wow, that was hot,' said Flood. 'But really delicious. That's the first time either of us have ever eaten Indian food.

'Not to mention the other stuff,' giggled Swan, arching his neck to look at the moon, which had appeared over the mountains. The silvery light radiated on the surface of the reservoir. Never in their lives had either seen the moon look so beautiful, so cool and alluring.

'Wow,' said Flood again. 'This is really something. Five minutes ago I thought I was going to die and now I feel like I'm in a dream or something.'

Swan was similarly affected.

'The bamboo looks like it's moving towards us......like it's almost talking to us or maybe whispering to the moon,' he said reverently.

'Hello moon,' he rambled on. 'I'm a piece of Chinese bamboo that will soon be a fishing rod in the National Geographic. Come on down and play.'

'The bamboo looks like a forest of fishing rods come to catch some trout,' added Flood. 'Hey brigadier.' He turned back towards the house where the brigadier sat enjoying the night. 'I haven't had a chance to thank you for everything.'

'Don't mention it, old boy,' murmured Western, enjoying the half-witted chatter of his two new friends and lost in his own dreamy thoughts. The brigadier spent most of his time fantasizing that he really *was* a brigadier-general, formerly of either the Indian Army's 45th infantry or the Calcutta Light Horse. Lately he had been cultivating the image of himself as head of an artillery brigade stationed on the Khyber Pass.

The reality was more interesting albeit slightly less picturesque. The only rank Western had ever held was that of a private with the Newfoundland Expeditionary Force during the Great War, when he and his fellow fishermen had set the dubious record of suffering the heaviest casualties among all British and colonial forces on the Western Front.

He hadn't been young then either. But unlike his fellow Newfoundlanders he'd fallen in love with all the pomp and swagger of the British army's officer class. After the war he had stayed in England and turned his hand to acting, as well as other more fraudulent enterprises, occasionally involving rich widows.

Various misadventures had taken him to Hollywood where, although a steady job had eluded him, he had perfected his guise as a retired Indian Army officer among some of the best pretenders on earth.

He had taken to importing hashish from North Africa and counted Errol Flynn, Flood's hero, among his customers. Trouble with the police had resulted in a sudden decision to visit Australia, which, to his dismay, had proved a trickier place than the United States to pass as a retired British officer.

Mokanshan was a form of early retirement for him, chosen for its remoteness and substantial American population. His menservants, who believed he was as advertised, had been hired in Shanghai; poor stranded sailors who had been practically starving when he came across them begging in the street. Touched by their plight and in need of some domestic help he had promptly hired them when he discovered they spoke some English.

At the end of their two-year contracts he had promised to repatriate them both to Bengal with a hefty sum of money, a reward for helping him start the business. Of course, he'd wiggle out of that when the time came.

With each move he'd made around the world his rank rose to correspond with his increasing age. He reckoned he had now probably reached his ceiling military-wise, it being too conspicuous a leap up to Major-General. And he had grown comfortable with his current status. He felt as though fate had meant for him to play the role of brigadier-general and he thought he played it well. He rarely thought of himself anymore as plain old Wally Flatt.

Unless something else came up, and in his line of work something almost always did, he was content to go straight for a while and work with young Flood and his money. He'd been living on the edge for a long time and thought he'd try to make a go of this fly rod business. His efforts at publicising his business with the photo he'd submitted to the English field magazine had been with an eye to raising a bit of capital. So far young Flood had been the only fish to rise to the bait. But it was early days yet.

No doubt there would be other, richer men sitting on some cash who could be enticed into something as alluring as the notion of making fly rods in China. But for now, Flatt was content to have access to Flood's money and his willingness to help hook other investors. Perhaps an advertisement in the National Geographic wasn't such a bad idea at all.

The laughter of Swan and Flood echoed around the pond. They had found two fly rods and it appeared they were having a competition to see who could come closest to catching the moon. Their rod tips were silhouetted against its light as sounds of their laughter carried across water into the forest beyond.

To Buchbinder and his minions, the moon was not proving nearly as obliging. Its light was almost completely blocked by the heavy screen of bamboo overhead and the policemen from the big city were completely lost. The maze of seemingly identical bamboo covered-paths surrounding the resort area had thwarted them for almost two hours. The electric torch wasn't working properly and Buchbinder was furious.

He coldly ordered the two Chinese to keep looking while he stayed at the centre of things, periodically trying to flash his cumbersome and unreliable flashlight so his men knew where he was.

There seemed to be no one about. After a short while Ming came back and reported that he had found some lights and heard some laughter by a pond. He had heard English words spoken and thought it must be the home of the English general. It was only minutes away.

The three policemen quietly began walking down one of the many paths, a revolver taking the place of the flashlight in Buchbinder's right hand.

Chapter 24

Dinner with the Chiang Kai-sheks was proving to be a relatively intimate affair, although rigidly split along lines of gender. Hahn had pulled a double take when the frightening looking gent sitting alongside the Generalissimo had been introduced as none other than the infamous Tu Yue-sheng, otherwise known as Big Ears Tu, ruler of Shanghai's underworld.

Hahn was sitting next to Madame Chiang Kai-shek, who was clearly in fine form, although her wrath had erupted tempest-like a few times already by the behaviour of the soldier-servants, most of whom seemed to be on the brink of falling asleep. The other dinner guests were senior officers in the Nationalist army and a couple of the Madame's aides.

Madame Chiang Kai-shek had the unnerving ability to turn her anger on and off like an electric switch, one moment cursing a sleepy soldier and the next brimming with coquettish goodwill towards her guests.

The Missismo had heard on the grapevine that a biography, this one on the cretinous Mao Tse-tung of all people, was to be written by the American writer, Edgar Snow. Although no one would be interested in a book on the communist leader, she was seeking to negate its influence by encouraging Hahn to write a hagiography of herself and the generalissimo.

Hahn had considered this but politely rejected it in favour of writing a book on Madame Chiang Kai-shek and her two famous sisters, Ai-ling and Ching-ling;

something she felt would be more interesting to people back in America. Their father, Charlie Soong, had been one of the first Chinese to graduate from an American college before returning to China and making a fortune printing and selling bibles, the most American of pursuits.

Like many self-obsessed women, Madame Chiang Kai-shek was reluctant to share the spotlight with her sisters, particularly since the eldest, Ching-ling, seemed to have taken up with the accursed communists. Since the death of her husband, Sun Yat-sen, the widow had acquired a certain aura of saintliness amongst the country's lefties.

Hahn was beginning to notice that for all of their marital strife, the Gissimo and the Missimo were totally committed to their mission of ruling China however they saw fit. They both loved power too much to let day-to-day discord between them prevent them from reaching their goals; too convinced of their destiny to let the fact they couldn't stand each other get in the way.

Down at the other end, the Generalissimo and Big Ears were having a heated discussion, punctuated by fists hitting the table. Hahn's Chinese was nowhere near perfect but it was much better than her hosts realised. Madame Chiang Kai-shek was fond of speaking English and spoke it well. Her husband never said anything to Hahn beyond a simple hello or goodbye, the only words he could manage in the language.

To Hahn's satisfaction, she had been able to figure out that the two men were discussing how to deal with the Japanese. Big Ears seemed intent on persuading his godson to broker an alliance with the communists. Or, at least, that's what she thought he was saying. It was either that or brokering a deal with the Japanese to take care of the communists. Nevertheless, something was clearly up and here she was, smack in the middle of it.

'The Japanese are cutting into our profits from heroin and opium and they are, of course, beyond the control of the Opium Suppression Bureau,' said Big Ears softly to the Gissimo. 'Need I remind you that it is these profits that are financing your regime?'

The Gissimo looked up before responding.

'If I can have six months I can destroy the communist devils forever—then I can turn my armies to face the Japanese,' replied the Gissimo through clenched teeth. 'If we join forces with the communists they will gain enough time to strengthen and reorganise.'

'But surely you are chasing a mouse while a tiger prepares to kill you,' replied Big Ears in velvet tones. 'You say the communists are not a threat and it is so. But the appetite of the Japanese grows larger every day—my spies tell me they are making plans to attack you in Nanking.'

'They wouldn't dare,' thundered the Generalissimo, stopping conversation at the far end of the table.

'Who?' asked the Missimo.

Her husband glared at her then glared at Hahn who was busy feigning ignorance. The Missimo, miffed at his rudeness, turned to Hahn and spoke in English.

'The generalissimo has too many enemies,' she said reasonably. 'That's why we need more friends. You are a friend of China?'

Hahn nodded.

'Then would you join our cause? I need someone to advise me on how to deal with the United States, someone who knows the proper channels of communication. I need your help to gain American support in our fight against the enemies of China.'

'Well I...would have to think about if for a day or two,' countered Hahn, wondering if she should change the subject by telling her about the negatives. She decided to hold her fire until she was sure they were the right ones. 'I'm just a journalist and it's usually not such a good idea to become so directly involved.'

'From what I understand in Shanghai,' said the Missimo, eyes narrowing. 'You have already become quite involved.' She paused. 'Very well, you can think about it overnight.'

A crash of cutlery startled everyone. One of the idiot soldiers, it seemed, had fallen asleep standing up and dislodged a tray of eating utensils. Begging forgiveness, the young soldier hurriedly began picking everything up.

Madame turned to her husband and spoke in rapid fire Chinese.

'With clods like this in your army it's no wonder you can't catch the communists.'

Her husband bared his false teeth at her but declined to respond.

Wu and his fellow soldiers had been in position for half an hour. As they still had more than an hour to go before the attack most of the soldiers had found comfortable positions on the ground. To prevent himself from falling asleep, Wu was sitting on a sharp stone and periodically pinching himself.

All was quiet except the soft rustle of the bamboo. Ahead in the distance loomed the small fortress of Chiang Kai-shek, well-lit but quiet. Wu wondered if the sleeping powder sprinkled on the soldier's food was having the hoped for effect.

This will be something to tell my grandchildren, he thought dreamily. Soon he was sound asleep, visions of his future family gathering happily in the reaches of his mind.

Buchbinder was advancing towards the dimly lit house when he heard some voices from across the corner of the reservoir. He motioned his accomplices to stop then listened long enough to determine there were two men there and both were Americans. Sounds like they're having a bit of a party, he thought.

The brigadier, who had gone inside to replenish his brandy, froze when he saw the three men advancing across his yard in the direction of the reservoir. He carefully slipped back into the shadows.

Swan and Flood were sharing a bottle of wine and laughing uproariously at virtually everything each other said. Swan looked over and saw some figures approaching them in the dark.

'Brigadier? Is that you?'

'Don't move or you're dead,' replied Buchbinder, anxious to get his hands on the negatives before opening fire.

'I'm with the Shanghai Police and I'm here to get the negatives,' said Buchbinder. 'Hand them over and you can both go free.'

The brigadier had returned to his house after dashing pell mell out the back door. A twinge of guilt—*this was no way to behave to his new messmates*—had brought him back. He'd quickly loaded a twenty-gauge shotgun, stepped outside and pointed it straight up into the air. He pulled the trigger.

Several things happened at once. The brigadier beat a hasty retreat as Buchbinder and his men hit the ground. When they looked back the two Americans had escaped and were crashing through the bamboo as fast as their legs would carry them.

Not pausing for breath, Swan and Flood heard shots from behind them as Buchbinder loosed off a couple of quick rounds before beginning his pursuit. Searchlights began shining down from the house of Chiang Kai-shek, followed closely by machinegun fire.

Buchbinder's capricious torch came to life, quickly attracting fire from the men in the bamboo as well as the now wide-awake soldiers in the fortress. A random bullet fired from one group or the other drilled a neat hole in his forehead. He collapsed where he stood, his men taking to their heels.

All around Swan and Flood dozens of soldiers suddenly materialised.

A rudely awakened Wu found himself facing two foreigners in uniform. Both slowly raised their hands as Wu jabbed his bayonet in their direction. He gestured with it towards the forest and away from the fortress home of the generalissimo. His fellow soldiers returned fire as they too retreated.

Swan and Flood, in uniform for less than three hours, were now prisoners of war.

Chapter 25

Swan and Flood's captors, apart from trussing them up and leading them with ropes all night, had otherwise paid them little heed except to occasionally give them water and urge them on. It was now dawn and the two Americans didn't have a clue where they were nor what their captors had in store for them.

Gone were the conspicuous scarlet tunics and with them the negatives of Wallis Simpson. These, however, were the least of their worries. Having written countless stories for the *Daily News* involving foreigners kidnapped by communists and bandits, Swan knew it could be a long time before they saw the lights of Shanghai again.

He had glumly whispered to Flood that the record for captivity was held by two German priests who had been prisoners for almost two years before they were finally released. Their photograph had appeared on the front page of the *North China Daily News*; gaunt, sickly looking men with long beards and a woeful tale to tell of living off the land with their peripatetic captors. Attempts at ransoming them had failed simply because no one had ever seemed to know where they were, having being lost and located so many times.

Their recollections of the previous night were a kaleidoscope of weird images, the hashish having heightened their confusion and fearfulness. Both men fervently wished they had surrendered to the policemen from Shanghai rather than escaping into the arms of the Reds.

The entire night had been one long march away from Mokanshan, sometimes along roads but more often along trails through endless thickets of bamboo. Shortly after dawn they were gagged, bound and left helpless against an onslaught of mosquitoes. Occasionally they would spot a warplane high in the sky, no doubt trying to find the whereabouts of the small force.

Obviously the communist plan was to hide during the day and travel at night by the light of the moon...Despite the fact that Swan and Flood were tied back-to-back and were uncomfortable and stiff, they still managed to doze periodically, although never in unison. As one fell asleep the other would inevitably feel compelled to stretch, thus waking the other. Their tempers were frayed and, unable to speak, they communicated by viciously elbowing each other in the back.

At around noon, the diffident young soldier who had captured them undid their gags to give them food and water. As Swan was drinking from a metal cup, Flood attempted to speak.

'Maskee! Maskee! We Americans! Americans!' he sputtered. 'We demand to be released chop chop!' he paused as Wu put the cup to his lips. Swan, refreshed by the water, took over in pidgin.

'My wantchee b'long Shanghai side,' he said slowly and more clearly. 'Bym-bye makee pay, makeum pay big time! No b'long proper! Makee pay number one! This side no b'long proper! He paused for breath. 'What fashion no can? B'long Shanghai side...oh fuck it!'

Wu, having never heard pidgin, imagined Swan to be speaking his native language. He smiled in response, not knowing what else to do. He began putting cold rice into Swan's mouth, effectively shutting him up.

'Number one dollah can do,' continued Flood hopefully, carrying on where Swan had left off. Getting no response either he gave up.

Whispering to Swan, still being fed by Wu, he continued.

'Where do you think we're going? Will your paper pay the ransom money?' Wu began feeding Flood as Swan replied.

'I don't know but sure they'll pay the ransom,' said Swan softly. 'I can write stories about all this once we're back.' He paused, envisioning their heroic return. 'What I'm worried about is how the police will react when we tell them we've lost the negatives. We can forget about Hahn and getting the car—that's for sure.'

Wu, wondering why fate had decreed he should spend so much of his time with foreigners, finished feeding them then politely allowed them to continue talking to one another. Obviously they had given up trying to communicate with him.

'I guess I'll never see Daisy again,' said Swan morosely.

'What's going to happen to my business while we're prisoners?' asked Flood rhetorically.

'Just when it looked like I might be making some progress with her.'

'Just when I'd found my feet.'

'What do you reckon the brigadier's going to do?'

'Well, I guess the police would have probably questioned him and figured out that from all the shooting and whatnot that the communists were there…what do you think they were doing there anyway?'

'Do you think they were going to attack old Chiang Kai-shek? If they were and we messed it up we could be in a lot of trouble,' whispered Swan nervously.

'Well, maybe. But the main thing is they'll have figured out we're prisoners of the communists and they'll start working on getting us free.'

'With the brigadier, the police and the newspaper behind us I think our chances are pretty good, don't you?'

'You bet—when these guys find out you're a reporter with the *North China Daily News* they'll realise it's better for them to let us go—I better not tell them

I'm with the Shanghai Defence Force though or they might try to pump me for military information...'

'Just what would that be?'

'Well they might *think* that I know some military secrets and that's the main thing.'

'When they captured us we were dressed up as British officers—do you think they might think that we're important military men?'

'We'll just have to tell them clothes like these are all the fashion these days—if we meet anyone who speaks English they'll know we're Americans—and I don't think these soldiers know too much about foreigners anyway—we'll just tell them the truth. We got dressed up for dinner like it was a costume party.'

'I see what they mean when they say smoking that stuff leads to trouble.'

'You can say that again.'

'Listen, we better get some sleep, maybe if we act like we're going to doze off he'll forget to put the gags back in....

'Shhhhhhh. He's fallen asleep. Do you think we should try and escape?'

'Well, there's really not much we can do right now, this isn't the talkies and I don't see any sharp rocks around—maybe later if we get a chance.'

The brigadier stayed in hiding most of the night in the bamboo grove behind his house. Returning home early the following morning he had been shocked to hear from his servants that some soldiers from the compound had removed a dead foreigner, a stranger, from his front lawn the night before. Whoever that had been it could only mean trouble.

He then showered and tucked into a big breakfast. He needed to build his strength for travelling. His dinner guests from the night before had vanished, perhaps taken by bandits or whoever had attacked Chiang Kai-shek's compound the previous night.

A man capable of making quick decisions, the brigadier decided things were not as restful as they'd once been in Mokanshan. The faint echo of distant bugles was beckoning him to fresher pastures and new adventures.

He sent his servants on a trip to Hangchow for some supplies then busily packed all his props, clothing and other belongings. Hiring a couple of sedan chairs, he made for the village where he promptly depleted Flood's funds from the bank. His messmates could fend for themselves. Pity about the uniforms though. They were hard to come by these days.

He had decided to catch a canal boat to nearby Hangchow then a train for Shanghai and find a boat heading south. To muddy his tracks he would use the name Wally Flatt for travelling and stow his military *persona* for a bit.

Perhaps Hong Kong and then Indochina? He was thinking that perhaps it was time to see if he couldn't set himself up in the antiques business somewhere. Apparently in the French colonies ancient stuff was just lying around the jungle. But speed was of the essence. He might not have much time before Flood found out he'd been embezzled.

Hahn was getting ready to meet with her hostess for coffee. She'd vaguely recognised Rolf Buchbinder's body when Chiang's soldiers had dumped it in the courtyard of the compound that morning. What was a Shanghai policeman doing with the communists? And where were those two ninnies, Swan and Flood? She'd called the hotel and been told they hadn't been back since the day before. If they'd been unwilling to meet with her last night why hadn't they contacted her?

More importantly, where were the negatives?

During dinner, Hahn had made arrangements to meet with Madame Chiang Kai-shek for coffee the following morning. Although she hadn't mentioned the negatives, it had been her intention to surprise her host with them when they met. She had hoped that this would distract Madame Chiang from trying to pressure her into writing a book about she and her husband.

'You didn't bring a notebook? asked the Missimo Chiang innocently.

'I'm still thinking over your proposal Ma'am,' replied Hahn evasively. 'Say what was all that commotion last night? It scared me half to death.'

Madame snapped her fingers and a soldier ran over to where they sat in a little outdoor alcove overlooking the valley. Without looking up she gave him an order. He returned a couple of seconds later with a notebook and a pencil. She smiled sweetly at Hahn.

'Perhaps this would be useful?'

'Sure,' replied Hahn, marvelling at the Missimo's thirst for publicity.

'On and off the record as you reporters say,' said Chiang conspiratorially. 'The dead foreigner they brought in this morning was a policeman.'

'I thought he looked familiar.'

'Well, you should—our security people say he and two Chinese detectives have been following you around for the past couple of weeks—do you know why?'

Hahn's guilty conscience offered up a wide array of reasons. She remembered entertaining both Mao Tse-tung and Chou En-lai at her Kiangse Road home; there was Sinmay and the opium. Then she remembered the negatives.

'Madame Chiang, I was hoping to give you a present this morning.'

The Missimo's cat's eyes narrowed suspiciously as Hahn reached inside her jacket for Swan's note concerning the negatives. She handed it over and waited while Chiang read it quickly.

'So what happened?'

'I don't know except Swan—the man with the negatives—didn't show up last night and hasn't returned to his hotel either.'

'What do you think is going on? Did last night's attack have something to do with the negatives?'

'I don't know.'

Madame snapped her fingers and another soldier appeared. She barked out a quick command and the soldier went running.

'I'm going to have our men scour Mokanshan for this fellow, what's his name?'

'Eli Swan—his partner is another American named Luther Flood. They have rooms at the Mokanshan Hotel.'

A senior officer appeared. Madame Chiang Kai-shek ordered him to search for the two missing Americans and to place them under arrest the moment they were found.

'What for?' asked the officer. Chiang shot him a poisonous look in reply. He scurried off to do her bidding.

An impressed Hahn sat poised with her notebook, pencil in hand.

'As for last night,' said the Missimo. 'It appears we were attacked by the venal communists and were only saved thanks, once again, to my husband's ceaseless vigilance.'

She paused and thought for a moment.

'Perhaps you could give a first person account of how we foiled the perfidious communists once again,' she suggested brightly.

'Sure, sure,' said Hahn scribbling away. She paused as two soldiers dragged a middle-aged woman, kicking and screaming, away from the basement where a large kitchen was located. Hahn raised her eyebrows, although Madam Chiang hadn't appeared to notice anything.

'The Generalissimo has a kind of sixth sense which alerts him to danger; there's just no other way of describing it.' She made a pretence of modesty. 'It's almost like he can detect the enemy's presence just by the sheer force of his mission.

'Do you know where this fellow Swan found the negatives?' she added, abruptly veering off topic.

'I really don't know. I was surprised when I read the note.'

'Where was I?'

'The sheer force of his mission.'

'No scratch that out. Something about his being a weapon, an instrument of God's will—I'd like to work in his strong Christianity in the front of the story and highlight our faith versus the faithless creed of the Reds.'

'I'll see what I can do,' said Hahn, wondering how the Missimo could appear to hate her husband whenever they were together but produce such drivelling nonsense about him in private. Sheer force of her mission, she decided, looking up at Madame Chiang.

'Excuse me for a second,' said Chiang. 'I just realised something—that gentleman you met last night, Mr. Tu, might be of assistance in finding out what happened to those two men.'

She snapped her fingers and another soldier materialised. Hahn wondered if she hadn't been a little careless in mentioning the negatives to Madame Chiang. The thought of Big Ears on the trail of Swan and Flood made her feel slightly queasy.

'So, after dinner the generalissimo took a walk and happened to notice something amiss in the woods below. He personally repelled the attack then launched a counterattack. If only more people knew what a heroic man he is! He is truly so humble and lives only to serve his country.'

The limit of how much of the Madame's propaganda Hahn could take at one sitting had been surpassed.

'So why do you think that policeman was in the middle of it?' interrupted Hahn.

'If you say that the men with the negatives were going to meet you here then perhaps this policeman was…' she paused. 'If he has been following you for the past two weeks then it's obvious that he was continuing his surveillance and got caught in the crossfire. That ought to teach those meddlesome Shanghai police a lesson.'

Hahn sipped her coffee and wondered whether the communists had attacked or if Chiang's soldiers had opened fire on the innocent policeman. It had sounded as though shots had been fired from the valley below so perhaps the Madame wasn't fantasizing for once.

'The generalissimo is both a man of action and a poet,' said the Missimo. 'Why just this morning he brought me a flower….' She paused, wondering if she had run this bit of nonsense by Hahn in the past. She decided she had.

Hahn was wondering whether Chiang's soldiers or Big Ear's gangsters would find Swan and Flood.

She hoped neither would.

Chapter 26

Inspector Givens was contemplating a transfer to the Hong Kong Police where the biggest struggle was determining acceptable levels of graft.

News of Buchbinder's death the night before had rattled him. Now Detective Chang was telling him that not only had Swan and Flood disappeared, but that the Generalissimo was reluctant to relinquish the body of the dead policeman.

Things were slowly becoming clearer. Buchbinder and his men had found the two Yanks near the home of Chiang Kai-shek just as fighting had broken out between the Government troops and some communists.

But that's not to say that the Americans hadn't opened fire on Buchbinder too. No one could say for certain yet who had actually shot Buchbinder.

As it might be politically difficult to blame Chiang's soldiers, and because the bandits had vanished perhaps the blame could be pinned on Swan and Flood. After all, Buchbinder had been chasing them when the shots broke out and it was these Americans who had nearly had Witherspoon killed as well.

What I'd really like to do, thought Givens, is to nail the person who is really responsible for all this. Wallis Simpson. But for now he'd settle for Eli Swan and Luther Flood.

His first priority was to get Buchbinder's body. An autopsy would perhaps provide some clues as to who had killed him.

Givens called in one of his men and told him to establish contact with someone in authority at Chiang Kai-shek's house in Mokanshan. Buchbinder hadn't been with the force long but certainly long enough to warrant a ceremonial funeral. This makes an even dozen men killed in the line of duty this year, thought Givens morosely.

Detective Chang had said they had been about to arrest the Americans when all hell had broken loose. What were they doing outside the home of Chiang Kai-shek at night anyway? Then he remembered that Emily Hahn was there too.

To make matters worse, his counterparts in London were under increasing political pressure to get the negatives, pressure which they had duly passed on to Givens in Shanghai. No less a personage than Winston Churchill had become involved.

The phone rang. A Captain Yang of the Nationalist army identified himself and asked what he could do to help. Givens explained that the body they had recovered outside the Chiang's compound was none other than that of a Shanghai policeman.

'A little far from home wasn't he?' asked the captain in perfect English.

'He was in pursuit of two criminals, Americans by the name of Flood and Swan. Do you happen to know where they might be?' said Givens.

'I think we're working at cross purposes here,' deflected Captain Yang. 'And I think I know why you were after the two Americans. If we had captured them I'm sure you know what we would have found.'

'Yes, I believe I do,' said Givens, impressed with the captain's candor.

'I regret to say that it appears that the two men have been taken by the communists,' said Yang. 'It seems they stumbled into a communist attack. We've searched for their bodies but nothing has come up.

'I can be honest with you as it seems that we're both out of luck,' he added.

'What about the body of my man?' asked Givens.

'I regret to say he was killed by a bullet from one of our machineguns,' said Yang. 'Of course, we'll blame it on the communists.'

'Of course. Or better yet, blame it on Swan and Flood.'

'Whatever. I'll leave that up to you to handle. We'll have his body delivered to you in Shanghai by tomorrow.'

'Captain, one more thing if you don't mind?'

'Certainly.'

'Why does the generalissimo want the negatives?'

'Who said anything about negatives? Good night, Inspector.'

CHAPTER 27

Flood and Swan were sitting face-to-face, ropes securing their feet and hands. They were no longer gagged nor tied back to back.

'Have you ever met a communist?' asked Flood.

'Never. Not a single one in my whole life then boom, I meet a whole army of them. Why do you ask?'

'Well, I'm thinking of becoming one.'

Swan burst into laughter.

'What are you laughing at? I've been doing some thinking.'

'Thought I smelled something burning.'

'Seriously, you've got rich people and you've got poor people right?'

'So far so good.'

'But you've only got rich people because there are poor people to compare them with. Because they're poor they make the rich seem rich. So why not simply get rid of the poor people? Then you'd just have people.'

'What do you plan to do with the poor people?'

'Well, that's the beauty of it, you take from the rich people enough to make them the same as everyone else.'

'Kind of like Robin Hood?'

Flood's attention was wandering. 'Do you know what I'd like right now?'

'Some green tights?'

'A nice thick steak with new potatoes, gravy and some fresh salt-and-pepper corn on the cob, followed by apple pie with ice cream and coffee.'

'I thought communists ate rice.'

'God, I hate rice.'

'These guys seem more relaxed now that we're away from Mokanshan.'

'I guess they know they're pretty safe and I can see why—we're in the middle of nowhere.'

'If we can get away what should we do?'

'Find a river then wait for a boat?'

'Makes sense; find a little stream then a bigger one and so on until we found something big enough for boat traffic. Do you really think you'll be come a communist?'

'Probably not. I like the good life too much. But I think I can understand why they're fighting. Old Chiang Kai-shek looks after the rich people and hasn't lifted a finger against the Japanese—the communists are trying to help the poor people *and* are fighting the Japanese.'

Their captors made no effort to begin the nightly march as the light began to fade. Small fires were being lit for the first time while other soldiers busied themselves making rough lean-tos and gathering grass for bedding.

'It looks like we're going to camp here for a while,' whispered Flood.

'Thank God for that—my feet are two big blisters and my shoes are ruined. Do you know what day it is?

'Thursday I think.'

Swan sighed. 'I wonder what Daisy is doing.'

'Don't you worry,' said Flood. 'I'll bet the brigadier has already organised a rescue party by now; this is just the kind of thing he'd be really good at.'

'And the police will have told the newspaper that we're prisoners,' added Swan. 'Say that policeman back at the brigadier's shot at us didn't he?'

'He sure did…those negatives must be pretty important if they'd send somebody from Shanghai to get them…. I wish we'd never gotten involved with Emily Hahn or the negatives.'

A soldier brought them some food and used chopsticks to feed them. From the darkness they heard the screeching tomcat sounds of a radio being tuned and someone speaking in a staccato bursts. The weird wailing sound was punctuated by silence followed by static and again by the high pitched voice.

Unbeknownst to Flood and Swan their group was taking orders from Mao Tse-tung and replying with details of the raid, including the information that they held two hostages. This information would be forwarded to Shanghai where sympathisers, as they had before, would arrange for ransom notes to be dropped off at all the foreign newspapers.

'Maybe they're getting orders,' said Swan softly, as Flood was being fed. 'Maybe they're trying to find out what they should do with us.' He felt a chill go down his spine. All of a sudden his exhaustion caught up with him. They hadn't slept properly since they were captured. He got as comfortable as he could and was soon asleep.

Flood stayed awake a while longer gazing at the moon and trying to work a way out of the predicament they were in. He guessed they had been travelling north and well away from the coast. Then it dawned on him that he had signed over permission for the brigadier to use the loan money as he saw fit.

If what Eli said was true they could be hostages for months and months. A year even. He thought of waking Eli to ask what he thought about this but decided against it. It could wait for morning and there wasn't much they could do about it anyway.

He wriggled around a bit and made himself comfortable.

The brigadier is a British officer and a man of his word, he consoled himself.

He's as solid as the British Empire, he thought, gaining comfort from the fact.

An air of truce reigned in the Chiang's granite mansion in Mokanshan, the result no doubt of the satisfactory dustup with the commie bandits a couple of nights before.

The Gissimo had just rung for a servant to convey his fresh plans of attack to his commanders and, like countless times before, he was lost in a daydream consisting of himself astride a horse with the head of Mao Tse-tung atop a rusty pike.

The clarity and vision of his bold strategies never failed to mesmerize him, at least until attempts were made to implement them and reports began trickling back, more often than not consisting of lame excuses involving either the weather or the communist knack of vanishing into thin air.

But his time he had them where he wanted them. His German advisors, von Falkenhausen and von Seeckt, had encouraged him to encircle his enemies with high barbed wire fences reinforced with blockhouses. This ploy had satisfactorily bottled up what was left of the bandit army in the northwest where they could do little real harm.

'The red bandit remnants are in their death throes,' he had written as a prelude to the orders and their recent failed attack represented the 'last convulsive snap of their bloodthirsty jaws'.

He had ordered up every available soldier and airplane to hunt down the impudent bunch that had attacked his mountain lair, warning his top leaders that they would be held personally responsible for their capture.

It was obvious the communists would try to return to their headquarters in Baijiaping in northern Shansi Province as quickly as possible. As the fastest route back to the northern mountains meant travelling along the Yangtze River he had also ordered his navy to check Chinese vessels heading upriver. His commanders had also been told to try to find the missing negatives.

Stretching contentedly in his silk robe, the Gissimo eagerly opened a letter from his youngest son, Wei-kuo, serving with the German Wehrmacht as a second lieutenant with the Ninety-eighth Jaeger Regiment.

Reading of his adventures, Chiang reminisced briefly about his own happy days as a cadet in Japan. Say what you will about us Chiangs, he thought with a touch of pride, but we always go with the winners.

His wife entered his study and interrupted his reveries, forcing him to hide the letter. Wei-kuo was the son of her enemy, Fat Cow, his first wife.

'What are you reading?' she asked.

'Just a report.'

'That Shanghai policeman who was shot by your men has got me thinking.'

He waited for her to continue.

'I thought it might be a good idea if we gave their leaders something to make them forget about him.'

'Like what?'

'Hmmmm. How about having the Ministry of War confer the Military and Air Medal on a few of them? The British love medals.'

'Why not? We had thousands of them made.'

'And I'd like to do the conferring,' she asked.

She was alluding to her desire to be officially named China's Air Marshall. Chiang had been pretending to consider it but was afraid that his warlord generals might laugh at him behind his back.

'Well?' she said, her voice hardening.

Chiang realised he owed a great deal to May-ling and her powerful family *and* she was proving to be a genius for gulling money out of the Americans. *And* he didn't have to share his home with nagging warlords.

He continued to mull it over. The communists didn't have any aeroplanes so it would be hard for her to botch that up; it would keep her busy and he as Supreme War Leader would still be in charge; the Americans would love it—their puerile press would go crazy at the thought of it—Wellesley graduate and all that nonsense.

'I'll draw up the orders tomorrow.'

'Good', she said. 'You can go back to reading the letter from the son of Fat Cow.'

'How did you know?'

'I know everything. By the way, we have lunch tomorrow with the Reverend Armstrong.'

'Who's he?'

'The one who made you a Methodist.'

'Oh him. Do we have to eat hot dogs?'

'To Americans hot dogs are very important. And I plan to have pictures taken.'

'And they say Chinese eat dogs.'

'How is the son of Fat Cow?' she asked, attempting to change the subject.

'Fine, fine—he likes the Germans. He plans on visiting Austria in the near future he says; although he didn't say what for.'

'Do you think I should wear a uniform as Air Marshal?'

'Absolutely not. I strictly forbid you.'

'Don't worry,' said the Missimo, already imagining herself in tight fitting leather aviatrix garb *a la* Amelia Earhart, complete with jodhpurs, white scarf and an aviator helmet. Charles Lindbergh and his wife had visited China a few years previously to help deal with floods that had washed over large portions of the country. Both the Gissimo and the Missimo had been nearly tongue-tied with envy at the swashbuckling image they'd cut.

The Generalissimo was already regretting his decision. His wife treated the Chinese Air Force like a glorified taxi service already and no doubt would soon insist on learning to fly.

Learning to fly? The idea of his wife at the controls of a large and unwieldy aircraft did immediate wonders to his mood. Foolish American women were forever crashing airplanes around the globe.

He would just have to make sure he wasn't a passenger.

The American community of Mokanshan was in a mild state of shock. After all, the reason they summered here was to *avoid* the consequences of China's erratic politics. Yet word that a battle had been fought, practically on their doorsteps, was like a wish come true for those who secretly longed for a bit of excitement.

Regardless of whether they viewed the battle and the kidnappings with alarm or titillation, everyone was galvanised into some sort of action. The more fearful of Mokanshan's inhabitants made plans to leave while others more resolute checked their supplies of ammunition, as well as the locks on their doors and windows. Family-imposed curfews were put into effect and drills practiced to ensure readiness in case of another attack. The entire Boy Scout troop, the only vaguely military force at hand, was practically insensible with excitement.

More than a few mothers and fathers remembered with impeccable hindsight how they had felt something like this was in the offing the moment little Alison Williams discovered the armed bandit lurking about the recent wedding.

A meeting was to be held at the church that morning. The Reverend Bradford Armstrong, *de facto* leader of the community, had swiftly placed himself in charge. As a muscular sort of Christian he shared the exact same happy outlook as the Boy Scouts, who he'd promptly put under his personal command. In addition, he'd also arranged an interview with none other than Generalissimo Chiang Kai-shek (a personal friend he assured everyone he could) to learn the whereabouts of the two missing Americans.

Daisy had alerted the community to their fate after they'd failed to show up at their hotel and it was remembered that the Brigadier lived *right* where the battle had taken place. A contingent of men visited his home and learnt from the Indian servants that Flood and Swan had disappeared just when the hostilities began. The brigadier's fate was rather more cloudy. In a mysterious twist, the Indians had wailed about being cheated by the missing man. Wisely the Indians had not mentioned anything about the dead policeman. Nevertheless, they'd been promptly locked up in the village's tiny jail as possible accomplices of the communists.

Daisy and her mother had checked into the Mokanshan hotel, in the very room vacated by Swan and Flood, and now spent most of their time in the dining room, Daisy bravely playing the role of the girl who came *that* close to being captured.

Her mother, who was only too happy to let Daisy claim the limelight, was not nearly as put out by their disappearance as was her daughter. Although drastic, the kidnapping of Swan meant she could relax her watch over Daisy's virtue and enjoy her holiday with the added bonus of having something truly exciting to tell her friends when she returned home.

In the fairy tale atmosphere that was Mokanshan no one actually thought that the two Americans were in any mortal danger. They were *American* and *Americans*, as everyone knew, didn't suffer the same fate that often befell less sensible or fortunate people.

While the Boy Scouts prowled around the woods surrounding the church, anxious looking men rode or walked up the hill from the village to the granite building. Others had remained behind to guard the women and children at the Mokanshan Hotel, giving the whole exercise the air of a wagon train under threat from hostile redskins. Armstrong was taking on the role of wily old wagon train leader, the man who would get them all through to safety.

He greeted the men at the door to the church and respectfully requested that all firearms, for he could see the odd revolver peeking out from under jackets, be left at the front of the nave. To his surprise nearly everyone had come armed, some with six shooters and others with ladylike little revolvers.

'Now men, as you know I'm off to see the Generalissimo soon,' he said plainly, as befitted his new role. 'I'll see what he can tell me about Luther and Eli and what is being done to effect their delivery back to us from the hands of the savages…er, communists. If that's where they are that is.'

'How do we know they're even alive?' asked a man named Andrew Field. 'I say we go after them ourselves on horseback. We've got men here who are good at following game trails. I say Americans should look after Americans.'

The Reverend immediately saw this as a threat to his leadership.

'Now hold on here Andy,' he replied steadily. 'You're a family man and you're from New York City. The Generalissimo, who I count as a personal friend, is in a far better position to get those boys back using his army and air force. So hold your horses.'

'Wasn't one of those boys a newsman?' asked another resident. 'Maybe we should contact his paper and they can put out some kind of bulletin.'

'How about calling the consulate and getting them in on this too?' said another.

'How about offering a reward?' piped up an older man during a brief lull.

The Reverend was getting hot under the collar. 'Hang on here,' he said. 'One thing at a time—and yes we should contact the paper—which one is it?'

'*The North-China Daily News*.'

'Thank you. And the consulate. And you Fred can start collecting a reward.'

Fred looked like he was already regretting his outspokenness.

'But first we've got to find out exactly what happened,' continued the Reverend. 'And we won't know what happened until I go visit with the Generalissimo. Those of you who are interested in finding out what he has to say can meet me later this afternoon at the hotel.'

And with this the Reverend concluded the meeting. Walking outside he called his Boy Scouts to heel and began marching in the direction of Chiang Kai-shek's little fortress.

The Boy Scouts sped up when the smell of hot dogs wafted down the trail, forcing the elderly Armstrong to restrain them. 'Hot dogs', he thought. 'Whatever can be going on?'

The guards at the gate were surprised by the appearance of the Boy Scout troop being led by an older man but had been told to let them through without delay. Madame Chiang herself met them at the doorway and led the group through the house to an outside garden where food was being prepared.

There stood a smiling Generalissimo clutching a hot dog, a photographer standing nearby readying his camera. The Missimo ushered the boys towards the waiting hotdogs as her husband looked on at the little soldiers in their flat brimmed hats and shorts. For once he was surrounded by Americans his size! He dutifully took a bite of his hot dog.

Reverend Armstrong was aghast. Hot dogs! And this a meeting to discuss the fate of two kidnapped Americans!

'Madame,' he said, his face colouring to a shade approximating that of the wieners. 'How can we possibly eat hot dogs when the fate of two American boys hangs in the balance!'

As his outrage grew, the Missimo shot a quick look at the Gissimo, causing him to immediately hand his hot dog to an aide standing nearby. The man clutched it reverently, as though it were a rifle.

'Perhaps we should go inside to talk about this,' said the Missimo consolingly, taking the reverend by the arm and leading him into the house. The Gissimo followed, eyeing the hot dog speculatively. He was acquiring a taste for the strange meat.

'It appears that the two boys were spirited away by communist bandits,' said Madame Chiang once they'd seated themselves comfortably in the drawing room. 'And as for the unfortunate policeman it appears that the rebels shot him as well.'

'The policeman?'

'Oh, I'm so sorry you hadn't been informed,' said the Missimo, eyebrows raised. 'You see it appears that a policeman, another American I regret to say, was with the other two when the firing began.'

From outside came the cries of boys happily devouring their food and soda pops.

'Do you mean an American was killed the other night?' muttered Armstrong, his face this time taking on the coloration of the inside of a hot dog bun. He hung his head, the responsibility of his position momentarily overwhelming him.

The Missimo grasped his hands in hers.

'Perhaps this policeman, Buchbinder I believe he was named, was a friend of the missing boys? Perhaps he was here visiting them?' she said, knowing full well he had been after the negatives.

The Reverend recovered his strength. 'What efforts are being made to rescue our two missing countrymen?'

'I can assure you sir that every effort is being taken to capture the fleeing bandits and that our airforce is patrolling the skies as we speak,' she said. 'It appears your two friends were helpful in spoiling an attack on the Generalissimo that night,' she continued. 'We are grateful and will not rest until they are safe and sound.'

'I see, I see,' replied the Reverend. 'Perhaps if you would be so kind as to let me use your telephone? I must call our consulate at once to let them know what has happened.'

As the Missimo led the Reverend away the Gissimo, giving an experimental chop with his dentures, took the opportunity of heading back to the barbecue.

From The *North-China Daily News*:

SMP POLICEMAN SLAIN BY RED BANDITS

Two Americans kidnapped during raid on Chiang Kai-shek

Mokanshan, Aug. 13

Efforts are being made to locate the whereabouts of Americans Mr. Luther Flood, salesman, and Mr. Eli Swan, formerly with the N-C.D.N, after a raid by communist bandits at the retreat of Generalissimo Chiang Kai-shek in Mokanshan on Monday. The retiring communists fled with the two men after killing S.M.P. detective Ralph Buchbinder in a gun battle with the Government troops. Reports say the Reds made a desperate attack on the residence where the Generalissimo and his wife were staying. Messrs. Buchbinder, Flood and Swan were staying at a nearby residence and were thus implicated. No ransom has been sent although a reward of $2,500 Shanghai dollars has been set for information concerning the location of the missing men. A funeral service will be held Sunday for Mr. Buchbinder, a member of the Shanghai Municipal Police since 1935, at the Bubbling Well Chapel.

CHAPTER 28

Messrs. Swan and Flood, former newshound and salesman respectively, were in the midst of a nightmarish forced march, the result of their camp having been discovered early that morning by enemy aircraft. The soldiers had quickly broken up into three separate groups in the hope that it would make it easier to avoid detection.

Although the two captives were unaware of the fact, scouts had also reported that two large groups of Nationalist troops were in close pursuit, supported by convoys of trucks and jeeps. To make matters worse, the communists were travelling through relatively open farmland under a blazing sun and cloudless skies. For once the Generalissimo's troops seemed to have all the cards stacked in their favour.

The stench of human faeces, used to fertilise the farms, mixed with Swan and Flood's sweat to burn their eyes and infect the air they swallowed as they were dragged along. For the communists, to remain where they were meant capture and death. There was no safe place nearby to hide from the airplanes. They had hoped their airborne pursuers would eventually run low on fuel but evidently they were being supported by other airplanes from a nearby air base.

In a small copse of trees the band paused to catch their breath. Swan and Flood's fine trousers and shirts were in tatters and their shoes had earlier been replaced by sandals made from discarded tyres.

'I'm no communist,' gasped Swan. 'But I sure hate those bastard airplanes.'

'We're fish in a barrel,' agreed Flood, lying down to catch his breath.

'Luther, I think we're going to split up. Those guys are pointing in different directions.'

'Maybe they'll just leave us behind. It's hours till dark.'

Everyone scrambled for cover as two warplanes came streaking down with the sun behind them firing bullets into the dusty ground, raising puffs of dust and finding soft bodies like hornets from hell. Before anyone could react the planes were past and banking to return for another attack.

To his astonishment, Flood himself praying out loud.

'Dear God, please let me live! I promise to be good. Oh Dad, I promise to change my ways.'

The planes came in again as Swan began screaming while curling his body into as small a shape as possible. After the attack the planes peeled off south.

A communist soldier jumped up and leaned against a tree. He excitedly began pointing to the direction they'd come from and yelling urgently to his comrades.

Along with the others, Flood and Swan sat up and looked. A long line of brown clad soldiers was cautiously approaching along a dirt track.

'Those are government soldiers,' whispered Swan. Realising it didn't matter if he whispered or not he continued in a normal voice. 'If we can get to them we're safe.'

A few of the communists began digging crude slit trenches as the rest of the group split into two groups. Swan and Flood were shoved into the smaller one, containing only a few men. The soldiers chosen to remain behind began taking shots at the ranks of the approaching troops. The larger group began running towards a nearby farm as fast as their legs would carry them. Just as they reached the rough buildings three more airplanes dropped to attack in a neat row, again claiming a few victims.

As the aeroplanes broke off to regroup, the men guarding Flood and Swan began running in the opposite direction from their fellow soldiers, pulling their captives along with them. They headed in a slightly downhill direction toward a row of trees lining the bottom of the shallow valley.

Behind them the remaining soldiers continued their fire on the cautiously approaching enemy soldiers as the warplanes continued their assault on the farm, adding high explosives to the attack.

Reaching a line of trees following a small streambed, the communist soldiers and their two terrified hostages ran downhill towards the protection of a small stand of trees. The unequal battle raged behind them with the warplanes lining up their attack in such a way that they could strafe both the small farm and the rearguard in one swoop. Fortunately, the pilots seemed to have missed the escape of the small group including Swan and Flood, now splashing along a stream under some slight cover.

As the sounds of the screaming planes grew less intense they paused and gulped water from the small creek, the soldiers filling their canteens and checking their weapons. One of the soldiers approached the Americans shyly.

'That was close calling,' he said shyly.

'You speak English,' burst out both Americans. Their initial capturer, Soldier Wu, took a proprietorial interest in the two kidnappees, moving closer to observe his fellow soldier speak the foreign language.

'A little goes a lots of way' said the young man, a radio operator named Lee, looking proudly in the direction of Wu.

'We're Americans, Americans!' howled Swan as quietly as possible as the leader of the group, a rough-looking older man, gave a sharp order for the group to begin gathering up their meagre belongings. As they jogged along the streambed both Swan and Flood tried to establish eye contact with Lee who was busy trying to settle the radio on his back and carry his rifle at the same time.

Soon the two captives were wishing they were back at the scene of the attack. At least they'd been able to stop moving. Each step they took now was carrying them further away from their rescuers. Dusk began to eat away at the light. Still they continued travelling, not stopping to trade for food as a precaution against informers giving away their location.

No talk was permitted but none of the party was capable of speaking anyway. Everyone, particularly the two Americans, was barely able to put one foot in front of the other. When they finally came to rest at dawn near a village the little group collapsed in heaps, too tired to do anything else.

NEWS OF AMERICAN ABDUCTEES

Shanghai, Aug. 16

A letter demanding ransom has been Received at the N-C.D.N regarding Missing Americans, Eli Swan and Luther Flood, kidnapped by Red bandits earlier this week after a gun battle in Mokanshan. In effect of their safe return, the Communists demand $60,000, two anti-aircraft guns, a wireless telegraph set, medicines and ammunition. These they expect to be furnished by Gen. Chiang Kai-shek.

'Do you want them back?' said Inspector Givens to his friend Dickson Hoste of the *Daily News.* The two were discussing the fate of Swan and Flood over drinks at the Shanghai Club's famous Long Bar.

'I should say not; the blighters put poor Witherspoon in the hospital where he remains, do you?

'Hardly, they were responsible for having my man Buchbinder shot in Mokanshan where I sent him to get those damn negatives of the Prince of Wales' tart.'

'Steady on old boy, that's the future King we're talking about.'

'Who happens to be bedding one of the all time great floozies; you should see her file. At any rate, I'd only want them back to charge them with something; not exactly sure what though.'

'What about the American consul?'

Givens burst into laughter. 'He's in no great hurry either. It appears young Flood installed a great number of air-conditioners at their consulate with guaranteed maintenance. Every single one of them has broken down. When they tried finding Flood he wasn't to be found. So no big hurry there either I should think.'

'Apart from presumably their mothers, does anyone else want them back?'

'I don't imagine old Big Ears is terribly happy at their having pulled the wool over his beady little eyes; he's after those damned negatives as well…and there's a bunch of Yanks up in Mokanshan, led by that meddlesome old warbler Armstrong, who have raised the princely sum of two thousand, five hundred dollars.'

It was Hoste's turn to break into laughter.

'Only fifty-seven thousand and five hundred to go!'

'And some spare anti-aircraft guns courtesy of the Gissimo!' Givens added, chortling.

'And would you be requiring some ammunition to go with your order, sir?'

'There's a special promotion on for wireless telegraph sets……' He began gasping for air. '……we're giving them away free this month to chaps who are sworn enemies.'

'Oh my word,' said Hoste, tears dribbling down his cheeks.

'I wish I could send a few more miscreants off to the Reds,' said Givens, signalling the barman for another round.

'What about the negatives; the ones they thought poor Witherspoon was holding?'

'Ah well, that's a good question. Poor Buchbinder was after the two Yanks who we think were trying to get them to Emily Hahn. Presumably she's acting on behalf of the Generalissimo and his lot.'

'But if that's the case then they've disappeared along with Swan and Flood.'

'Presumably you'd pay to get them back?'

'I suppose so. But what worries me is that the Gissimo might provide what the Reds are asking for if they throw in the negatives along with the hostages.'

'So the negatives are actually worth more than the two Americans?'

'Absolutely, they've no particular value. You know how eager Chiang is to win favour with the Yanks.'

'Quite disgusting really.'

'Well, I must be pushing off. Give me a call if you hear anything.'

'Right you are.'

CHAPTER 29

The small group of communists had no money to buy food but they did have something almost as good as silver and certainly better than paper money. During the recent Long March, stocks of opium had been seized from rich traders and these were useful to barter for food from peasants.

One of their group went off to see if he could exchange a large chunk of opium for some food. It had been more than a day since they'd last eaten and all were famished. Even Flood was having kind thoughts about rice.

Soldier Lee approached Swan and Flood and recited a ditty in his strong singsong English.

'I am a radish gone to seed,
I am the thinnest of my breed,
Roots and fruits and asparagus shoots!
Come all ye heathen, come and feed.'

'Where on earth did you learn that?' asked Swan.

'I am working for missionary family when boy and they taughted me English. You are from what for country?'

'The United States of America and we demand to be released immediately,' said Flood indignantly.

'Oh no I am think not. You are meat ticket!' said Lee laughing.

'What's a meat ticket?' asked Swan.

'Chiang Kai-shek give us plenty meat and you the ticket!' he said.

'Oh I see,' said Swan glumly. 'Say, where are you taking us?'

'Big secret but maybe go with ship on Yangtze River?'

'But how can Chiang Kai-shek give you plenty of meat if he doesn't know where you are?' asked Flood.

'Maybe use radio. But first must becoming safe from soldiers,' he added. 'I living with American family. Call me Billy.'

'OK Billy…'

'No my name is Lee. Soldier must Chinese name now.'

'OK Lee. Have you contacted people in Shanghai? Foreign people? Told them where we are?'

Lee looked puzzled. 'You here'.

'I know but do people in Shanghai know we are prisoners?'

'Pris-on-ers?'

'Yes, that we are with the communist army?'

'Ah yes I am seeing. No talk English long time. Yes for you we are having many things and big money.'

They were interrupted by the member of their party returning with a supply of cooked rice, meat and vegetables. A portion was divided equally between the six men who wolfed it down using their hands. As Lee went off to do guard duty, Swan and Flood began discussing the information he had shared with them.

'If we get on the Yangtze or on a boat maybe we can jump off it when we get a chance. I'll bet we can out-swim these guys pretty easily,' said Swan.

'I don't want to try out-swimming a bullet though,' replied Flood.

'I don't think they'll shoot us—remember what he said about us being meat tickets? I think they sacrificed some fellows back there so we could get away clean.'

'I could sure do with some meat—I think I've lost about twenty pounds in the last few days.'

'And there's bound to be some of our boats or British ones on the Yangtze so maybe we could try to get to them.'

'I'm game if you are but what about waiting until they send the ransom?'

'Those Germans I was telling you about; the ones who were gone for two years?' said Swan softly. 'They'd collected the ransom but the communists were never in one place long enough to collect it—I remember hearing that Chiang Kai-shek hates it when anybody gives the Reds money or anything that would help them.'

'Let's try to get as friendly as we can with them so that they'll think twice about shooting us,' said Flood. 'I'd rather be a hostage than a dead man any day thank you very much.'

'Let's agree on a code word we can use if we decide to try to escape.'

'OK, what about one, two, three, Mickey Mouse?'

'One, two, three, Mickey Mouse it is.'

'I just remembered something,' whispered Flood. 'The prof told me that the river moves something like fifty million tons of rock and sand and stuff every second or every day—I can't remember which—but anyway it's pretty powerful, maybe the most powerful river in the world. Are we sure we just want to hop in and hope for the best?'

'I don't know but our best bet is go in where the river is the widest so we can avoid rapids and suchlike; maybe try to grab something to float with.'

Soon the group had arranged themselves in the shade to sleep until nightfall.

They heard the river long before they caught sight of it, a vast roaring sound reminiscent of Niagara Falls, the only place of any note ever visited by Swan and Flood before their trip to China.

The air was becoming damp and fragrant and soon a deep, chanting sound was heard above the constant roaring of the river, an eerie and monotonous chant interspersed with the slow beating of a drum. For Swan and Flood, the sound conjured up a dark religious ceremony involving human sacrifice. Both felt chills go down their spines, as the chanting grew steadily louder then without warning abruptly stopped.

The roaring of the river was now quite deafening and mist could be seen rising above the nearby forest. The group quickly gathered branches and plants to make a simple hidey-hole where, once again, they divvied up some food. After the meal, Soldier Lee and the leader of the group went off to scout the river and determine what they would do next, taking with them a much larger ball of opium.

Swan and Flood spoke together quietly. Their captors had indeed grown friendlier and no longer gagged or tied them together, although their hands and feet were expertly bound. They seemed unbothered when the two spoke, although they still spoke in hushed whispers.

'Man, that chanting was pretty spooky,' whispered Flood. 'What do you think it was?'

'I don't know but I've got a feeling we're going to find out soon. I don't think Billy was lying when he said we might be travelling by boat; my guess is that we'll be going upriver to put some distance between us and the government troops.'

'How far do you think we've travelled in the last week?'

'Hard to say, maybe a hundred and fifty miles or so as the crow flies. It looks like we've reached the Yangtze though.'

'Do you know Eli, there's not much left of these fancy pants we got from the brigadier; I can see your bum through the back of yours.'

Their shirts were hanging in strips and provided almost no protection against rain and insects. Both men had scraggly beards and their skin had been fried red and was pocked with mosquito bites. They looked utterly unlike the two *faux* British officers who had been swanned about in the brigadier's house back in Mokanshan.

'I don't know how much longer I can go on,' said Flood wearily. 'All this endless running and hiding and eating awful food and sleeping on the ground and the mosquitoes…'

'Cheer up, I think we'll be travelling by boat soon; we'll do the 'Mickey Mouse' and arrive home as heroes and settle back into our old lives.'

'Do you think so?'

If truth be told Swan didn't actually think things would be that simple. After the aborted mission against Chiang Kai-shek the communists obviously realised that the only way to salvage anything from the campaign was to return with the two 'meat tickets' for the purpose of ransom.

Secretly he was thinking about writing a book about their experiences with the bandits. Something with a sure-fire title like 'In the Hands of the Reds' or 'I Was a Communist Meat Ticket.' Like many people who have been in China for just a short while, Swan felt he was more than qualified to write a book about the country through the prism of his own experiences. This, he decided, would be his ticket to fame, fortune and perhaps even the hand of Daisy Munro.

'Sure, look at it as the adventure of a lifetime; something to tell your grand-kids.'

'I'd just as soon forget all about it,' sniffed Flood. 'And I wouldn't want to frighten the wits out of them either.'

'Fine, but let's keep talking to Billy; see if we can find out what their plans are and where we're going.'

The chants and the drumbeats resumed.

Meanwhile, Soldier Lee was being chastised by his leader for getting too friendly with their captives and for speaking to them in their language. Where had he learnt to speak like that anyway?

The two soldiers had made a deal with the owner of a small cargo boat who would soon be travelling upriver with some pigs. They were on the bank of the swiftly flowing river below Mirror Mountain, a huge cliff which forced a narrow pass in the charging river. Opposite the rocky face of the mountain was a small island called the Little Orphan which Lee found auspicious since he'd once been an orphan himself.

His family had disappeared in the general upheaval that was China's recent past and he had found himself begging for food in the streets of Hangchow where an American missionary had found him and given him the means to work, eat and get a rudimentary education. But most of all, a chance to survive. As a result he hadn't any hatred for foreigners—quite the reverse although he knew they didn't belong in his country.

Alongside the Little Orphan a gang of nearly naked men pulled long bamboo ropes attached to a boat they were dragging steadily upstream through the rapids. As they chanted they moved in step to the beat of the drum. They were called *chow-fu*—trackers—and men like them had worked the Yangtze since the time long ago when the Yellow Emperor had built a mountain that forced the river to dramatically change direction, turning it eastwards to enrich the Chinese people.

These days many boats didn't use the trackers and their numbers were slowly decreasing. Foreigners had dynamited the large rocks in the river that had previously funnelled the water into narrow and dangerous channels. Of course, many of the more powerful engines were able to go against the current quite easily. But many of the boats had poor engines and some had no engines at all.

Despite the danger of travelling by boat—sailors coming downstream had spoken of an increased government presence on the river and many inspections being made—the leader decided that it was necessary to rest his men and to make better time travelling on the river. They would travel for one full day and night unless they were forced to flee from the nationalist navy or soldiers.

They would hide their passengers among the pigs and stow most of their weapons so they wouldn't be visible to passing traffic. The price was high—almost all the opium they had left—but travelling by river would be immeasurably faster than trying to scale mountains where they would be visible to aeroplanes and vulnerable to spies.

They would sail—or rather be pulled—when there was just enough light for the trackers to do their work.

Aboard the *HMS Sandpiper* near Nanking, Sub-Lieutenant Billy Beloe was having the time of his life. Having been stationed with the Yangtze Flotilla for only a few weeks, the increasingly plodding work of river patrol had been suddenly interrupted by an urgent message from the Commander-in-Chief, Hong Kong: Prevent warlords acting on behalf of the Chinese Government from interfering with the lawful traffic of British boats.

Now the HMS Sandpiper was steaming west and upriver to set things right.

Although it boiled the blood of all patriotic Chinese, the Yangtze was by legal treaty an international river and British, as well as American, Japanese and European boats were not subject to the same laws that applied to Chinese vessels. This, of course, was much the same in the forty-odd treaty ports that dotted the country's coastal regions and lined the huge river.

Although the rights of the foreign powers were somewhat tenuous, the punishments they meted out to Chinese craft were severe. After all, this was gunboat diplomacy so if push came to shove on the Yangtze Station, the Sandpiper would shove very hard indeed.

Beloe was about to engage in his first action on the high seas—or rather high river at any rate. Weaned on tales by G.A. Henty, Percy Westerman and the like, he was almost agog with excitement at the prospect of battle.

The *Sandpiper* was little more than a jumped-up riverboat but her big guns fired explosive shells six inches in diameter. Her arsenal also included Maxims and Lewis guns which packed a strong punch, particularly when compared to Chinese guns. And everyone knew that the yellow blighters couldn't shoot for toffee anyway.

The greatest danger on the Yangtze was the wildly fluctuating depth and flow of the river. Beloe was learning a great deal about the river by hanging about the command bridge and keeping his ears open. The previous night he'd overheard a cautionary story of another gunboat that had run aground a few years before during a flood. A sub-lieutenant like himself had been sent off in the fog in a twelve-ton cutter to get help but had gotten lost then 'neaped' in the mud himself.

The next morning the unfortunate sailor and his Bluejackets awoke to find the water had dropped considerably and their little boat was stuck hard and fast in a paddy field almost two miles from the river. Hundreds of coolies were then rounded up to dig a canal to the nearest creek so the boat could return to the Yangtze.

One action that did make Beloe's superiors nervous was the possibility that Chinese pirates might 'accidentally with intent' set a couple of junks, secured to each other by a long cable, on fire then let them drift downriver and across the Sandpiper's bows. Gun crews were in a state of permanent readiness to blast anything which posed a threat.

The little ship made a steady ten knots up the river, bordered on each side by a monotonous expanse of marshland teeming with waterfowl. The Sandpiper 'hogged it' straight up the river, blithely trusting that sampans and other Chinese craft coming downriver would swerve to avoid the gunboat's reinforced steel bow. Even a warship as little as the Sandpiper was capable of destroying wooden boats without slackening speed.

Swan and Flood gazed at the little boat. 'This doesn't look too bad,' said Swan. 'And it'll sure beat walking.'

'What's that horrible smell?' replied Flood, wrinkling his nose.

'Whoah,' said Swan, pinching his nose. 'Pig shit I think.'

The soldiers pointed down into the sampan's hold, indicating that the two Americans should go below.

'Forget it,' said Flood. 'I've never smelled anything this bad—this boat hasn't been cleaned for twenty years I'll bet.'

Two of the soldiers, Lee and Wu, climbed into the hold uncomplainingly. The others pointed their rifles at the two captives and made threatening noises.

'It is OK,' said Lee, smiling bravely despite the horrible smell.

'Shoot me if you will but I've got a thing about pigs—I'm afraid of them,' said Flood.

'C'mon Luther, they won't hurt you.'

A soldier used the stock of his rifle to try to push Flood into the hold. With the soldiers pulling from below and the others pushing from above he was forced into the evil smelling place. A few large pigs milled about nervously.

The owner of the boat fired the small, asthmatic sounding engine and the trackers, waiting impassively nearby, rose from their haunches and started gathering the coiled bamboo ropes. The drummer, an amazingly wizened old man, began beating slowly as the boat began moving against the current.

'God damn Emily Hahn and god damn the King's girlfriend,' swore Flood. 'I hate China, oh do I hate China.'

A rain began to fall and, mixed with the pig shit, soon had them both gasping for air. Without asking permission they both pressed their faces to small portholes where they could breathe a bit more easily.

'I'm feeling sick,' said Flood, yelling outside.

'How do you feel about Mickey Mouse?'

'The sooner the better; can we get to the shore in this kind of water?'

'Let's try to go where it's wider.'

Fishing weirs dotted the shorelines and pagodas looked down on the river from their cliff top perches. Flood wondered how far they would be travelling upriver and whether they would have any chance to escape. He grew tired of standing with his face to the porthole so he sat down and pressed his nose and mouth against his tattered shirt to block the stench. After a while he grew used to the smell although Flood remained glued to the tiny window.

This *would* make a good book, he figured, and of course he'd jazz it up a bit and make he and Flood seem more heroic and dashing and all. The pigs had settled in near the back of the boat and both soldiers had their heads and shoulders above deck.

The owner of the boat obviously was a believer in never throwing away anything that might prove useful later, including an assortment of old bottles. Manoeuvring under the watchful eyes of the hogs, Swan managed to kick two bottles up to where Flood was standing at the porthole.

He nudged Flood's legs to get his attention. Flood turned inside the hold but was unable to adjust to the lack of light. Swan whispered to him that they should try to break the bottles without attracting the notice of the soldiers standing nearby.

Outside the rain was picking up. Swan used his feet to wrap one of the bottles in a piece of canvas then bent down and picked up a second heavier bottle with this bound hands. Flood, ignoring the smell, stood between Swan and the soldiers to block the sound of breaking glass. Swan dropped the bottle. It missed the other one and rolled a few feet. Swan used his feet again to get it close then dropped it a second time. This time the smaller bottle broke.

Swan had stopped cutting and was sitting innocently when Soldier Wu brought down some cooked rice and vegetables. Flood turned away from the window to indicate that he wasn't hungry so Wu turned to feed Swan. When he was finished with Swan he went and sat close to the pigs and soon fell asleep, oblivious to his surroundings. Swan returned to his task of freeing his bound hands. When he had finished, he rested for a few minutes before slowly and carefully stretching his legs, which had fallen asleep. He reached over and tapped Flood on the leg.

'I'm free,' he whispered.

'Now what do we do?'

'I'm going to hit him on the head with this bottle then free you.'

Swan crept over to the soundly sleeping Wu as the pigs stirred restlessly. Taking a deep breath he swung firmly and Wu went over on to his side. He rushed back to Flood and began cutting him free.

'Good going Eli,' he said rubbing the circulation back into his hands. 'What next?'

'I hadn't thought that far ahead.'

'Let's tie him up and make it look like he's sleeping.'

Flood quickly tied up Soldier Wu in a large tangle of granny knots while Swan stood near the hatch with the bottle in his hand. He figured he'd have a second or two before the eyes of the soldiers could adjust to the dark. Flood threw a piece of canvas over Wu's bound hands.

All of a sudden the engine of the sampan stopped. The two Americans froze on the spot and looked at each other. A pair of legs appeared swinging in the hatch. As Soldier Lee came down Swan hit him on the back of the head with the bottle. He collapsed in a heap and they began trussing him up as well.

Flood, who had forgotten all about his fear of pigs in the excitement, went forward to look out of the small porthole.

'There's a roadblock or whatever and a British passenger boat is tied up to the shore,' he hissed. 'It looks like the government army but they're all running around like crazy. We're floating backwards too I think.'

A loudspeaker boomed from behind them.

'This is the HMS Sandpiper,' a voice said in English. There was a brief pause before a translation boomed out in Chinese.

'You are engaged in a hostile action against a British warship.' Again a Chinese speaker echoed the statement. 'You have no right to detain His Majesty's ships. Desist immediately or we will fire.'

Swan began tugging at Flood's elbow.

'C'mon, here's our chance!'

They crept back to the open hatch and Swan peaked out quickly, drank in the scene then dropped back into the safety of the hold.

'There's a British Navy boat coming up behind us pretty quick with lots of guns.'

'So what do we do?' hissed Swan.

'Let's get out of here. Just hop off the back of the boat before they know what's going on. The British will save us.'

They both cautiously raised their heads into the daylight. Facing the backs of the soldiers and crew they launched themselves up from the fetid hold and jumped off the stern of the sampan, both screaming loudly for help.

They emerged sputtering from the depths, Flood facing upstream and Swan down. Flood screamed abuse at the sampan then spun around and screamed much louder. A British navy gunboat was bearing down on them at full speed. Swan had already begun pulling hard for shore.

Flood began thrashing madly in his wake, as the prow of the ship, its snout thrusting upwards through a watery moustache, grew larger, drowning their screams.

Suddenly, the gunboat's engines stopped and anchors were dropped from the stern. The Sandpiper was now facing the blockade with its guns broadside. The bow wave, however, was close enough to the two Americans that it picked them up and flung them downriver and slightly towards the southern bank of the river, a couple of hundred yards away.

Again they surfaced then drifted past the gunboat, screaming at the top of their lungs. Briefly they tried swimming in the direction of the moored ship, yelling for help. But all attention aboard the ship was upriver and the current was carrying them downriver and away.

Tired by their exertions the two let the current carry them along while they figured out what to do.

'Do you...think the...Reds are...coming...after us?' sputtered Flood.

'Can't see...past the...British boat,' replied Swan, gasping for air.

The current was strong and they floated away from the gunboat at the rate of a few knots. After a few minutes they could see their former captors in the sampan sneaking back along the shore away from the nationalist river blockade. Swan and Flood began angling for the opposite shore. There was a bend in the river where some fishermen had tied long bamboo ropes connecting their small pointed skiffs to the trees on the riverbank.

They started swimming as hard as they could for the ropes, periodically turning to check the progress of the sampan. They were nearly at the ropes when the sampan turned to give chase, spurring their efforts.

Flood, the stronger swimmer of the two, reached the rope first and began hauling for the shore, less than fifty yards away. Swan was right behind him but the sampan was rapidly closing the distance. The communist soldiers began taking shots over their heads in an attempt to discourage them.

'C'mon Eli,' yelled Flood as his feet found the slidy bottom of the river. He turned and pulled his friend along and they scrambled on shore, realising as they did that there was nothing left of the brigadier's evening wear. Naked, they ran barefoot into some cover and then upriver towards the *Sandpiper*. The sampan ran aground, the sound of pigs echoing in the hold. The soldiers leapt onto the shore and began the chase.

Sub-Lieutenant Beloe had been ordered to take some men and a couple of Lewis guns to ensure that the Chinese didn't cause any mischief from the shore behind the gunboat. It was not unheard of for bandits to take pot-shots at foreign ships from the riverbank.

Beloe was cursing his luck. There was little happening in the direction downriver from the blockade. Upriver, the government troops were using the Jardine passenger ship as insurance against the Sandpiper opening fire. It was a stalemate of sorts although one which wouldn't last long. Another, much luckier, sub-lieutenant had been ordered to take a party of Bluejackets up to the blockade and force the nationalist troops to release the passenger ship.

'Look sir! 80 degrees, 300 yards!' A Bluejacket pointed towards the shore where a chase of some sort appeared to be taking place. Beloe hoisted his binoculars. Two naked white men were running full tilt in their direction, chased by perhaps half a dozen armed Chinese. 'By Jove, those chaps are really hogging it,' Beloe said exditedly.

'Fire a round over the heads of those yellow jossers,' he said, trying to remain calm as he gave his first ever order to fire. 'Careful not to hit those two chaps in front.' A scrap of submerged training surfaced in Beloe's mind. 'The element of surprise is a strong factor for success in minor operations against savage or semi-civilized enemies.'

'Spray the water then swing it in front of them,' improvised Beloe. 'Let them see what we've got!'

The machine gun rattled satisfactorily, giving the two naked white men fresh steam while checking the progress of their pursuers. The gap between the two parties widened as the two foreigners approached the gunboat. 'What can this be about?' said Beloe, now hearing them screaming something about kidnap and Americans.

'Fire a round a little closer to the ground at the coves with the rifles. Look, that chap's firing at us!' To be under fire was adding immensely to Beloe's afternoon. A bullet *tinged* off the superstructure just as a senior officer, quickly ducking his head, came around to see what the fuss was about.

'What in blazes are you firing at?' asked Lieutenant Derek Graham, incidentally the former sub-lieutenant who'd had the ill luck to land a cutter out of sight of the Yangtze a couple of years previously. Beloe explained the situation quickly.

'Take a life boat and go pick those chaps up,' said Graham sensibly. 'I'll carry on here.'

Within seconds, a lifeboat was lowered and Beloe and two sailors were pulling for shore as the two naked scarecrows collapsed to the ground, obviously at their physical limit. Intermittent fire continued from the Sandpiper as the two ragged escapees got to their feet, huge smiles breaking out.

'Boy, are we glad to see you,' said one of them as they nimbly hopped into the lifeboat.

'Did you chaps swim the Yangtze?' asked Beloe politely. 'I've never heard of anyone doing that before. Perhaps you're the first ones to do so.'

And thus were Swan and Flood delivered from the hands of their communist captors.

Chapter 30

The trip downriver to Shanghai passed like a pleasant dream. The *Sandpiper* had quickly freed the Jardine riverboat *Ewo* and the two former hostages had been warmly received onboard where they were clothed, fed and toasted in quick order, basking in admiration for the pluck they'd shown escaping from the fearful communists.

Slightly tipsy, they'd been shown to the captain's stateroom and tucked into beds by his personal servant, a young Chinese. Flood had expressed his determination to get back to Mokanshan to resume work while Swan had already airily begun discussing his forthcoming book. It seemed the nightmare was over.

This happy state ended the moment they returned to their apartment in the French Concession to find two caskets in the living room resting on sawhorses. Chen the maid was nowhere to be found.

'Ha,' laughed Flood. 'What are these doing here?'

Swan's face went white despite his sunburn. He released a moan.

'Luther, this means we're dead!'

'Steady on old boy,' countered Flood in a passable imitation of his hero, the long departed brigadier.

'Oh shut up with that accent,' barked Swan. 'The gangs deliver these to people they plan to kill; they're so sure of themselves that they feel free to let them…us…know beforehand.'

Swan's panic, as if by osmosis, transfused into Flood.

'Let's get out of here!'. He ran towards the door.

'No, no, out the back!' Swan cried, grabbing his chequebook as he ran though the house.

They raced out the back door and hurled themselves at the six-foot wall, the effects of fear overcoming gravity. With no clear destination in mind they ran down the twisting alleys behind their former home, emerging onto a street where they flagged a taxi.

'Where do we go now?' asked a dazed Flood.

'Shut up. I'm thinking.'

What about Herbert Armitage?'

'Of course,' agreed Swan, turning to the driver and telling him in pidgin that they wanted to go to St. John's University.

They slouched down in their seats, gradually becoming calmer as the car took them in the direction of the American university, surely one place where the Green Gang wouldn't have much influence.

The two Americans asked for directions to the history department where they found Herbert Armitage behind a desk in a small office, pipe clenched between his teeth and an opened book in his lap.

'Good God,' said Armstrong, getting to his feet. 'Where did you two come from?'

Swan and Flood quickly filled in their friend about the kidnapping, leaving nothing out including their misadventures with hashish and finishing with the two coffins in their sitting room.'

'That means the Green Gang are after you.'

'What do you mean?'

'I hate to be the bearer of bad news but the police dropped by—it seems you're in quite a lot of trouble.'

'Those damn negatives again,' said Flood.

'Well probably, but I think it's more than that,' continued Armitage. 'I called your old paper and spoke with your old boss—the police seem to be after you—something about another reporter at your old paper, a fellow named Witherspoon.'

'What do you mean *old* paper?'

'Apparently you no longer work there.'

'I do now I'm back.'

'Apparently not, you see it seems this Witherspoon fellow was put into the hospital with some dreadful injuries by some thugs who thought he was you. That fellow Hoste mentioned something about criminal charges because of it.'

Swan looked at Flood, then dropped his head.

'Maybe I gave that priest one of Witherspoon's cards but I never thought......'

'That would explain the coffins,' interjected Armitage, earning a dirty look from Flood.

'And the fact that Hoste made it very clear you were no longer employed at the paper,' he continued.

'Herbert, can I use your phone?' asked Flood. 'I want to check in with the brigadier.'

Flood made the call using the local exchange to reach the operator in Mokanshan.

'That's funny,' he said, hanging up the phone. 'The line doesn't seem to work.'

Flood, the penny beginning to drop, grabbed the phone again and called his bank, asking to speak to the manager. After speaking for a couple of minutes and waiting for a few more he softly hung up the phone.

'The money has all been taken out, it's gone, all gone.'

Armitage coughed quietly. 'Perhaps you'll be safe for a few days hiding at my apartment.'

'Luther, this means you can't pay the money lenders right?'

'Right, and um, I guess I may as well tell you but they made it pretty clear that if I tried any monkey business I'd be answering to the Green Gang.'

'Ah, that would explain the second coffin,' said Armitage helpfully.

Both shot him dark looks.

'I hate to say it but I think you guys should think about leaving Shanghai,' said Armitage more carefully. 'Not that I don't want you to stay…'

The realisation that they would have to leave Shanghai immediately struck them with force. Swan sat down and put his face in his hands as Flood paced the small room.

'But I can go to Mokanshan!' he protested.

'Luther, you have no money,' said Swan through his hands. 'In fact, you have less than no money and the Green Gang want it back.'

Swan turned to Armitage.

'I've got a little money left in the bank, enough to get us to Hong Kong at any rate—could you cash a cheque for me?'

'Sure, no problem—I can even try to find out what ships are leaving.'

'That would be swell,' said Swan. 'You'd better try to get one leaving tomorrow, perhaps first thing in the morning.'

'Fine, fine—hey, I'm really sorry to have to tell you all this. When I heard you were kidnapped I went to the *Daily News*—that's when I heard about this Witherspoon guy. You gave the gang his namecard?'

'No, no,' replied Swan, showing signs of life. 'We tracked down the negatives—the ones we showed you—at a church. I guess I might have given Witherspoon's card to the priest we got them from. It wasn't meant to get him in trouble or anything.'

'Well, the important thing is you escaped from the communists,' said Armitage. 'Let's go over to my apartment and you can tell me about it; I still have that bottle of whiskey you gave me up in Mokanshan.

'First let me make a couple of phone calls,' he said, reaching for the phone. 'I take it you don't want me to give the shipping offices your names right?'

'They might be expecting us to leave,' said Swan, his mind awakening to the difficulties they now faced slipping by the police and the Green Gang, not to mention the loansharks.

'Maybe we should get some sort of disguise organised,' said Swan. 'Can we afford to get aviator's glasses and hats?' he added, knowing that Flood had long wanted a pair of dark glasses.

The three took a circuitous route to Armitage's small apartment, just off the campus. Swan and Flood rested while Armitage went off to enquire about passages out of Shanghai and to buy some dark glasses and hats. Flood ranted a bit about the duplicitous behaviour of the brigadier, though oddly both confessed that they still rather liked the old man.

'Do you reckon he was really a brigadier?' asked Flood.

'I doubt it,' replied Swan. 'He was a bit, well, too much—more like something you would see in a movie than in real life.'

'Well, he sure took me in hook, line and sinker,' said Flood. 'He made it seem like I was the one taking advantage of him somehow.'

'I guess that's why they call them confidence men,' said Swan.

Armitage returned after dark grinning importantly and clutching some shopping bags. He had arranged for two passages on the Royal Mail Ship *Stanley*, leaving first thing in the morning from the port of Ningpo, some eighty odd miles south of Shanghai. The ship made a weekly milk run down the China coast and Armitage figured the smaller port would be a safer embarking point than Shanghai. He'd even arranged a car to drive them south that night. Spirits restored, the bottle of whiskey was opened to toast their friendship and, hopefully, a successful journey south.

CHAPTER 31

A rumour had quickly spread throughout the American community in Shanghai that Swan and Flood had escaped from the Reds and were back in town. As a precaution, Patrick Givens had ordered some of his men to keep an eye on their apartment, as well as the *Daily News* and a few of their former haunts. By pure blind luck, Swan and Flood had not been spotted by any of Given's men.

Armitage realised that the longer Swan and Flood stayed in Shanghai the more likely it was they would be discovered. He apologised for rushing them along, but both seemed keen to be on their way, the coffins having accomplished their goal...They'd had enough adventure for a while and now looked forward to putting their lives back together in Hong Kong, where they hoped they'd be safe from trouble, at least for a while.

The taxi arrived soon after dark and the two desperadoes, Fedoras and aviator glasses firmly in place, made their farewells to the professor.

'Thanks for everything Herbert, we'll send word from Hong Kong to let you know we're safe,' said Flood, giving Armitage a hug.

'You'll be famous when my book comes out,' said Swan, warmly shaking his hand.

'One thing that I forgot to mention Eli,' said Armitage carefully. 'Daisy would sure love to hear from you. I know she's been worried and all. She wrote asking for news and gave me her address back in the States in case you turned up.' He handed over a scrap of paper with an address scribbled on it in a girlish hand. Armitage had deliberately not mentioned Daisy earlier in case Swan decided to risk staying in Shanghai in order to see her.

Swan's heart turned over at the mention of her name. 'That's, that's wonderful!' he said, his brain feverishly churning over the possibilities of a reunion. He hugged the embarrassed professor.

'Give her my love if you see her and tell her I'll write her soon.'

Armitage gave Swan an envelope containing some additional money. 'You can pay me back when you get back on your feet, maybe when your book comes out.'

They thanked him again. Suddenly eager to leave, they slipped out the door, adopting ridiculously stealthy moves as they slunk off in the direction of the unmarked taxi. Armitage discreetly waved from the doorway as the large black Ford roared off towards Ningpo. Behind glasses and under hat brims, their faces could be faintly seen peering out the windows as Swan and Flood took a long last look at the city that had been their home.

Passports were unnecessary to either enter or leave China so all Flood and Swan had to do the next morning was to show their tickets and board the ship, hiding in their second class cabin for the trip south along the coast. The boat would stop in Amoy then at the crown colony of Hong Kong, a place much belittled by Shanghai residents for its staid atmosphere, law-abiding populace and lack of fun.

Already, Swan and Flood were discussing moving south to Singapore if things didn't work out in Hong Kong, especially if they still thought that the Shanghai police, gangs or moneylenders might be able to find them there.

'The problem with these Chinese secret societies is they're kind of international,' said Swan, who had cadged some paper and a pen to start his book. He hadn't actually started, a state of affairs that would last a very long time.

'Not like it's Fu Manchu or anything, but they're kind of like big businesses with branch offices all over the place,' he continued airily. 'And I'm sure the Shanghai police keep in touch with the police down in Hong Kong.'

'Maybe we should change our names or something,' said Flood, who'd been wondering if the brigadier had done so and whether they might catch up with him one day.

'Do you reckon the brigadier uses different names?' he added.

'Oh I'm pretty sure he has a few of them, although I bet he likes to pretend he's a soldier,' answered Swan, who rather than writing about his adventures preferred dreaming about how he would deal with fame or who would star in the movie version. Thoughts of Daisy, now that he knew she really cared for him, competed with his visions of fame and fortune.

'I reckon if I'm gonna get a job at the newspaper there, it's the *Morning Post*—definitely a step down from the *Daily News*—I'll have to change my name to something else—at least until I get my book done.'

'Are you using your real name to write the book?'

'Sure, by that time everything will have blown over and I may be back in the States anyway,' he said, conjuring up visions of how Daisy would fit into his life on Easy Street.

'I might go by the name of Frank for awhile,' said Flood. 'Frank Steele maybe.'

'Frank's good,' said Swan. 'I'm tending towards Ralph myself—say do you want to have a look around this boat?'

'Why sure, I reckon we can show our faces now, get some fresh air.'

There weren't many passengers on board the RMS *Stanley* but Swan and Flood enthusiastically greeted everyone they encountered, revelling in their return to civilised society. They approached a middle-aged woman sitting on deckchair with her back to them. She seemed to be knitting something vaguely familiar. At the sounds of their approach she turned her head. It was Mrs. Munro.

'You,' she said accusingly to Swan. 'What are *you* doing on this boat?'

Swan, immensely flustered by her sudden appearance, croaked in reply.

'Um, going to Hong Kong. Is Daisy on board?'

'No, you young fathead, she isn't,' replied Mrs. Munro.

She barked out an unpleasant laugh.

'She jumped ship just after we boarded this morning and left me a note,' said Mrs. Munro, suddenly looking very pleased.

'She'd heard somewhere that you had escaped and wanted to welcome you back personally—little did the ninny know you would end up on this ship.

'At least I can be sure she's safe from the likes of you,' she continued. 'And I can assure you that you will never see her again.'

'But, but I love her,' whined Swan.

'Oh you *are* an idiot. I'm getting off at the next port and returning to Shanghai,' she said coldly. 'I understand there are some people there who might be interested to learn you two are on your way to Hong Kong. Isn't that right?'

Swan gulped some air and nodded miserably.

'So here's the deal—you promise to never have anything to do with Daisy ever again and I'll forget that I ever saw you. And you too,' she added, pointed her knitting needle at Flood.

'I guess we don't have much choice do we,' mumbled Swan miserably.

'Well, no you don't, but good luck to you both,' said Mrs. Munro, turning back to her knitting.

Although it was unknown to Swan or Flood, the police had lost interest in them now that they had received word that the negatives had passed to the communists, information that was relayed to them from Pockmarked Huang to a Chinese detective working for Givens. Using a radio broadcast, Pockmarked Huang traced the negatives to the small band of communist soldiers who had finally managed to evade the Kuomintang and return to their base far to the north.

Sitting by a fire later that night, the exhausted communist soldiers had made their report to their leader, Mao Tse-tung, telling him about their aborted mission against Chiang Kai-shek and the strange prisoners who had managed to escape on the Yangtze.

Mao sat on his haunches, a toothpick in his mouth. He'd forgiven his men for their poor results and was in a good humour. Holding the negatives to the light of the fire, he turned them this way and that, squinting to get a better look at this woman of loose morals.

Finally he grunted.

'She is the ugliest woman I've ever seen in my life.'

With that he threw the negatives into the fire where they flamed briefly before vanishing forever in a spiral of blue smoke.

978-0-595-36201-
0-595-36201-X

Lightning Source UK Ltd.
Milton Keynes UK
26 January 2010

149122UK00002B/99/A

9 780595 362011